My Name is Margot!

My Name is Margot!

Lisa Talbott

Lineage Independent Publishing

Marriottsville, MD

ISBN (Paperback): 9781088016893

Publisher: Lineage Independent Publishing, Marriottsville, MD, USA

Maryland Sales and Use Tax Entity: Lineage Independent Publishing, Marriottsville, MD 21104

lineagepublishing@gmail.com

For my siblings...

Contents

Foreword

Once again, I find myself writing a foreword to a Lisa Talbott novel. This one, her third, delves deeply into the skeletons hidden in one family's closet. Lies, psychopathic and sociopathic behavior, and family dysfunction are all laid bare in the story that Lisa weaves. The story is at times raw, at other times unnerving, but always riveting – in Lisa's typical free-flowing style.

Life can be a messy business, despite our best efforts to keep everything "sunshine and rainbows." There are things we just can't control, no matter how hard we try. People's minds break, addiction and substance abuse take over, others die before it is their time, and relationships are soured by revealed truths once hidden in the strangest places. For some families, that's just life. Good or bad, it becomes a matter of survival in the long run.

When Lisa first proposed this book to me early in 2021, I was intrigued. Could she craft a believable story about a family, and in particular a child, who was broken at a very early age? Could she have enough twists and turns to keep it interesting to the very end? The answer is a resounding "Yes!"

I will be the first to admit that there were places in the story that made me squeamish and evoked very visceral reactions. Some readers might not be able to deal with the raw presentation of events in the story, and I caution those readers in advance. Others won't be able to put the book down until the very end. I found myself in the latter camp.

I congratulate Lisa for making this book a reality. It took a lot of courage to write Margot's story. It is my hope that readers will remember that it is *just a story* from the author's vivid imagination.

Michael Paul Hurd
Editor/Publisher
Lineage Independent Publishing

My Name is Margot!

Prologue

There was a box that was hidden, buried deep. No, that's wrong, there IS a box that's hidden, in fact there are hundreds and hundreds of boxes.

It is a cause of wonder to come across such a thing, inventing scenarios as to what lies inside. Perhaps it is empty? In which case one asks why it has been secreted away from prying eyes.

Secrets are stored in such boxes by those hoping the contents will never surface, truths and lies never to be revealed.

It could be a fancy box, highly decorated, exciting to stumble upon. Or it could be less fanciful, and therefore considered boring. Moreover, it could simply be a box in one's memory where painful or shameful events are tucked away, their nostalgic revival too discriminating to recollect. Don't we all know of such boxes?

What to do? Open it and discover things you weren't meant to... or leave well alone to remain thereinafter in ignorance?

Pandora came across a box, and curiosity got the better of her. She decided to open it and nothing was, or could ever be, the same again.

Chapter 1: Margot, Aged Eight
(In her own words)

I didn't like Steven. I don't like Simon that much either, but at least he's not smiling and laughing all the time, like Steven was. Steven was always laughing, and smiling, and Mum and Dad were laughing at them both, all the time.

I didn't like my mum and dad much then, either. Why did they have to get Steven and Simon to come and live with us? It was better before. Before those horrid babies came to our house. When it was just me, and Mum and Dad.

'Steven's gone to live in heaven now, with Jesus', that's what my mum told me. 'He's gone to live with Grandma and Grandpa', she said. And I smiled. I knew that.

I'm glad he's gone to live somewhere else. Simon will go and live with him soon, I hope! And then everything will be back to how it used to be; it will be just me and Mum and Dad - again.

But I don't like Mum and Dad right now because they're always crying, and they don't smile or play with me anymore. It makes me angry.

I hate boys. Why did they have to go and get some more kids to live with us?

Aunty Sue is my favouritest person in the whole wide world. She loves me. She buys me things and lets me put lipstick on, like *she* does. She laughs a lot, does Aunty Sue.

When I go to stay at her house, we watch Frozen and other DVDs and eat pizza and we sleep together in her big brass bed with a feather mattress that's soft and squishy and she reads me stories from a book that my grandmother used to read to her when she was little, like me. Her pretty brass bed used to be her mum's, my grandma's. She got it from an auction but I'm not sure what an auction is.

I like hearing Aunty Sue's stories of when she and my mum were little. I think they used to be best friends, years ago. But I don't know now because my mum doesn't ever get birthday cards from Aunty Sue even though Mum sends them to her. I don't really know. But at least I got to go and stay with my aunty every now and again and it was always only me, never Steven nor Simon. Me, and my aunty.

One day I found a photograph album – 'cos I went looking in her cupboard for something to play with - she was in the bath. The photograph album was full of nice, happy pictures of Grandma and Grandpa, Mum, and Aunty Sue. They looked different, so young. How could my mum be that young? She doesn't look the same now. Her hair is different and she's taller. She had a dog, too. Not a real dog, it was a pretend one. I wish I could have a dog.

Grandma and Grandpa died a lot of years ago and went to live with Jesus, in heaven, and that's where Steven is, too, so he'll be ok! He's got my grandparents to look after him, now. He's so lucky.

And I'm lucky and Mum and Dad are lucky that we don't have him anymore. Hmmm, I wish Simon had gone with Steven, too.

Chapter 2: Bath Night

Eight-year-old Margot leaned against her grieving mother who leaned against her husband, Doug, as their two-year old son, Steven, was lowered into the ground. Steven. Their pride and joy. Twin brother to Simon.

United in their grief, they huddled under the umbrella as the cold rain continued to pour down on them and the rest of the mourners. It offered little protection against the rain or their sorrow. Rose was somewhat aware of her daughter leaning on her side, but her grief was too raw and selfish to concede anyone else's. She just wanted to get the day over and done with so that she could return home and wallow under the comfort of her duvet. A large gin and tonic or three would help pass the hours until sleep overtook her.

Simon - Steven's twin - had been left with the next-door-neighbour as Rose and Doug hadn't been able to function properly since the loss of their son, and a funeral wasn't the place for a toddler.

Deb and Alec had been wonderful, everything a neighbour could be expected to be, and had helped in abundance. Their two children had long fled the nest. One at university studying archaeology and the other had joined the RAF. Deb was the neighbour you could depend on and relished having young Simon admitted into her care. She'd loved both the twins and was as heartbroken as everyone else in their street and surrounding neighbourhood when young Steven had been found dead at the foot of the stairs. She would never forget that night, that Saturday, just after the X-Factor had finished when she heard a primal scream coming from the house next-door. It was strange, that guttural scream, and she wondered what on earth was going on.

A short while later both she and Alec noticed flashing lights outside the house – a police car, an ambulance, Doug (Rose's husband) rushing outside, barefoot, in his joggers, to usher them all inside.

Her curiosity found herself going to see what the palaver was and noticed young Margot sitting in the upstairs bedroom window, looking down on everything going off all around. She waved at Deb and smiled. Deb waved back.

She decided not to venture further, assuming she would hear it all, later, from Rose.

*   *   *   *   *

Deb and Alec were overjoyed having the young family next door as neighbours. It was delightful hearing those gorgeous little boys running around the back garden, laughing, and screeching. It reminded her of the days of her own children growing up, finding their voices and feet in the big wide world.

First, they'd had Tim, and next came Katy. She was so thankful to have a daughter; a little girl with whom she hoped she would develop a friendship. A daughter who, in years to come, would be a shopping companion, a confidante, a best buddy. Alec had had that with Tim. They'd had the male-bonding thing over the years before Katy arrived. The football matches they'd both gone to and the ATC (Air training Corporation) events, and so when she birthed a daughter, she felt complete.

Katy was her double, too. Not only in looks – that was evident – but in personality, likes and dislikes, ambitions, aspirations, taste in music, men, archaeology, the whole caboodle! Her cup runneth over.

And now, with both of her offspring venturing out living their own wonderful lives, she and Alec were left desperately waiting to become grandparents. For now, though, she resolved to enjoy watching the little kiddies next-door fulfil their dreams as they grew up.

*   *   *   *   *

The ambulance and police car remained outside for the longest time. Deb never considered herself a 'curtain twitcher' but she admitted to being so now. What on earth was happening next door?

She was a concerned friend and neighbour, but would Doug and Rose construe their concern the same way? She would hate for them to think of her as 'nosey'. To go or not to go round? Luckily for Deb, Alec made the decision, and they walked round together.

As they approached the front door they halted and turned to look at each other as Rose's sobs and high-pitched wails hit them. They crossed over the open threshold, bewildered to see a gathering of uniformed personnel.

A young, blonde-haired policewoman sat aside Rose, not looking at her face but writing in a little notepad. Doug, still barefoot, was walking round and round in circles, his hands covering his face and then his head, seemingly not knowing what to do with them. His pained facial expression recognised his friend and neighbour ,and he strode across to Alec, flinging his arms around his neck, sobbing and shaking.

"It's Steven," was all he said.

Rose continued to sit there, not noticing nor acknowledging either of them.

Deb was confused. *What* was 'Steven'? Where was Simon? She had already seen that Margot was upstairs in the window, so was Steven hurt? Is that why the ambulance is here?

A police officer at the Foster household ushered both Deb and Alec outside as forensics needed no further contamination whilst they were working. He enlightened them with the basic details of the situation and asked if Deb could give a brief summary of her opinion of the Fosters.

"Steven is dead?" she gasped. Her hand rose to her chest in shock, "Oh dear Lord! But how? Why? What about Simon, and Margot?" The Police Officer said no more other than to explain that a devastating accident had occurred, and the family would be afforded every assistance possible.

As they left, Deb looked up to the window where she'd seen Margot only moments earlier. She was still there, playing with the lace curtains, wrapping it around her hair, looking like a bridal veil. She looked down at Deb and Alec, and the police offer, and gave another little wave.

"If there is anything we can do, Officer. Anything at all, please let us know," said Alec. "I can't imagine what those two are going through, right now. They adore their kids. Good God, what a nightmare for them."

Alec put an arm around his wife as they both walked, despondently, back to their home, next door, selfishly relieved it wasn't them it was happening to.

* * * * *

The silent mourners left the cemetery drenched, dejected, cold and miserable. It was unthinkable that little Steven, gorgeous, happy, delightful Steven, was left behind in that earth pit, as everyone walked to their cars to go to a venue booked to host his wake and celebrate his pitifully few years on this earth. No mother should have to bury a child, and no mother would ever consider such few years a 'celebration'. A celebration is a birthday, a milestone, an achievement. Some *thing* to celebrate not a heart-breaking loss!

Rose didn't want to go to the local pub where the locals had congregated together and organised some farce of a memorial for her boy. She didn't want to listen to their condolences or their profound statements of pity when they had no possible inkling of what it felt like - to find your beloved child lifeless and twisted at the bottom of the staircase that was supposedly the route to rest, sleep, and pleasant dreams.

Going upstairs was the penultimate to the day. The bathroom was at the top of the stairs, the big white cast-iron bath where she washed her three children in readiness for their beds. It was a fun time, and she loaded the bath with bubbles, toys, sponges. All three of the children would get in together and she and Doug would sit at the side of the tub, showering them in warm water as they spluttered, coughed, and laughed.

It wasn't always a nightly ritual, usually every other night. But it was a joint thing, bath-time. All five of them, together, in the bathroom.

Margot was always the last one in and the first one out. She didn't like being in the bath with her baby brothers. She preferred it when it was just her, all those years ago when Mum and Dad sat beside her and played with her. They'd pile her soaped hair on top of her head and take pictures of her. She didn't like being photographed with her brothers, there were two too many faces in the pictures.

*   *   *   *   *

This was Saturday night, bath-time night. She didn't want to be in the bath, so she soiled herself, deliberately. She considered herself too old to join her brothers and she was determined to make her parents realise.

As she defecated in the water, everyone squealed in horror, except Margot, who sat there, laughing, picking it up in her hands as it leaked through her fingers and fell back into the bath water.

Rose was furious and was verbally scolding her daughter. Steven was already trying to clamber out of the bath while Simon remained there, ambivalent as to what was happening, a bar of soap between his hands and his teeth!

Rose demanded that Margot get out of the bath and go to her room. Steven had already left the bathroom, leaving Rose to haul Simon out of the putrid water. She began to rinse his little white body with the showerhead that was too high for the children to reach and washed away the pieces of floating poo that covered her little boy's lower regions.

"What on earth had come over Margot?" she thought to herself as the shower blasted away on Simon. She was so angry and vowed the little madam would go straight to her bed without a story!

As Doug and Rose worked together cleaning up, they heard a loud bump, bump, bump, bump, and a little patter of running feet.

Chapter 3: The Perfect Mother

Rose had lost so much weight since Steven's accident. She was encompassed with guilt and felt the whole blame lay at her feet. She should have been there when Steven got out of the bath; she, or Doug. She should have dried him herself and left her husband to wash Simon. Why had she remained in the bathroom?

She cursed herself over and over, as well as Margot! Her daughter had never done such a disgusting thing! She felt if she had gone after the two of them, Steven wouldn't have tumbled down the stairs in his wet feet.

She couldn't eat; her appetite as diminished as her will to carry on trying to be the perfect mother. Even though she blamed herself in many aspects, she couldn't shift the feeling of resentment towards her daughter.

Margot hadn't shown any signs of remorse; no tears, no questions. Nothing. Rose tried to discuss her lack of empathy with Doug, but he reassured her over and over, concluding that Margot was too young to digest the enormity of Steven's accident. But it seemed too big a pill to swallow for Rose, and her guilt was further compounded at her daily endeavour to distance herself from her daughter.

Bedtime stories were now undertaken by Doug, but when he left to go to work in the mornings, Rose tried desperately hard to revert to the caring, devoted mother she used to be.

She never let Simon out of her sight. With him, she'd now become over-protective, and her routine was bordering on extreme obsession.

*   *   *   *   *

Rose had a younger sister, Suzanne, and they were very much alike in many ways, particularly in their physical attributes. They were both the same height, five foot seven. They both had shoulder-length auburn hair that they both wore tied back in a ponytail. Brown-eyed, freckled faces, and button noses.

As young girls they were best friends and where one was seen, so was the other, as they seemed to be joined at the hip. There were only two years difference between the sisters but as they grew older and socialised together, many assumed they were twins.

They worked at the same factory too, albeit different departments. Rose worked on the shopfloor, overlocking, whilst Suzanne worked as Receptionist at Bent and Sons, knitwear manufacturers. That's how Rose came to meet Doug. He worked at an engineering company on the same industrial estate and Rose had noticed him drive by her whilst she and Suzanne waited at their bus stop every evening. He'd never so much as made eye contact with her, though she sent silent prayers that one day he would do. Nine whole months of wishing for him to look her way, her prayers were answered as he pulled up at the bus stop and asked if he could offer her a lift somewhere.

It was raining, and it had been raining fitfully the whole afternoon. It was exceedingly windy, too, and she was struggling to keep her umbrella from blowing inside out! She was on her own that day as Suzanne had taken the day off to attend an interview for another job elsewhere.

Rose felt and looked like a drowned rat as the rain and wind whipped around her. She desperately wanted to accept his offer of a lift but was conscious as to her appearance! Damn and blast he would offer on an evening such as this! No chance of applying lipstick now, she looked like the 'Wreck of the Hesperus'.

"No, thank you," she replied, reluctantly. "Look, here's my bus now. But thank you anyway."

He laughed, leaning across to open the passenger door, "Get in quickly before that bus driver accosts me for stealing his fares."

She hurriedly jumped in and buckled up, sitting next to him, a broad grin on her flushed face.

"No sister with you today, then?" he sang.

Ah, here it was, she thought. The offer of a lift was just a ploy to get to know her younger sister.

"No!" she answered, more indignantly than she had intended, "as you can see, it's just me!" She wasn't about to indulge him.

"Good," he said, smiling across at her, "fancy a drink?"

That first drink at The Pineapple became a regular event and they went there every night after work. Suzanne didn't get the job she went after and so she would join Rose and

Doug most evenings, much to Doug's dismay - as he wanted to spend time alone with Rose - so one evening he invited a friend of his along. A work colleague, Stuart, who had just left working on the trawlers and joined the workforce at Ferwell Engineering, working as a sprayer in the paint-shop. Stuart was over the moon with Suzanne and felt he'd won six numbers on the lottery! He was quite besotted.

His fascination with Suzanne was not, however, reciprocated, and her aloofness only enhanced her appeal.

Stuart didn't drive a nice new Audi like Doug - he owned a small, older, Renault Clio. Suzanne liked motorbikes. She loved the roar and power of the engines and the liberating feeling of the wind wrapping around her on the occasion she rode pillion on a friend's Kawasaki or Honda.

Stuart was the dependable boy-next-door type who would do anything to please – but he wasn't the unpredictable, good-looking bastard that her sister had managed to hook! She tried *not* to be jealous of her older sister, but it was becoming increasingly difficult!

Doug was gorgeous! He had that square-shaped, chiselled look about him. His body was to die for! Doug was a sportsman; he did amateur boxing and played football for the county. He was charming, witty, clever. Doug was sex on legs, and Doug wasn't hers!

He had everything that Suzanne wanted! How could poor old Stuart compare? He couldn't, and so – after stringing the poor chap along for as long as she could bear – she eventually had to send him the dreaded text message, which she felt incredibly guilty doing. It was cowardly of her, and she acknowledged that, but she simply could not stand going along as a foursome when she only had eyes for the one man who was besotted with her sister!

*   *   *   *   *

Rose took stock of her surroundings. The washing machine had finished its cycle and needed emptying, hanging outside on the line and the next pile needing loading. The boring, mundane rituals necessary to maintain equilibrium, normality, in an otherwise dysfunctional life.

In the grand scheme of things what did it matter if the washing was done or not, the dusting and vacuuming, the ironing and cooking? Had anyone ever died through being dirty? Did anyone else notice the dust on top of the mantlepiece? Who, but Rose, would deem to scrub the toilet and bleach the seat and underneath? No-one, that's who.

Would her wonderful husband care if she bought fish and chips from the chip shop instead of making them herself? The times she'd peeled the potatoes, par-boiled them before submerging into the boiling oil to make the perfect chips. Lovingly made the batter to coat the expensive cod she'd bought from Morrison's to deep fry. She'd even soaked the box of peas overnight to make mushy, chip-shop-style-peas to go with it all. What did it matter, now? Who cared?

Rose didn't care. She didn't even care whether or not Doug cared.

She was thankful that it was Thursday, and that Margot was at school. She was alone with Simon. It was supposed to get easier, she'd read, as time went on. But it wasn't happening like that, the way it said in all the books.

When Doug had left the house to go to work and Margot had been dropped off at school, Rose sighed with relief. She could withdraw her feigned enthusiasm and plough her whole being into her son, Simon, and when he had grown tired and she'd put him to bed for a nap, she could go to the garage where she kept her secret supply of gin and tonic and wallow alone.

She realised she must have been drinking too much and she hated herself for being so weak. Doug had no idea. He wasn't a drinker and never had been. The odd shandy was his tipple, and sometimes a red wine or two, but nothing to class him as a 'drinker'.

Rose had been sick for the past two mornings, and her breasts were tender. She poured the remaining gin into the Yucca plant that Suzanne bought her before they had that 'falling-out' session. "Drink that and die you Mother-Yucca," she laughed.

But die, it never did!

Chapter 4: Suzanne

My sister and I have that 'love-hate' kinda relationship. Odd really, I suppose. You see, I love my sister and I'm pretty sure she loves me too, deep down, but we don't talk much now.

We used to tell each other, all the time, we loved each other. It's true, we did. She was my big sister and according to Mum and Dad, Rose was over the moon when I appeared. She was the very first person to hold me when I was born. It was a Tuesday night and Mum was having a home-birth 'cos she didn't like hospitals; she had a real phobia of them.

Anyway, apparently Rose held me before my parents had the chance, and we bonded, so the story goes. And I don't dispute that, at all, 'cos we really did grow up 'as one'.

We look the same, (well, we used to look the same, but I have tattoos now that Rose would cringe at if she knew!) and we shared many same interests. We were the same size, and we always wore each other's clothes, every day.

In fact, our mum would often dress us alike when we were younger so that folk could not mistake us for twins. Ha. Good memories.

She's two years older than me so it's easy for anyone to mistake us for twins, but we're not, and the older we both get the wider the gap between us.

When we were kids, we shared the same friends in our street and neighbourhood. We played together, we walked to school together, we had ballet lessons together.

I remember one Sunday afternoon after we'd come home from Sunday School and I was playing at my friend's house, Rose came to bring me an ice cream cone. It was melting down the sides and she'd licked it 'cos it was running all down her fingers. That's the kind of good-hearted sister I was privileged to have. She wouldn't even have an ice cream without including me!

And when we became teenagers... well, we just got closer than ever. I could tell Rose anything and everything and she could me, too. We never had any secrets between us.

Do you know how good that felt? It's a fantastic feeling to be so comfortable and at one with, where there's no falseness, no pretence, no need to dissect any thoughts or actions. It's pure sisterly adoration.

I'm glad we never had any brothers. A lot of our friends had brothers and they never spoke kindly of them! Our next-door neighbour, Judy, had a brother, and he was vile! We hated him with a passion and felt really sorry for poor Judy for having a horrible brother like she had. He was cruel, and very ugly!

I guess you could say that Rose and I had an idyllic childhood. Our parents adored us and were forever taking photographs of us both. It didn't matter what the occasion, our dad would get the camera out and we'd all have to pose for him. Christmas, birthdays, holidays to our caravan at Skeggy, visits to Theme Parks, first day back at school in our new uniforms, you name it, there's a photograph of it!

When our dear, beloved parents died in a car accident, all those years ago, Rose and I started to clear out their house in readiness for its sale, I found their photograph album. Albums, not singular! Mum had four, and I have two of them. Rose took the other two.

That was shocking, when Mum and Dad died. Rose and I were still living at home then, and our beautiful, perfect world was shattered.

Our parents loved antiques. They used to sell at antique fairs every month. They had the most exquisite antiques, believe me! Mum loved her nice things, and I think that has rubbed off on Rose and me. Mum and Dad went to a lot of auctions and they bought wisely, but usually the things that Mum liked. Dad was just happy to pay up!

She bought a brass bed once – I have it now. She got it for a song and the headboard was embroidered in the finest pale-green silk, so intricately worked. She loved the old Victorian bed linen too, the drawn-thread work and the crocheted edgings. She always had a bolster with proper bolster cases!

Dad collected old clocks, all sorts. Grandfather clocks, grandmother clocks, cuckoo clocks, you name it, Dad had one! It would drive us bonkers when they all started chiming at once and I could never sleep in a room with a ticking clock! I hated them, still do!

You see, Mum and Dad were coming back from an antique fair they'd been at when they had their accident. It was just a couple of weeks before Christmas. They were excited because Christmas was the time when the punters would be coming to spend their money.

We were told that Dad jumped a red light and an oncoming vehicle had ploughed straight into them. Mum and Dad were dead and everything in their van was scattered at the traffic lights. Rose and I were never given the money they must have made at the antique fair, nor anything salvageable.

And that's our background, Rose and mine. We didn't sell the house for a long time, we stayed there because neither of us had been in position to buy our own place. Besides, it was our home and we were happy to remain there . . until she started getting serious with Doug.

Chapter 5: In the Beginning

Margot's sixth birthday was approaching, and Rose could barely contain her excitement. Christmas had passed just three months before and of course she had been spoilt rotten, like all good five-year-old little girls should be.

Rose and Doug had been like kids themselves, brimming over with joy at wrapping all the presents they'd bought for her. They waited until she had been bathed and in bed before they gleefully got all the boxes on the living room carpet and began cutting up Christmas wrapping paper, lavishly embellishing every one with huge festive bows and ribbons.

Margot was at that delightful age when the whole Christmas season was full of magic and fantasy. She had made a snowman picture at school which was now proudly on display on the door of the fridge. It would eventually be framed, packed away with all the other decorations, and resurface every following Christmas.

Rose couldn't wait for the week before the big day when they would all go out together and buy a "proper" tree, one with roots that they could plant in the garden afterwards. They would adorn it together, as a family, with stupidly expensive ornaments she'd been collecting from the garden centre for weeks.

She was planning a colour scheme this year. Silver and Purple. Margot loved purple. There were one or two ornaments that had a lot of sentimental value attached to them, some that came out of the Christmas box year after year, from the days of when she and Suzanne were little. Their dear old dad was a big softie where special, family occasions were concerned, and he'd made some exquisite birds for his two young daughters. Rose's bird was a robin, Suzanne's was a budgie. Their dad had moulded the body out of thin wire and wrapped cotton wool around, shaping it to look like a bird. He'd then glued various feathers to the forms and painted a red chest for the robin, and blue and yellow for Suzanne's budgie.

The girls had been thrilled with them and they would never – in a million years – dream of parting with them, getting them out every single Christmas and reminiscing about their own magical times.

This Christmas was going to be extra special, for Margot. Rose had told Doug that she was pregnant and that her doctor had made an appointment for her to have a scan. This concerned Rose, she worried something was wrong, but her doctor assured her it was routine, she was just a little larger than her dates suggested, and her baby might be a week or two older than she thought.

And that's how they discovered they were going to be blessed with twins! Doug was over the moon. He was going to have - not just *another* child - but two sons!

The scanned image of the baby boys was placed in a special, polished-mahogany box Rose had found in a charity shop, possibly previously housing an expensive wristwatch, or bracelet, lined with gold satin. She then placed it in an even bigger cardboard box, wrapped it up in gold shiny paper, and were going to get a helium-filled gold balloon tied to it, which had 'Big Sister' printed on.

This was going to be her big surprise present. She was going to have two baby brothers to help her parents look after. What an exciting gift was this going to be for her.

They'd also bought her her very own baby doll with its own baby buggy. Everything sat in a huge box surrounded by baby-doll clothes, nappies, changing mats, the whole caboodle. They would play 'mother' together and Rose and Doug were ecstatic.

But their planned surprise failed. The gold, helium-filled balloon wavered miserably, misrepresented by the atmosphere of the proverbial lead balloon when the realisation sunk in with Margot.

She stared, bewildered, at the smiling enthusiastic faces of her mum and dad as she opened the little polished mahogany box. What a boring Christmas present! A boring black and white photograph of nothing recognisable or interesting!

Thank goodness for Aunty Sue's present, she thought to herself. Another huge box that was decorated with cartoon caricatures from all her favourite DVDs. She tore the wrapping, opened the box, and squealed with delight when she found the most beautiful Cinderella dress. It was lilac lace, her favourite colour, and it was adorned with sparkly sequins all over the bodice. She had a silver tiara in another box, from her aunty, one she'd bought from a bridal shop!

Her aunty had made her into a real live princess, and she couldn't have been happier.

Margot climbed out of her Frozen pyjamas and donned her new Cinderella dress. She couldn't wait to phone Aunty Sue to tell her how much she loved her Christmas present.

'Why couldn't my mummy and daddy have got me something this?' she thought to herself.

None of her friends at school was going to have a *real* crown like she had, full of rubies and diamonds and emeralds!

Rose and Doug laughed at her in her fancy-dress costume. She did indeed look like a beautiful princess.

"Here's another big box for you to open. Look!" said Doug as he pushed over the biggest box next to the tree. But she wasn't interested in anything else. Her parents had already made the fatal mistake of giving her a boring present. What other boring thing was in the big box?

She opened it. Slowly, at first, until Rose began to encourage her to be quicker! And it was beautiful, this gorgeous baby doll sitting in its own buggy. It was lifelike too; she now had her very own baby to look after. She grimaced as she picked the doll out of the buggy, studying it.

"What are you going to name your baby, Margot?" Rose asked.

"Lilo" answered Margot, picking up her doll, turning it this way and that.

"Lilo?" laughed Rose.

"From Lilo and Stich! She looks like Lilo."

"You mean Lila? Lila and Stich," Rose corrected.

"No. It's Lilo." Rose and Doug howled with laughing. Margot's 'baby' was thus named Lilo!

They were worrying about this impending birthday of their daughter's. It was her sixth and was going to be the last birthday to be celebrated with being just her. The two of them had showered all their love, devotion, and time to their only child, but imminently the family was going to be larger and two more babies to nurture was going to take up a lot of the time that had previously only been bestowed upon Margot!

Their daughter had shown no interest whatsoever, in being pronounced 'big sister', even though Rose had included her in every step of her pregnancy.

She'd placed her little hand on her ever-expanding stomach to feel a kick. She'd humoured her by asking an opinion on names for the babies, maternity wear, colour schemes for the bedroom.

She'd searched on-line for guidance on how to include older children through the journey into siblinghood! And she had done everything by the book. Nothing, yet, was working, so she was pinning all her hopes that this birthday would be the ultimate ace card.

Rose was very creative, and artistic. She sat down one night, a week before the birthday, and made a dozen party invitations so that Margot could hand them out to some of her schoolfriends that she wanted to invite to her birthday party. When Margot was having breakfast, Rose gave her the invitations and told her that she could invite twelve of her friends, whoever she wanted.

She smiled, begrudgingly at her mother as she stuffed them in her school bag, her mind running through the names of the children in her class, that she thought she ought to include. There would have to be Chloe – the little girl who lived a few doors away – and Nathan, the boy whose mother had appeared on one of those reality TV shows before he was born. She would like Jolene to come, too, because Jolene had long blonde hair that she wore in a bun at the back of her neck, and she went to ballet classes every Monday and Friday night. She decided she would give an invitation to Lily because Lily had a Golden Retriever puppy dog named Benson and he was the most beautiful puppy she had ever seen in her whole life. *She* wanted a Golden Retriever puppy dog for her birthday, like Lily. She was going to ask her dad if she could have a dog instead of baby brothers.

She didn't want any babies, she already had Lilo; she only wanted a dog. What was so hard to understand?

Chapter 6: The Birthday Party

Their daughter's apparent lack of enthusiasm over her birthday party was overshadowed by her parents' who had gone absolutely overboard!

There were pink and purple balloons everywhere, hanging from the four corners of their living room. A "Happy 6th Birthday" banner hung precariously over the tea table as the brown tape applied to the corners became unstuck. It dangled on top of the birthday cake - the bright pink mass of butter icing in the shape of a butterfly... it had taken Rose two whole afternoons to make, shape, and decorate.

The obligatory photographs were taken that would be stored on a photo-stick probably to be viewed once in a blue moon.

Margot had confirmed that she'd given out her invitations but showed no willingness to divulge the names of her intended guests. She had repeatedly asked for a Golden Retriever puppy and had already decided she was going to name her Doris. (*Doris was the lovely old lady who read stories to the children at her school. She wasn't really that old, she was 65; widowed, and a retired schoolteacher herself. She enjoyed participating at her old school and this was her way of maintaining some sort of contact with her former life.)*

There was no way she was going to have a puppy for her birthday, especially a purebred which would cost a fortune! They were pregnant, two more babies were on their way and Rose was going to have her hands full, she wouldn't have the time to look after a demanding puppy as well!

Her husband, however, didn't share her lack of enthusiasm and quite liked the idea! He could picture the whole scene, the typical family, three children, and the dog. It would enable him to make a little escape in the evenings, walking a dog. But no matter what picture-postcard image he threw at Rose, she was steadfast. It wasn't the right time. She knew only too darned well that the responsibility would be laid bare at her feet, and hers alone. It was all very well and good, Doug saying he would take it for walks, he'd take it to the vet for its inoculations, and it would be good for the children to be brought up with a dog...

HE – was barking! And barking up the wrong ruddy tree! *HE* was going to be out at work, every day. *SHE* was going to be the one that had to clean up after it, teach it to go outside for its business, clean up the dog hair! *HE* had another think coming if he thought for a second that she was going to give in.

And Margot had heard all their excuses, over and over. Her parents were cruel! All they thought about was their precious baby boys that were coming. They must really hate me, she thought.

Out of the twelve birthday invitations she had distributed, only two turned up. Young Chloe, the little girl who lived a few doors away, and Wilf, a boy from her class that nobody bothered to get to know or play with because Wilf was deaf, and he spoke 'funny'. Nathan, the boy with the 'celebrity' mother hadn't bothered to show up; nor Lily, the prima donna ballerina who had Benson - the perfect puppy.

Margot, dressed in her Cinderella dress that her aunty got for her Christmas, was angry. She was supposed to be the star turn at her birthday party and she hadn't been given the opportunity to be that.

This was the worst birthday party, ever! She hated her birthday, she hated her parents for subjecting her to this humiliation, and she was infuriated that she they hadn't even acquiesced to her most demanded present. The dog!

The whole event was ludicrous, a fiasco. The lack of guests was embarrassing, and Rose was at a loss to understand why Margot's friends hadn't turned up. What had she missed? All kids love a birthday party so why had no one turned up for Margot's? She decided to get on the phone and call some of the other mothers, just really to confirm they'd received an invitation?

Nathan's mum, after talking to him, said he hadn't been invited. Erin's mother said that Margot HAD given her an invitation but had taken it back – due to some squabble over whether their teacher, Miss Benniston, was really a man! Erin had been terribly upset when Margot had pointed out that she wore glasses and had facial hair!

"She's got no boobs either," Margot had exclaimed, loud enough for the whole class to hear and causing a great deal of hilarity. Poor Miss Benniston was mortified.

Josef's father answered the phone after the third ring. Jack was a single dad, bringing up Josef alone after his wife, Paula, died of breast cancer two years previously. Not only was Jack drop-dead-gorgeous with his coffee-coloured skin, his muscular body, waist-long dreadlocks, pearly white teeth enhanced even more when he gave off his enigmatic sexy smile (phew!). He was an amazing dad. He was a great guy too, a good neighbour, an excellent car mechanic, and fit as a butcher's dog. He also had a big crush on Rose! No, he knew nothing about Margot's birthday party, if he had, he would have made sure that Josef was there and had the perfect birthday present for her.

She could not understand what had happened. And here they were, trying to salvage what was left of a supposedly special birthday party.

Margot threw a tantrum, the likes of which her parents had never seen before. She yelled at Chloe and told her to go home because she hated her. Chloe cried and ran home. Wilf was playing with two balloons; he had one between his knees and was jumping down the garden path. Because of his hearing impediment he hadn't heard the altercation between the two girls and was suddenly surprised when a

43

beautiful bundle of golden fur bounded over to him, jumping up on his back and its little razor-sharp paws piercing the balloon. Bang!

The startled puppy ran away trying to find another source of entertainment.

Suzanne stood watching apprehensively by the back garden gate, wondering if she dared enter.

Chapter 7: Rose

I am absolutely fuming! In fact, 'fuming' is not a strong enough word to describe how I felt seeing that ruddy puppy running around our garden and my daughter's whole demeanour alter from the miserable, ungrateful little bitch, she'd been - turn into the most ecstatic, happy, grateful child.

Once again, my sister has made me look like the baddie while she – once again – gets to be the best damn auntie in the whole world!

Please don't tell me I should be grateful for this surprise birthday present she didn't even ask my opinion on, because I am not! How can I have possibly said no?

You should have seen Margot's face. And my husband's! The pair of them all gooey gooey over it, making me look like the mother from hell. Don't get me wrong, the puppy is absolutely adorable (what puppy isn't?) but I am going to be the one that looks after it, and I'm going to have two babies in a couple of months' time and I'm going to be pulling my hair out!

Suzanne hasn't considered me at all. I *know* she loves Margot and honestly, I'm happy they have such a great relationship, but a dog is a big thing to include in a house and shouldn't have been given as a gift to someone as young as Margot. Dogs chew when they're puppies, they need a lot of walking, and they grow up!

Anyway, Doris is here to stay by the looks of things, but I'm telling you now, she is going to Sue's with Margot every weekend! I'm going to be far too busy.

I had to secretly chuckle, seeing my sister hovering at the gate after she released the puppy into the garden. She did look worried, ha ha ha. And she had every right to be!

It's sad that our relationship isn't the same anymore, especially with what we've been through, together. I've tried. Tried and tried so many times, but Sue is really cold towards me. I haven't received a birthday card from her in... well, actually I can't remember how many years, but I still send them to her. She's my only sibling and she is a great aunty, and I'm hoping she will love the twins as much as she loves Margot. I can't see that, though. It's as though Margot is hers. She knows I'm having twin boys but I don't think she's all that interested. She's not that 'maternal' - though you wouldn't think that if you watched her with Margot - no, Suzanne is more career-minded, she hasn't the inclination.

She's a writer, you know! She doesn't broadcast it though, she's actually very modest about her writing and I don't even think her neighbours know. And because she's a writer, she's able to work from home. How lucky is she? She went from being a humble receptionist at a knitwear company to a really renowned author!

I'm dead proud of her, and our parents would have been chuffed to bits. She writes novels about children, ironically. Goodness knows how she knows so much about children when she doesn't have any of her own, but her books sell, and that's how she makes her living. A darned good living, too! My younger sister drives a BMW and she lives in the prettiest chocolate-box cottage that has red climbing roses over the front door. She has marble-topped work surfaces in her untidy big kitchen with a Rayburn cooker that I doubt she ever uses. A microwave is more her style.

She only lives about two miles away. Two miles away, can you believe that? And we hardly ever cross paths. Don't you think it's sad that two sisters that grew up so lovingly together now find it difficult to even wish one another a happy birthday? I hope my children don't turn against each other and lose the love that Sue and I once had. I'd hate that. I don't think that will happen, though, I think Doug and I will make sure they're all loved equally and treated exactly the same.

We didn't have brothers, Suzanne and me, thankfully, but I'm sure that Margot is going to be a proud big sister.

I am not, however, letting the dog situation go by without having my say. Like I say, I'm fuming. She should have consulted us, Doug or me, but she wouldn't because she knew we would say no. And once it's here, all fluff and an abundance of cuteness . . . well, whose heart wouldn't melt?

Chapter 8: Doris

There is no such thing as an ugly puppy and Doris was no exception to that statement. She was beautiful, an armful of cuteness in every respect.

She was nine weeks old and came with a pedigree as long as your arm. She had huge ears, big brown eyes, a wet black nose, and the most beautiful pale golden fur. Who could fail to fall in love with her? Margot could!

It was beyond anyone's belief after the constant pestering for a dog the same as her schoolfriend, that the novelty could wear off as quicky as it had done. The opposite had happened with Rose, she fell head-over-heels in love with the hound!

She amazed herself at how quickly she had bonded with Doris and was overjoyed with her only taking five days to become fully house-trained! The kitchen floor no longer needed to be covered with newspapers overnight because the minute she got up in the morning, she would open the backdoor and Doris would run outside and oblige.

One pair of Doug's underpants had been chewed and one of her slippers, but so far, that was it!

Every afternoon Rose would get the lead hanging from the door, and go to meet Margot out of school, with Doris. She concluded that her sister must be stark raving bonkers not to have kept the puppy for herself. It was a magnet to the opposite sex! The amount of wolf-whistles she had been receiving since walking the dog was uplifting! People would stop her and ooh and ahh over Doris and it was so funny to watch grown men bend down and talk soppily like the dog could understand everything they were saying. If her sister had kept the dog for herself, she would be inundated with prospective suitors! Stuff those on-line dating sites for a lark, get a puppy! A guaranteed winner to attract a roving eye. Even though it was obvious she was heavily pregnant, her adorable puppy attracted them in their droves. What a boost!

Rose could not understand her daughter's lack of interest in her much-wanted dog! Doris was a pure delight and did everything possible to make everybody love her. And everybody *did*... well, almost everybody. She decided not to make an issue of it and played down everything. She wondered if Margot was worrying about the responsibility of becoming a big sister to her two brothers - which was hypothetical, really, as they were yet to be born.

It was Friday afternoon and Margot was going to spend the night with Aunty Sue, as she often did. For all their misgivings, the two sisters never deprived Margot of family integration. It was a special time for the two of them, and indeed for Rose and Doug as it freed up a night for them! It had become their 'date-night' and even if they didn't actually go out, out, it meant they had the whole glorious night to themselves.

Rose walked with Margot and Doris to Suzanne's house. As she unlatched the gate to let Margot go forward, Doris ran behind her. Margot turned round and kicked her, sending her squealing and sprawling. Rose was horrified! She hurriedly bent down to pick her up, cuddled her, and stared at her daughter in disbelief.

"Margot!" she cried out, "what are you doing?"

Margot, totally ignoring her mother and her puppy, ran off and banged heavily on the front door of her adoring, doting aunty.

Rose and Suzanne had an understanding where Margot's visits were concerned. They rarely made telephone calls, they usually corresponded via text messages, emails, or Messenger, thus alleviating the need for personal contact.

That evening, Rose had made dinner for her and Doug. It was smoked haddock, chips, and sweetcorn. Nothing too fancy and nothing too difficult that warranted her spending hours over the stove. They both loved smoked haddock with sweetcorn and would never tire of having it.

"Honey, I'm a bit concerned about Margot."

He looked up at her with his mouth full of chips, "Hmmm? What? Is she ok?"

She didn't pull her punches, "She *kicked* Doris this afternoon, Doug. She hurt her."

"Oooh, poor Doris! Why did she do that?"

"You tell me. Why would she want to hurt her? She was only running after her."

Doug continued masticating on his mandibles. He loved using this phrase over and over and laughed every single time he used the expression. Rose had heard it that often it no longer had the same humorous effect, but she did manage a feeble smile.

"I'm a little worried, Doug, to tell you the truth. I thought the Christmas reveal was going thrill her; I assumed she was going to be excited at having two babies, two brothers. But I'm not so sure she is. Look at Doris. She'd been going on and on about us getting her a dog and now she doesn't want to have anything to do with her. Doris actually cowered in front of her yesterday. Doug, Doris is a pup, she has had nothing to fear or be afraid of and yet I'm telling you, that dog cowered! Why is she cowering in front of a little girl?"

"Perhaps for that very reason Sweetheart. She's just a little girl and sometimes they can be a bit too boisterous for a puppy. Maybe Doris had been startled by something, who knows? Rose, what are you trying to say?"

"I'm trying to say," she emphasised her words, "I'm worried about our daughter. It's not normal behaviour, surely?"

"What's not 'normal behaviour'? Oh, kicking the dog? yes, yes. I agree, Love, she should not kick the dog. You need to tell her that it isn't right to do that. Explain to her that it's not kind. Margot isn't cruel; she loves animals. Look how excited she was when we took her to the zoo, and she saw all the animals there. She loved it. I think you might be wrong, Love. It IS normal."

Rose did remember that day they'd all gone to the zoo, and yes, Margot had been really excited to see all the animals. But there was a niggle at the back of Rose's mind, like an itch that she couldn't quite reach to scratch, that wouldn't go away. She'd witnessed poor Doris getting the uncalled-for kick and running away whimpering. She'd also noticed how Doris had started to back away from Margot, running behind *her* legs, when she entered the room.

She'd omit this piece of information for now, telling herself she'd take a more positive monitoring of the situation, hoping she was being unnecessarily paranoid, and blame it on her hormones!

Meanwhile, Margot was enveloped in the adoration of her beloved Aunty Sue. By six p.m. the pair of them had donned their PJs, eaten pizza and ice-cream, and were lounging on the huge sofa about to watch a new DVD that was a 'surprise'. It was a surprise because Sue had bought it from the local charity shop and the sleeve was missing, but the shop assistant assured her it was suitable for young children, so they had no idea what was about to appear on the TV screen.

Margot found this hilarious. This was fun. Aunty Sue was fun. The film began and they snuggled closer. The lights in the living room were dimmed to make the ambience more like a cinema, and she'd had candles burning in little glass dishes everywhere. It was cosy.

Sue began to smile when the film started. It was Bambi! But not an original, someone had copied it. Nevertheless, it was at least watchable, and they loved it. They sang together at the songs, dancing and swaying on the sofa, laughing at the hilarity of the cartoon characters.

When Bambi's mother died, at the end, Sue was sobbing like a baby and had to keep blowing her nose into a tissue, like she had done the very first time she watched it. Margot showed no emotion.

Chapter 9: Every Loss Adds to the Pain

Doris eventually became Suzanne's dog. After only six months of her arrival, the situation didn't improve, and poor Doris had become a nervous wreck. The deciding factor came after one morning when Rose was getting ready to walk with Margot to school and Doris bounded up to them with a doll in her mouth. It was one of those hand-knitted dolls, dressed as a ballerina. It had been sitting on Margot's toybox, along with all her other toys, and Doris had proudly showed off with it hanging from her mouth.

Margot screamed at her to drop it, trying to pull it from her mouth. Doris wee'd, and then Margot screamed even louder at her for wetting on the kitchen floor. She ran off with her tail between her legs.

It was Monday morning, and Rose was not only feeling very fat and frumpy in her pregnant state but also very frustrated. This was not an idyllic start to the morning, or indeed, the week!

She had sobbed as she walked over to Sue's house with Doris on the lead. She'd bonded with her, adored her, and hadn't contemplated doing so. But the poor dog didn't deserve what was happening to her, and although Rose had tried to get her little girl to treat her with more kindness and patience, nothing was working.

Doug wasn't being all that helpful either! He hadn't witnessed as much of the cruelty towards Doris that Rose had. In fact, he had begged Rose to persevere a little longer, give Margot some more time to understand the needs of a young dog, take her to puppy training classes.

But Doug hadn't been around to see Margot shoving a fork up her little black nose, nor had he seen her poking her in her eyes! He hadn't heard the yelps when she pulled her ears or seen his daughter throw a tantrum when she couldn't get her own way.

By the time Doug got home from work there was only a couple of hours before she was having to get ready for bed, by which time Margot was angelic! He would sit and read her a bedtime story, tuck her in and kiss her goodnight. Normality.

He was of the opinion his wife was exaggerating and that was totally understandable considering her hormones were all over the place! But he could neither comprehend nor accept that his darling daughter was at fault, in any aspect. She was a child, for goodness' sake.

His suggestion that Rose get some sort of counselling had been welcomed with the same enthusiasm as if he'd suggested a three-some to improve their diminishing sex-life!

Simply, he was just not 'getting' it, (*the situation with Margot, not the sex*!) and so Rose made the heart-breaking decision to take Doris to the foundation of the problem – her sister!

Doris had been with Suzanne for only three months when she somehow 'escaped' from her garden and ran into the road after a ball. She was hit by a car and the poor mite hadn't stood a chance.

It had been a weekend that Margot was staying with her aunt. Her aunt had left the two of them playing outside for a few minutes and she knew the gate couldn't have opened by itself. Suzanne picked up her glorious golden lifeless body as tears streamed down her face. She sent a text message to Doug asking if he would come over and bury her and would he please take Margot back with him because she was too distraught to entertain her. She wanted to wallow, alone. Margot didn't cry, nor did she display any sign of upset.

That was well over two years ago, but Rose still felt that awful guilt, as if somehow it was her fault. Her GP had said that grief could be behind her unpredictable periods, which had been as regular as clockwork since her late teens. She bought a pregnancy test anyway. If it was positive, how was she expected to feel? A new baby wasn't going to replace her sunny, smiling boy who tumbled down the stairs and lost his life, was it?

Margot was now approaching her tenth year and Simon was three. Six whole months previously, she was the happiest she'd ever been. Her family was complete, with a girl and two little boys. They were a happy family. Or were they?

Rose had tried to put her doubts about their daughter behind her. She was a little girl who had been the apple of their eyes, and the princess of their castle. She'd been spoiled, of course she had! She was their first child, and as Deb – next door – had said on a couple of occasions, 'you'll always have a best-friend with a daughter. Remember that adage, *A son is a son until he takes a wife, but a daughter is a daughter, and a friend for life*, or something like that'.

She loved that old quotation and envied her neighbour's relationship with her own grown-up children. They came home often, usually bringing a new girlfriend or boyfriend, or any friend really; and good old dependable Alec would get the barbecue going and invite a few of their immediate neighbours round to join in their obvious glee, making everyone welcome.

Deb and Alec were good people. They were party people too. Any occasion was an excuse for a knees-up, and both of them had loved her three children, *especially* the boys, with Deb often just 'popping in' to have a peek and a 'hold'. She would pick one of the twins up and smother him with kisses until he laughed so much it seemed painful. She couldn't remember, now, which twin it was, but it was a wonderful memory.

As she sat holding the little stick that boomed loudly 'YES, YOU ARE PREGNANT' she knew what Doug's response was going to be before she even told him. He would say 'you can't be!' and she would look at him with the same contempt as if to reply, 'how can I *not* be?!'

Men! How annoyingly stupid and dismissive can they be sometimes? Like it was all her fault! *'Rose, you need to be more fastidious when you take your pill. It's a bit irresponsible of you to be so lackadaisical.'* Women have been known to murder husbands for less!

Simon sat in his playpen, piling brightly coloured plastic blocks on top of one another, then knocking them down and laughing as he did so. It was excruciatingly painful to watch him play, alone, without the joint companionship of his brother. Rose wondered if he missed him, as twins were known to have that 'special' connection, a unitedness that a single child didn't have. Would he grow up to feel a part of him missing?

What if she was pregnant with twins, again? That was something else; surely not? She doubted she could handle the fact that she would have another set of twins!

Parenting was not the easy occupation her own dear mum and dad had made it look, or was it that she and her sister were easier and more grateful for everything? She couldn't ever recall either of them having to be chastised for anything they did, and never were they smacked! They only wanted to please their parents, 'the look' was all they needed to know when to stop!

So where was she going wrong with her own daughter? Yet again her thoughts came back to Margot. She was supposed to be enjoying Simon: she desperately wanted to enjoy Simon, but her heart was aching as she watched him, singularly. It was always 'the twins', or 'the boys', Steven and Simon . . . now it was just - simply - Simon!

Simply, Simon. Simple Simon? She would dismiss that! Like she also tried to dismiss saying 'before Steven had his accident', or 'just after Steven's accident'. Making everything seem like life was revolving around that timeframe. It wasn't healthy, but she needed to keep remembering him in any way possible.

Since Steven's accident (*there she goes again*!) she couldn't help but notice Margot's slightly changed demeanour. Or perhaps *changed demeanour* was the wrong phrase, it was quite difficult for her to put into words, but happier she definitely seemed. Margot was changed but barely noticeable to anyone who didn't know her as well as she did. Doug hadn't noticed a thing! She contemplated sending an email to Suzanne to ask for her opinion but worried that her sister would read too much between the lines and make a great big mountain out of a molehill. She was curious as to how 'things' were between the two of them.

Sue had been extremely disappointed with Rose when she turned up at her house that afternoon with Doris on the lead, telling her she was over-reacting and Margot wouldn't dream of hurting her puppy. She assumed, like her perfect brother-in-law, that Rose's paranoia was a case of escalating hormones, due to her being pregnant.

Well, Rose wondered what her thoughts were afterwards, when the dog was hit by the car, escaping out of her 'unescapable' front garden!

And now, *six months after Steven's accident*, here she was pregnant again... Time to tell the hubby!

Chapter 10: Delayed Reactions

She was putting off making the dreaded announcement, hoping that the pregnancy testing kit was faulty – it happens! She began exercising... jogging on the spot... picking up and carrying heavy loads... She even suggested she join Doug at his gym, one night in the week. Maybe the foetus would dislodge and there wouldn't be the need to tell him. Maybe she could ignore it for a while, and maybe she ought to stop thinking the way the was thinking and accept what cannot be undone!

A new baby is a gift and though they were all still raw with their grief, surely this was a blessing? Might Margot be different with a sister? She could have that best-friend relationship that she and her sister had. *Had*! Oh dear! What if Margot didn't want another brother or sister, like she'd said on MORE than one occasion?

"You and daddy don't love me any more now that those babies are here. I wish they hadn't come."

Rose had remembered that little outburst! Doug had laughed out loud at Margot's disgust, picked her up in his arms and spun her round, "you will always be our number-one-princess, even when you're an old, old lady, like mummy." The little love!

Whilst Simon was having his afternoon nap, she decided she would go up into the loft and get down the 'Baby Box'. It was actually an old-fashioned suitcase that her mother had lovingly restored by decoupaging the whole thing. She *thought* it may have belonged to her dad many moons ago; a small, brown leather 'weekend' case, and it was beautifully decorated in little cut-out Christmas cards, birthday cards, cherubs, Victoriana pictures, then varnished on top. Rose kept all her baby memorabilia in this, which she now referred to as her Baby Box. Birth certificates, first pair of shoes, first haircuts, congratulations cards – all the type of things that doting mothers keep forever! She really could do with a bigger suitcase.

And when she found it within arms' reach of the loft, she carefully took it downstairs and poured herself a glass of red wine while she sat alone and reminisced.

This was great therapy! She hadn't considered that this was just 'what the doctor should have ordered' as it was overwhelmingly satisfying.

There were photographs of her being pregnant, first Margot, then the twins. There was the first scan of Margot, another of the boys. Their children's very first photographs taken in the hospital seconds after they were born. An envelope containing fingernail cuttings, another containing hair, a little box of Margot's teeth with notes inside with the dates she'd lost them.

Tears ran down Rose's cheeks that she hadn't even realised were there. This Baby Box was *more* than that, it was a Memory Box, it was their lives. It represented happiness and it did not deserve to be shoved up in the loft, out of sight.

She closed the suitcase and smiled; tonight, she was going to give Doug the glad tidings and they would have cause to celebrate. She closed her eyes and sent up a little prayer to her mum, thanking her for the beautiful decoupage case, wishing both her parents could have been here to meet their grandchildren.

She felt guilty now, having that glass of wine. She ought to have waited for Doug so they could drink together. There was no more in the house, so she'd have to buy a bottle from the 'off-licence' when she went to collect Margot from school. She wanted to make the night a little special, something to add to the Baby Box for their new addition.

She didn't have time to think about finding a nice recipe, buying the ingredients, cooking everything, etc., etc., and then she had an idea! They'd get a take-away and the menu would be the first memento of their new child! She was chuckling to herself at her great idea, 'it will be our take-away baby'. How she would have loved to have had a friend – or a sister! – to share this silly, happy moment with. Oh! She could go next door and tell Deb. Would that be all right? Telling your neighbour before your husband? No, of course it wouldn't be all right! Husband first, everyone else later.

*　　*　　*　　*　　*

"You're smiley today," said Margot, looking up and anticipating her mother's reply as they walked back home.

"Am I?" Rose queried. "Aren't I always?"

"No," replied Margot, frowning. "You're never this smiley."

Rose was saddened by Margot's forthrightness and felt ashamed that her own daughter had had to point this fact out. She was too young to understand what it felt like to lose a child, how could she? Only a mother who had lost a child would totally comprehend.

She felt like her bubble was wilting. The previous elation she had been feeling was evaporating into the ether, and she blamed her daughter for deliberately setting out to deflate her. The little bitch!

"Margot, I'm sorry that I haven't been smiley, I really am, but I've been very, very sad. Dad and I were heartbroken when Steven fell down the stairs. We miss him so much. We would have been just as sad and not-smiley if it were you, or Simon. One day, when you're grown up and you have babies of your own, you will understand."

Margot glared at her mother in utter contempt. "I will *never* get married and have babies! I hate them!"

Rose was shocked at the vitriolic way she spoke her words. "You don't hate babies, Margot. You don't hate Simon and you didn't hate Steven. You won't... " She didn't finish her sentence. "You love Lilo," she quickly altered her tack. Margot didn't answer.

"Anyway, Sweetheart, you have your whole life ahead of you with hundreds of exciting things to look forward to. You can travel all over the world and see wonderful things, experience different cultures, meet lots of people. You can do anything you want to. What *would* you like to do when you grow up?"

Margot shrugged. Then after a few seconds later she said, "I want to work with babies."

Rose's face lit up; she was thrilled! She'd just declared she 'hated babies' and in the next breath she said she wanted to work with them. She was overjoyed! This contradicted her feelings just a split second ago, now she couldn't wait to tell her that she was having another baby and that she could help her with it, become more involved from the start. She would make sure she did everything right this time and not leave her out for a single moment!

What a turn-up for the books! She told herself she was a despicable mother for even thinking of her precious daughter as a 'bitch' while all the time she really *did* love babies. How beautiful! She was SO proud; everything was going to work out perfectly.

"I want to see them in their coffins. You didn't let me see Steven in his."

Wham! Rose fell even further back. Her legs trembled as she tried to push Simon in his pushchair, eager to get to the safety of her home, frightened beyond belief at what she had just heard coming from her young daughter's mouth!

When she arrived back home, she unbuckled Simon from his pushchair and he stepped out, running into the living room where his tricycle sat waiting for him. Margot threw her school bag on the floor where she always left it, never hanging it up on the hook where her mother had placed it every single day, then ran up the stairs to her bedroom.

Rose looked over at Simon, watching his face contort in concentration as he manoeuvred his legs to straddle his toy. She was still trying to analyse Margot's statement but eventually had to conclude that it was a normal reaction, surely? They *hadn't* let her see Steven in his coffin as they felt it was inappropriate for any child to witness seeing a dead sibling in a coffin. She was far too young to understand that the body was no longer her little brother, and that he was going on a journey to heaven.

Rose started to remember *the* night. The night of the accident. Bath night! It was as if she was watching a DVD in slow motion, and it all came hauntingly back. She could smell the bubble bath, hear the chuckles of the boys, then their squeals when Margot defecated in the water and trying to leave the scene, and Steven hurling himself out of the bath, the water splashing on the bathroom floor. Her, reaching for the showerhead to rinse off all the poo from Simon while hearing Steven's footsteps running across the landing, and then the bumps as he hit the steps... and then... What? *WHAT?* What did she hear?

She opened the bottle of wine she'd bought before collecting her daughter from school and poured herself a large glass, then went and stood outside of her back door, looking around her imperfect garden. The lawn was desperate to be mowed, the weeds were in abundance, the shed needed creosoting as well as the fence panels, it lacked nurturing, it needed someone like Alec, next door, to put it all right.

She raised her head upwards, concentrating on the clouds above and sent a prayer to her parents. 'Tell me I'm wrong, Mum. Please, tell me that I'm wrong.'

"Yooo hooo!" came a cheery distraction from over the fence. It was Deb. "Ah, the sun's gone over the yard arm, I see," she chuckled heartily, "mind if I come over and join you?"

Rose felt as though her mother had answered her prayer. "Oh Debbie, PLEASE do! Come round and I'll get you glass."

Deb was still chuckling when she appeared in the garden. She was like a breath of fresh air and a much-needed respite for Rose.

"And here's my favourite little munchkin in the whole wide world," she exclaimed when Simon cycled up to greet her. She leapt up from her seat and hoisted him off his bike, wrapping her big arms around him. As per usual she subjected him to the never-ending kisses all over his face as he tried, unsuccessfully, to push her away.

She never asked about Margot, or if she did, it was rare. Rose wanted to have a deep and meaningful conversation with her but was worried about how the revelations would come across. Would Deb be discreet and keep what she said to herself? Would she think that Rose was being paranoid, like she felt she was being, and like her husband did? Was this the right time, and was Deb the right person she ought to be talking to about her doubts, insecurities, suspicions?

Alcohol has a lot to answer for. It loosens ones' inhibitions, it liberates the tongue, it throws caution to the wind, and an hour later poor old Debbie had been subjected to the lot! It was almost as if Rose had had her own mother sitting next to her, hearing her pour out every preposterous, unimaginable, crazy thought.

The bottle of wine was empty by five o'clock and Rose panicked. She had dinner to arrange, children to feed, a husband to look after, an announcement to make! The time had passed so easily with having someone to listen to her that she had been oblivious to the time!

Debbie just waved her alarm away, reminding her that she was going to order a take-away, and she would go back to her house and replace the bottle of wine they'd both enjoyed. Doug need never know! (How naïve. He would most definitely know!)

"Are you pissed?" was the first thing he said when he leaned over to give her a kiss as she was trying to sort out the various food containers.

"No, I am not!" she said indignantly, lying through her back teeth. "I've had one glass, with Deb." (It wasn't a barefaced lie, 'cos she *did* only drink from the one glass!)

"I've got us a take-away tonight, for a change," she smiled, anticipating his expression when she revealed her news.

He appeared not to have heard her, "have you heard from Sue today?"

"No. Should I have done?"

"Hmm. Don't know why she text me and not you as well. She's going away for two months tomorrow, her new book launch. She said she won't be able to have Margot stay over again until she gets back."

Ooh, that was a blow. A bitter blow! She'd have no reprieve! No special time for just her and Simon. Her sister was so lucky to live the single life with no family ties, to be able to just up and go at a minute's notice and have no other person to consider but herself.

Doug looked around the empty kitchen where Rose was placing the crockery and cutlery on the table, "where are the kids?"

"Margot!" she yelled, rather coarsely, Doug thought. "Simon, Sweetheart, come and get some dinner."

Simon cycled into the kitchen, dismounting his bike when he saw the table full of aluminium containers that smelled delightful. He climbed up onto his chair and grabbed his beaker of water, taking a big gulp. It was Chinese, and Simon loved chicken and mushrooms with Chinese chips.

There were various dishes ranging from prawns, ribs, chicken, noodles, rice, and of course there had to be chips! Margot had still not condescended to make an appearance, even after a couple of yells. Rose was trying to contain her frustration because she needed the night to run smoothly; she had knowledge to impart to her husband!

With her non-attendance, Doug marched upstairs to her bedroom where he found her lying on her bed, listening to her iPod on her earphones. He was taken aback; he didn't know she *had* an iPod!

"Margot, come downstairs and eat with us. What are you doing with that?"

She removed the earphones and stared at her father, disgusted that he'd interrupted her. "What?" she said.

"It's dinnertime. Your mum's got us Chinese. Come downstairs before it all gets cold."

Grumpily, she followed him and sat at the table. Doug put her plate in front of her and went to pour her a glass of water. He picked up the take-away menu from the work surface and went to throw it in the rubbish bin along with the some of the paper lids.

"Oh no, don't throw the menu away, Honey. I want to keep that."

He looked at her, amused, wondering why she would deem to keep the menu when they ordered the same things time after time. They even had the restaurant's number in their phones!

At long last the children were in bed and Rose poured her and Doug a glass of wine. She was smiling, stupidly. She'd had too much to drink but was never going to admit it. She plonked herself down next Doug on the blood-red leather Chesterfield settee. It was old, well-worn, cold – but well-loved. She waved the take-away menu in front of his face, and he patted it away.

"This is to go in our Baby Box!" she slurred, ever-so slightly.

"A Chinese take-away menu is going into our Baby Box?" he echoed, sarcastically.

She jumped up from the settee and stood facing him, "Yes! Look!" she said, putting her hands on her tummy, "Ooops, we did it again," she sang to theme music of Britney Spears.

Doug stared at her, dancing like a loon in front of him. "You can't be!" Precisely the three words she would've placed a bet on him using!

Unbeknown to the pair of them, their daughter was not asleep in her bed, she had crept downstairs on the pretence of asking when Aunty Sue was expected back, and she had overheard everything, the laughter and the joy. There was going to be *another* baby coming into their lives. Another Steven!

Chapter 11: The Book Launch

Suzanne's two months' book launch trip was going very well. Her new book was proving to be another success, not that she doubted it would be, she had an amazing publisher. He was encouraging without being pushy, constructive but not critical, and the pair had a mutual respect for each other, too.

Adam was in his late forties and, like Sue, childless. Married with a secret mistress that Suzanne knew all about but feigned interest. She couldn't blame him in the slightest, seeing as though Beth had been diagnosed with dementia over five years ago, at such an early age. It was tough for him, she concluded, to slowly lose the woman he loved, day by day. She admired him, actually, for staying with her, a lesser man would have taken to his heels and skedaddled, abandoning her in her time of need, but not Adam, he was 'old school', where his vows 'in sickness and in health' had meant exactly that… but apparently the 'forsaking all others' part had been totally overlooked!

Beth would never know; and Suzanne doubted she had the wherewithal to be able to even *care* if she did find out.

He did talk about his personal life with Suzanne sometimes, as she did hers, but their conversations mainly revolved around their writing, the books they produced, and other authors' books too.

Her latest book, *In Sickness, Not In Health*, was, she felt, her best yet. It had taken her just over nine months to complete, and she had poured her heart and soul into it. She sat at her PC for hours, sometimes until the small hours of the morning, bashing away at her keyboard, deleting, rewriting, researching, remembering. Being a writer enabled her the capacity to put all her thoughts, ideas, and opinions into novels which, she hoped, would appeal to her fans, of which she had a huge following.

In Sickness, Not In Health had been available on pre-order for two weeks prior to general publication and had already amassed over two thousand orders. She had been planning how she was going to spend her royalties: a tombstone – for Steven; it was far too long overdue.

She had spent an entire afternoon signing her books and at last the queue was receding. She was looking forward to getting back to her hotel room, having a glass of wine before heading out to grab something to eat, and just as she was picking up her bag to leave the bookstore, a spotty-faced teenaged boy plonked himself in front of her with a copy of her book. "Please Miss," he asked like he was addressing his schoolteacher, "I've got all your books. Would you sign this one for me?"

"Of course I will," she answered, "what's your name?"

"Aaron."

"Aaron, is that with two As or one?"

"Two."

"Great name," she smiled at him. "So, you say you have all my books. Tell me, which do you like the best?"

"Finding the Negative," he answered without hesitation and blushed right down his neck. She was sure it was nothing to do with the mention of the book; he looked uncomfortable, sitting in front of her, like he couldn't wait to get away yet at the same wanting to stay and talk.

"Yes. The negative. I like your play on words, and the way you lure the reader into thinking the obvious, but then you come to realise it isn't obvious after all." He stopped talking to look at her face, "That's what I mean with 'Finding the

Negative'. Your reader presumes 'the negative' is a reaction, but it isn't, it's the negative to a photograph. I like that. It was clever. And that negative was just what Lizzie needed to find, to know about what happened to her, and why she'd been adopted. It's important for someone who's been adopted to know, isn't it?"

"I can see you are a very ardent fan, Aaron! I'm impressed," she told him.

"I am, yes," his eyes alternating looking at her and his signed book, "is this your *real* name?" he asked, pointing to *Suzanne Barsby*.

"Do I look like I'm not real?" she answered coolly.

He laughed, "it's been 'surreal' to meet you, Miss Suzanne Barsby. Can't wait to read this one," he said, tapping his new acquisition. "I'll send you a personal review, on your website. Bye, now."

And with that, the gawky teenager rose from his chair and left the store.

Suzanne chuckled to herself. Teenage boys were always predictable and so easy to make fun of - torture, even. How many times had she done a similar thing to the boys at school? She took great pleasure at ridiculing them, especially the shy, unconfident ones, making them blush or squirm whenever the opportunity presented itself.

She was still smiling to herself as she was walking to her hotel, thinking of the young lad's awkwardness, he looked a little familiar too. His naivete had given her a kick, and this encounter had conjured thoughts of a liaison she'd had with a boy not too dissimilar in age to this Aaron lad, and not all that many years ago.

She was twenty-five at the time. Marcus had just turned sixteen. His mother would have *killed* her if she'd had the slightest inkling!

He'd been impossible to have gone unnoticed with his casually-styled blond hair, his 'come-to-bed' blue eyes, and he was *far* too mature for his meagre sixteen years! A dead-ringer for Leonardo DiCaprio... and he bloody-well knew it.

She saw him at the gym. Him, and his two buddies, she forgets their names now, but she used to watch him watching her. It was funny – actually, it was hilarious at how he couldn't take his eyes off her - and she decided to throw caution to the wind and play the dangerous game.

She supposed most teenage boys fantasised being with an 'older woman', the more *experienced* that could teach them a thing or two! She got 'turned on' imagining herself being the teacher, the one to indoctrinate *the young Leonardo DiCaprio* into manhood.

She listened to Bobby Goldsboro's 'Summer, the first time' over and over and wanted to be that woman for Marcus; his first, the one he would never forget. You never forget your first time.

For four months, sweet-sixteen-year-old Marcus enjoyed numerous evenings of unbridled passion behind the seclusion of Suzanne's four walls, until he found his new sexual expertise too much to keep to himself, launching into bestowing his skills to the younger uninitiated, opposite sex. That was a pretty hard pill to swallow for Suzanne, being 'dumped' by a youngster.

She felt like she'd been tossed into the scrap heap and was beyond miffed. Standing naked in front of a mirror, she studied her body. There was no cellulite in her thighs. Her face was largely unwrinkled. Her breasts were still perky. Her teeth sparkled and her gums were pristine. She was only twenty five, damn it! How had she managed to become so insignificant?

She was feeling sorry for herself and then remembered how poor old Stuart must have felt when she cast him aside without so much as a by-your-leave. So, she did the most ridiculous thing ever and sent him a text message to apologise for the way she dumped him, a lifetime ago!

And she didn't know what had depressed her the most, the fact that she *still* had his number in her phone or the fact that he'd replied "*Sorry, who is this*?" She deleted his number.

Suzanne was leaving Brighton in the morning. Her next port of call was Dulwich, to a little bookshop that Adam had promised was frequented by many household-named celebrities, the comedians, singers, actors, and actresses. An old friend of hers lived on Consort Road so she had arranged to stay with her for the night, to catch up on the last twelve months. According to her Facebook posts she was having a bit of a hard time getting over her ex. A night out in Leicester Square was going to be the perfect tonic for them both.

As she knocked on her friend's front door —a bottle of Prosecco held high in her left hand - which was opened almost immediately, she walked inside and instantly regretted her decision. It was one she would come to regret for a long time!

Whack! Everything turned black.

Chapter 12: Margot's Thoughts

Where are you, Aunty Sue? I haven't seen you in ages and I miss going to stay at your house. You've been gone a long time. Don't you love me anymore?

Did you know that my mum and dad have a secret? Has dad told you? I bet he has. They're having *another* baby. Aunty Sue, I don't want them to get another baby! Can you tell them that I don't want them to do that? Please! It's not fair! They've got me and they've got Simon, we don't need another one.

You haven't got any babies so why do they keep having them? When I grow up I'm going to be just like you. I'm going to smoke and drink wine, like you do. I'm going to be famous like what you are and everything in my life will be perfect like what yours is. I can't wait till I'm old, like you.

I've asked my mum if she will buy me a phone so that I can be the same as everyone in my class at school. All the kids have phones, but Mum says I'm too young to have one. I'm not, am I? If I could have a phone I could text you and call you every day.

Do you know what? I got stung by a wasp, on my foot. It's really big now, and hurts a bit – my foot, I mean, where the wasp stung me. I squashed it. And then I went round the garden to find all the horrible wasps and I killed them all so they couldn't sting me ever again.

I hate wasps! I hate spiders and bees, slugs and snails and everything that's horrible, like Debbie next door. She just pretends to be nice, but she isn't really. Why can't everybody be like me and you, Aunty Sue?

We're the same, aren't we? I'm your other little 'twinnie'.

I wish you were my mum. Why can't you be my mum? If I could come and live you then Simon and this new baby that mum's having can all be together and I won't have to hate it, like I had to with Steven, will I??

Chapter 13: Doug's Story

I thought they were twins, Rose and her sister, Suzanne. We all did, and when I say all, I mean all the lads at work. We'd see the pair of them at the bus stop in the evening, we saw them in the canteen at break times (*Taylor Hobson - the factory next door - had a massive canteen that everyone in all the surrounding factories went to at lunchtimes*). They were always together, and it was a bit off-putting for any of us guys that wanted to talk to one of 'em, to get one of them on their own. You know what I mean?

I think we assumed they were twins because they looked exactly the same. They dressed alike, wore their hair in ponytails. I was a twin myself, and even I couldn't tell which was the younger, or older! You would think I would know, wouldn't you?

But when I say I was a twin, that was yonks ago, before I was adopted. My twin died, so I didn't have that connection that comes with being a regular twin. My parents were great, and I never once had the inclination to find out anything about my birth parents. Hence my intrigue with the sisters, and when I saw just the one of them at the bus stop that night, when she was on her own, that was my cue to make a move!

If I said I was a tad disappointed it wasn't the other one, I'd perhaps not be lying and I have no explanation why, only to say that the lads had claimed Suzanne was the more accommodating – if you get my drift.

I was young, fit, and liked a bit of skirt that was deemed 'accommodating'. Some nice totty on the end of my arm for a week or two was gonna do wonders for my street cred!

I was considered good-looking I suppose. I worked out at the gym, played football, did a bit of boxing, and I didn't drink or smoke.

The lads on the shopfloor reckoned Rose was a bit prim and proper, weird, but I didn't find her at all weird. In fact, I liked her. She had a surprising uniqueness about her that I never found in other girls. Rose wasn't the type of girl who seemed on settling for second best, yet she was just an overlocker at the knitwear factory. It surprised me because she spoke as if she had ambition, drive, dreams. Perhaps these were pipe dreams because she didn't have a dazzling career.

She was funny, too. I remember when I took her to The Pineapple for the first time and we never stopped talking or laughing. It was a great night, that. I didn't want the night to end but then Rose looked at her watch, stood up like she was Cinderella gone way past her curfew, announcing she had to go. Wouldn't even let me drive her home, *insisting* she got a taxi.

She was definitely bewitching, and then we spent night after night together after that.

I fell. I cannot lie, I was well and truly besotted with Rose. I'd never met anyone like her, and I used to fantasise bedding her, and I tried my hardest, but she dangled me on a string for ages! My mate, Stuart, was a lot luckier with her sister, Suzanne, when we all paired up! Sometimes he'd turn up really late for work, hungover and shackered!!! At it all night, that pair! Lucky bar-steward. I thought perhaps I'd made a big mistake with my choice of sisters, picked the wrong one, never getting any further than a fumbled grope! Fair play to Stuart, he never bragged, only to me!

Neither Stuart nor I were invited into their house for ages though, it was almost like it was taboo, a secret, so I'll leave it to your imagination where their sex took place! But then one night, totally out of the blue, Suzanne sent me a text message to tell me that she had 'dumped' my mate, Stuart.

We all had each other's numbers because we had become a foursome, so it wasn't unusual to receive a text from Sue. However, the content confused me. I was just reading it when Stu sent me a text, telling me he had been given the big Spanish Archer (*el bow!*)

I was as gobsmacked as poor old Stu was gutted! Rose hadn't given a hint that she knew anything was – what you'd call – not working out. And Suzanne further rubbed salt into the wound by saying she was going over to Spain for the unforeseeable future, needing "time out" to *find* herself. Bullshit by the bucket load if you ask me - but nobody ever did ask me!

I felt sorry for my mate 'cos it was me who'd introduced the two of 'em. Imagine how I felt when he told me he'd been text-dumped! That is so emasculating, so bloody cruel and unnecessary. She should have told him to his face, Stuart was a decent guy. And that's when I decided I really didn't like Suzanne anymore and was glad I'd fallen in love in with the nicer sister, Rose. Those two were like chalk and cheese, and I was glad when she went away. It wasn't my Rose who was the weirdo, it was the other one!

Strange though, 'cos she didn't go to Spain, like she told Stuart - she went to London!

Chapter 14: Suzanne

When Suzanne came to, she was disorientated for a minute or two. She was sitting on her friend's settee in her living room with the mother of all headaches. She reached up to her throbbing nose and was horrified to find her hand covered in blood. A huge, fearful brute of man walked in holding a glass of water. He was tall, over six feet if she calculated correctly. His whole demeanour portrayed "thug" without a shadow of a doubt. His navy joggers had seen better days and his tee-shirt was covered in blood. What little hair he had was scraped back into a greasy ponytail, and he sported at least a week's worth of stubble.

"Here," he announced gruffly, shoving the glass of water in front of her. "Where is she?"

Suzanne looked around the living room, trying to see if her friend was hiding. She stood up in panic and then felt the brute's massive hands push her back down.

"I said 'where is she'?" he boomed loudly.

In that split second Suzanne recognised the man and her stomach recoiled. She was scared and had every reason to be.

"Garth!" she whispered. Saying his name out loud would have been too intimate, too familiar. "Where's Corah? What have you done?"

"I'm asking YOU the questions!" he bellowed.

"The blood on your shirt. Garth, what have you done to Corah? CORAH! Corah, where are you? Call the police!"

She felt another blow to the side of her head which sent her sprawling the whole length of the sofa. She could see the contents of her handbag emptied on the coffee table in front of her. Her suitcase was opened and all her underwear on display. She knew that Garth would have done what men do, as it was obvious with how all her clothes had been placed. She wanted to die from embarrassment. Garth was a pig – *and that was being derogatory to pigs* – he was scum. Shame, he hadn't always been.

"Garth. Where is Corah?"

"That's what I would like *you* to tell *me!*" he answered, sarcastically. "What brings you back down to the 'smoke'?

Did she ask you to come and do a bit more damage, a bit of 'for old time's sake', hey?"

Suzanne stared at him, fearful of upsetting him with any answer she had to give. She remembered his tolerance level, or lack of. She'd borne his wrath before and that's why she'd had the tattoos, to cover the scars!

"I've come down for my work, Garth, and that's why I got in touch with Corah to ask if I could touch base with her again, but no, not to do damage. Just to catch up, like I said."

"Ha," he howled. "You? Not do damage? Just by breathing *you* do damage," and he spat his venom right up close to her face.

She was determined not to break eye contact. She wanted him to think she was no longer afraid of him, even though she was! He could physically do her a lot of damage, she knew that only too well. He was out for revenge by the sounds of things, and Corah wasn't there to help. Her heart was beating ten to the dozen. Garth had neither patience nor tolerance and if Corah wasn't at her house at the time she said she'd be, why not? Where the hell was she?

"I expected Corah to greet me at her front door, not your fist. If I had known you were out, I wouldn't have bothered coming down here."

"Just what you deserved. She'll get some of the same when she decides to show her face. I can wait. I'm used to sitting and waiting patiently."

The hours ticked on and Corah didn't show up. The clock showed it was seven thirty. By now she had anticipated the pair of them would be getting ready, dolled up to go out on the town, visit a few fancy bars, try a nightclub, but her friend hadn't returned home.

"Let me call her," Suzanne suggested.

The thug was sitting in one of the big armchairs, just staring at her. "So that you can warn her?" he smirked, looking through some photographs that he'd found in her handbag. He held one out to show her, "your daughter?" he asked, turning it over and seeing Margot's name on the back. "Poor thing. Bit of a nutter like her mother, is she?" he laughed.

"Yes, she is. She is a nutter just like her mother," she answered.

Just then, they heard the sound of a key unlocking the front door and whilst Suzanne panicked, knowing what Garth was capable of doing to Corah, he beamed his triumphant smile.

"It's like a friends' reunion," and he leapt up off the chair and went to greet her.

Corah stood stock still in the doorway, then two police officers from behind, moved in front of her and Garth's sarcastic grin was instantly replaced with a look of cold shock.

"Mr. Payne?" enquired one of the officers, "I believe you've broken the terms of your parole, again. Be a nice boy and come along with us. Let's leave these lovely ladies alone where you won't do anything you'll live to regret."

"Lovely ladies?" Garth scoffed viciously, "two words that don't apply in this room!"

Suzanne was trembling; she wasn't sure if it was from relief or the fear she'd had. Discretely, she checked her knickers to be sure she hadn't wee'd herself. As Garth was led away by the police officers, the two friends fell into each other's arms, laughing, crying, both trying to talk at once.

Corah broke away first and darted for the bottle of gin she had in her cupboard in readiness for their reunion. They both had a very large and very-much-needed glass, and Corah began answering her friend's questions: how did she know he was there? Why was he there? When had he been let out?

"Payne by name, pain by nature" she laughed. "I was just coming back from the shop, I knew we'd need a bottle of plonk to have before we went out, and just as I turned into the street, I clocked him looking through my window. I had no doubt he would find a way to break in. Old habits die hard, hey? So I went straight to the Old Bill. I was terrified we wouldn't get here before you, but they had to do all their checks before they would come with me. That's when they ascertained he'd broken his parole. Oh, Sue, what a horrible experience for you! I bet you wish you hadn't come!"

"No, no, don't say that Corah, I'm glad I was here and that you were out! I shudder to think of what he would've done if you had been here alone. You must leave, Corah. Get away, leave London."

Corah nodded, "I know, and that's what I intend doing," she replied. "I'm going to move away from this place," she said, glancing around her living room then reached out to the gin and poured themselves another. It seemed as if 'going out' had now lost all its appeal. They were settling for a night of reminiscing, a bottle of Gordon's, and a take-away.

"I'm going to take a leaf out of one of your books," she laughed at her quip "and move to somewhere totally different. I might stick a pin on the map of Great Britain and see where destiny takes me."

"You know," Suzanne reflected despondently, "he wasn't always a bad guy. I remember when he was a sweetheart, before the drugs."

Corah stared into her glass of gin and tonic, nodding. "Hmm, you and me both. I feel sorry for him, he's been in and out of prison for years now, and we both know why he started doing the drugs."

Suzanne shrugged, "Chinese or Indian?" That part of the conversation was over as far as she was concerned and started to put all the contents of her handbag - that were strewn over the coffee table - back inside.

Corah picked up the photograph of Margot, her cigarettes and lighter. "This little girl," she enquired, "she is beautiful, who is she?"

"My niece, Margot. My sister, Rose's, daughter. Do you mind awfully if I smoke?"

"Not at all, I'll Join you. After this evening's shenanigans I don't think any holds are barred. Give me one."

Later, as Suzanne lay in the single bed in her friend's spare room, her head buzzing from the amount of alcohol she'd consumed, the memories came flooding back. The room started spinning and she lay on her back trying, unsuccessfully, not to throw up. At that moment she couldn't have given a damn that she'd just spewed her guts up over her friend's cream carpet, she couldn't have made it to the bathroom if she'd had an ounce of 'care' in her body!

Guilt is another powerful emotion. Hate, guilt, love, regret. They all counted in her make-up, along with secrecy and revenge, of which she had an abundance.

She lay there, trying to erase such thoughts from her spinning mind but the demons wouldn't go away. They taunted and ridiculed her, reminding her that her past was still as ever-present as the day she left London.

Poor old, sweet Garth, he hadn't deserved her. She wondered if the young, spotty teenaged Aaron who'd been at the bookstore yesterday, had read between her lines and sussed that 'Finding the Negative' was personal. That encounter had unnerved her slightly. Her writings invariably included personal stuff but she always tried to camouflage reality under an umbrella of make-believe, never thinking – for a moment – that anyone would take the time to analyse it! The kid seemed to have a knowing expression on his face, he even remarked he would message her via her website!

It was her fault that Garth was the way he was. And it was her and Corah's fault that he'd been banged up!

She heard the sound of retching coming from the bathroom, next door to where she lay awake, glad it wasn't only her that their alcohol consumption had affected.

She forced herself out of her bed to go to her friend's aid, then took a step back from the bathroom as Corah vomited repeatedly down the toilet, the smell making her feel even more queasy!

"Black coffee," she mumbled. "I'll go downstairs and make us some coffee."

She filled the kettle and switched it on, picking up the empty bottle of Gordon's in disbelief that it was all gone, before noticing yet another empty bottle of Chardonnay. She cringed, forgetting that they'd had wine, too! Mixing drinks was never a good idea and now they were both suffering. She checked her phone next, praying they'd not been stupid enough to start texting or even, heaven forbid, facetiming old friends. They hadn't, but there was a text from Rose, letting her know that Margot wanted to wish her well with her book launch.

Even in her after-drink stupor, she knew that Rose was just being Rose. Maintaining contact, even if it was on the pretence on behalf of Margot.

If only she could turn all the clocks back, but of course that was impossible. She could never remove that bridge, the walls, the façade. It's like words; once spoken or written, they're there for ever, stored in the memory bank of life, more painful than a wound.

Rose. The perfect English Rose! The wonderful, adoring, doting sister, Rose! Her, with her perfect marriage, her perfect husband, her perfect life. But then she felt that feeling again, guilt. Guilt, because Rose *hadn't* got the perfect everything, had she? She may indeed feel she had the 'perfect' husband, but she hadn't got the 'perfect family' had she? Rose herself wasn't perfect!

"Don't put any sugar in mine," said Corah, hoarsely, as she slumped into a chair at the kitchen table. The pair of them had smoked three packets of menthol cigarettes between them and Corah was feeling the effect. Suzanne was a bit miffed as fags were not cheap, disregarding the fact that it was Corah who had paid for their gin, etc!

Suzanne shoved a mug of coffee towards her. They both sat in silence for a few minutes, neither of them wanting to raise the subject they had both neglected to address earlier.

"He only came to me because of what you did to him," Corah eventually admitted while trying to sip at her scalding-hot coffee. She hiccupped.

"Corah, it's history, it's past," Suzanne answered, laughing as Corah constantly hiccupped.

"Is there any more o' that wine left?" asked a bleary-eyed Corah, still hiccupping.

They erupted into fits of laughter, and the more they laughed, the more Corah hiccupped. This was so reminiscent of the nights they spent together, the times they got plastered into oblivion and had a job remembering what they'd actually done!

They sat together with their mugs of coffee, howling with laughter at nothing, other than the fact that this is how they always ended up after a night of debauchery! It felt good, it felt like being young again.

"But I did really like Garth, Corah. He was sweet..."

"Yeah, you keep saying. So sweet that you wanted to break him."

Suzanne gasped at her friend's harsh truth. "And break him, you did. Can you blame him, Sue? I loved him, always did, but I was never *you*. And every time he came to me for comfort then went back to you, I hated you! Sorry for the harsh reality check here but you know it's the truth. Garth would never have taken drugs if you hadn't encouraged him to. Those scars you've tried to cover with those flowery tattoos are gonna fade as slowly as your memories, his too. But hey, like you say... it's history. You and I have to live with what we did to that man, and I know he deserved to go to prison for what he did, but Suzanne... we have to take our share of the blame."

The silence was profound. They sipped at their coffees not daring to delve any deeper. It was a mistake, thought Suzanne, coming back to a place she'd tried to forget. She'd leave immediately and would break all ties with Corah. She had a different life now, a successful career and the last thing she needed was ghosts of her past coming to haunt her. Guilt can be a painful curse, especially when hearing the truth.

She put her empty mug in the sink and went back to her bedroom. She packed everything back into her suitcase and waited until she heard Corah walk back upstairs and close her bedroom door. She tiptoed down the stairs, opened the front door, and left. She walked out of Consort Road in the early hours of the morning, the mist clouding like halos around the streetlamps, not giving a damn how rough she looked, and hailed an approaching taxi.

Chapter 15: Aaron, the Spotty Teenager

He left the bookstore with his new book in his hands. He loved books, all books of all genres and was a regular visitor to the local library in Brighton *and* the bookstore. He was in possession of another signed copy and was feeling chuffed with himself, it was an addition to his collection, and this one was extra special!

He didn't have friends, not in the physical context anyway, all his friends were in the books he owned, of which he had hundreds. He would lose himself in the mystery and magic of words and make-believe. He would analyse them all, dissecting every chapter, every character, cross-referencing dates, statistics, questioning this and disputing that.

If an author had written about a battle being on Sunday, 5th of whenever, he would know if that was correct or not and would rejoice in finding such an anomaly because that gave him the blissful opportunity of being able to write to said author – via their website - and notifying them thus. The feeling was orgasmic!

He was fourteen, he had teenage spots – not acne, just 'spotty' through, basically, lack of a bit of soap and water! Aaron had better things to do with this time than wash and look after his appearance. He didn't care, and he had no one to care whether he did or not.

He was a bit of a freak, so he was thought, but he didn't even *care* what his peers thought of him. His author friends appreciated him, thanked him for his support, his input, and his scrutiny. He was *valued* in the literary world of writers and one day he was going to write his very own book. It would be perfect, too; flawless, faultless and a best-seller, might even be made into a film. He kept a notebook - right next to his PC - where he made lists and notes of all the hundreds of errors he'd encountered in the books he had read, the emails he'd sent and the replies he received. It was his bible and his most prized possession.

He didn't want to read his new book just yet; it was too new and smelt too fresh. His collection of signed books was to be savoured for just the right moment, almost like anticipating Christmas, seeing all the wonderful, gift-wrapped parcels underneath a decorated tree and having to wait until after breakfast to open them all. That build-up of excitement and wonder, and that was enough, that euphoric anticipation of what's inside.

Not that Aaron's experience about the 'wonderful, gift-wrapped parcels under a decorated tree' had ever been a reality, it was only what he'd read about in his books.

He looked at the cover of *In Sickness, Not In Health* and ran his fingers over the author's name – Suzanne Barsby. He opened it to read the words she written especially for him, smiled, then placed it on his bookshelf along with all her others.

Chapter 16: A Growing Family

Rose was getting bigger and bigger, and the baby was due in just another six weeks. They were having a girl, a fact which was a relief as a boy would have been too much to bear. Margot had still not shown any sign of acceptance of the new baby, and she distanced herself further from her brother and her parents.

It hadn't helped with Suzanne being away for such a long time and even when she did return, she didn't resume their weekend stayovers immediately. She'd sent Rose a text to say she was 'busy' and when she had time, she'd send for her. Always the elusive, was Suzanne.

It was early August, and the weather was getting hotter by the day, Rose was finding it difficult to cope with. She was wearing bigger, baggier, looser clothing but still she sweat bucketloads. Her little garden was suffering from lack of water because she was too mithered to do anything about it. How she used to wish they lived in a house that had a swimming pool. She and Doug would lie in bed sometimes and dream about when they retired and the kids had flown the nest, the pair of them would buy a little 'place in the sun' somewhere where they could have lots of fruit trees and a big swimming pool!

She'd bookmarked some pretty cottages in Italy she found on the internet, feeding her imagination, and there were many! Enough bedrooms for the kids to come to visit for however long, *with* grandchildren! And a pool was an absolute must-have. She'd been trying to persuade Doug to take another trip back there, to Italy, to get a better feel for the place, and plant the seed.

Doug humoured her with as much enthusiasm as he could muster. Rose had big ideas, too big, it was going to be years before they could even *think* about retiring.

He did like her idea of getting a pool, though, a small one that could be dismantled during the winter and stored away in the garage. It wouldn't take a lot of maintenance and it would be great for the children; the neighbours would be green with envy! In fact, he had already decided to get one, but was keeping it as a surprise.

A work colleague of his was taking a very early retirement after bagging himself a nice little win on the lottery. He told no one exactly how much he *had* won, but he'd given in his weeks' notice at the factory and was heading off to do exactly what Rose had been dreaming about for years – the sun! George was only fifty and his son, Kieran, was twenty-eight. They were leaving Blighty to go and live in Portugal where they planned to find a nice plot of land – preferably near a river – where they could hold reggae nights, jamming sessions, holistic weekends, and as such he was selling his house, its contents, his Honda Goldwing, the lot!

He hadn't been surprised that Kieran wanted to join him in his venture as after his mother walked out on them when Kieran was diagnosed with special needs at the tender age of three, George had been his staff and his safety net.

Anyway, George had a pool, the type that dismantled. He'd bought it for Kieran years ago to help with his mobility skills and now it was going to be Doug's and he was collecting it on Friday evening when George was anticipating an influx of potential buyers round his house, hopefully getting rid of the entire lot. What didn't sell was going to be dumped outside the charity shops!

Doug and Rose spent the entire Saturday and Sunday morning trying to erect the pool without the joy of instructions that George had lost years ago. They'd tried to print some off from the internet but even so, it was causing disagreements and raised voices. Temperatures were accelerating every which way, to the point where Rose stormed off indoors to cool down, leaving Mr. Know-it-all to do it 'his' way!

She was actually thrilled to bits when he came home from work with swimming pool parts hanging out of every window in the car, the boot, the roof rack, the seats, eager to get it in situ so they could all get in and enjoy it.

They decided it would go right in the corner, just outside the back door where it was out of the way yet easily accessible – for now - to water and electricity. The lawn would benefit from the backwashes and rinses too, as the waste would just pour out on the garden, rather than simply going down the drain. Hopefully, they could get a barbecue in before Doug returned to work, and Margot, school.

She would have to go out and buy some inflatables for the children to play with, a pool-noodle, arm bands for Simon, and a new bathing costume for Margot, then gasped in horror as she realised she hadn't got anything decent for herself. No way was she going to wear a bikini, she'd look like a bloomin' beached whale! She'd have to make do with a large tee-shirt to cover her huge bump.

By late Sunday afternoon it was ready to be filled and it was obvious that it was going to take many hours, and their forthcoming water bills were going to be horrendous!

"Margot, I don't want you or Simon going in unless me or Dad is here with you. Do you understand?" she'd instructed.

The next weekend...

Both Rose and Doug had been monitoring the weather forecast all week, praying it was going to remain hot and sunny so that they could make-believe they were in their little Italian retirement villa – with a pool – and make a weekend full of glorious memories. She bought Margot a divine costume trimmed with big purple flowers, arm bands for Simon, a blow-up flamingo to sit in, and a pool-noodle. She'd bought sausages and chicken drumsticks for the barbecue, salad, and crusty bread.

It had taken almost the whole week for the pool to fill but it looked fabulous, crystal-clear, and they both agreed it was money well spent. She'd dressed the children in readiness for their initiation and Doug had taken photograph after photograph.

It was blissfully refreshing, the coolness of the water after the heat of the sun, and Rose had to keep reapplying sunscreen to ensure the children didn't get burnt.

Doug had had the barbecue going for a while, the embers were settled enough to start cooking and he placed the pre-cooked chicken on the rack along with the sausages. The table was already out on the lawn, along with the crockery and cutlery.

Everyone was happy. It was what the weekends were all about, spending quality family time together. It didn't matter that the kitchen floor was swimming in the water that had dripped from Margot's swimwear as she went backwards and forwards, inside and out, and it didn't matter that Doug's beer had lost its fizz while he was turning everything over on the barbecue – oh, hang on, it did!

"Rose," he shouted while she had gone inside to fetch the bowl of salad to bring to the table, "get me another cold one from the fridge, this one's gone warm," and he emptied the remnants of the bottle into a plant pot.

Rose walked back with the bowl of salad and a bottle of cold beer, as requested, and skidded on a little pool of water, right at the foot of the steps of the patio. The bowl of salad flew into the air, the beer still in her hand, whilst she went crashing flat on her enormous belly, her legs in mid-air, behind.

She screamed the loudest scream imaginable, and every eye turned towards her. Doug took a split second to register what had happened; barbecue utensils in his hands, he ran over to his wife who was wailing in agony. His instinct was to get her back up on her feet but she couldn't move, her pain indescribable.

"Doug," she screeched, "the baby, get an ambulance. Quickly!!!"

Simon walked tentatively over to where his mother lay, writhing in pain, "Mummy's bleeding" he said softly.

It was an horrific scenario. Doug's clumsy fingers were clammy as he frantically tried to call 999 whilst trying to keep Simon away from Rose, at the same time desperately trying to console and offer support to her, while his daughter continued to play unheeded in the little swimming pool that had only minutes earlier been the hive of fun and laughter.

Rose was still prostrate when the paramedics arrived, ten whole agonising minutes later, her legs pooled in her own blood, her screams reduced to pitiful moans, her will for her children not to witness what was happening as negligible as her need to mop the floor from their dripping swimwear. "*Next time*," she told herself, unbelievably she found herself thinking of the next time, she'd "*put a towel down, a mat...*"

The medics hoisted Rose onto a stretcher and loaded her into the waiting ambulance. Doug climbed in too, not giving a second thought to Margot or Simon as the ambulance doors closed, and they sped away under the piercing urgency of the flashing blue lights.

"Are you hungry, Simon?" Margot asked her brother who stood looking very bewildered at the now absent scene of parents and ambulance crew, "do you want a sausage?"

He walked over to join her at the barbecue. Everything smelled delicious, everything looked good. "Sausage, please," he replied, a little half-heartedly. "Cut it for me and put it on my plate."

"Suzanne, it's me, Doug. Look, I'm sorry to do this to you but Rose has had an accident, we're at the hospital, and I was in such a panic I didn't think about Margot or Simon! They're on their own and you need to go over and be with them. We've just had the bloody pool installed and I'm worried sick that something else might happen. Yeah, I know that Margot's old enough to know better, but please Sue, please go over and be there for them until one of us gets back. I don't know if Rose's fall has damaged the baby somehow, God, I don't know shit, Sue, but please, be there for our kids!"

Suzanne listened to her voicemail message and pressed replay at least half a dozen times . . . *'please, be there for our kids'*.

Oh yes, it suited him now to need her, didn't it? Good old *'Aunty Sue'* to the rescue whenever the need arose, whenever they needed a babysitter, a lifeline! Well, too bad; she had a life too! She was busy right now, writing. She'd condescend going over when it suited *her*, not him!

She sent a text message in reply. *"Will do. Collect them from my place later. Hope everything's ok with sis and babe."* She poured herself a glass of wine and sparked up a cigarette, pondering Doug's frantic message, wondering why he didn't think of the easier and more obvious option, to ask their next-door neighbour to look after them!

When she eventually arrived at her sister and brother-in-law's house, she was surprised to hear loud music blasting away from inside, familiar music that she remembered from one of Margot's many DVDs. She walked round the back and let herself in, noticing the newly installed swimming pool, the remnants of the barbecue, the table with crockery and cutlery - a replicated scenario of the Marie Celeste - the bloodied patio, and she approached with a sense of foreboding, trying to recall the last time she'd actually been inside her sister's house!

"Margot!" she shouted, "hey, Angel, are you there?"

"Aunty Sue! Aunty Sue . . ." she squealed over and over as she came thundering down the staircase towards her. "Oh, Aunty Sue, I've missed you SO much!" She wrapped her arms around Suzanne's waist and held on tightly. This was what being a 'best aunt' was all about. The joy of having one's niece proclaim such love.

"Where's Simon? You're to come with me until your mum's better. She's had a little accident and your dad has asked me to take you both to my house and he'll pick you up later. Where is he?"

She shrugged her shoulders dismissively and started to run outside to where she knew Suzanne's car would be parked.

Suzanne shouted out to her nephew whom she'd had minimal contact with but received no reply. She ascended the stairs and peered intrepidly into her sister's bedroom, cautiously venturing inside, taking everything in. She smirked at her bedcover that matched the rose floral curtains, remembering them on their parents' bed, amazed she still had them and what great condition they were still in. She felt guilty trespassing into their intimate quarters, inhaling the perfume her sister always used – Agua Di by

Giorgio Armani — it smelt fresh and cool, sweet but not overpowering. They'd both loved it.

"Simon!" she called out again. Where on earth was he? Boys! Who'd have 'em?

She looked inside the bathroom and noticed nothing other than Rose's meticulous OCD. The towels placed strategically, the toothbrushes in the holder, the sink and taps shone without a trace of spit or toothpaste! Nothing at all like her bathroom!

"Margot," she yelled outside after coming downstairs, "where's Simon?"

A friendly face appeared over the garden fence, "Helloooo, are you looking for young Simon?" she asked Suzanne. "Don't worry, he's here, with us. We rushed round as soon as we heard the commotion, but they'd left in the ambulance before we got there. Here he is, look," she raised Simon up so that Suzanne could see he was ok. "I'll pop round. Hang on a tick."

Seconds later, a jolly Deb appeared with Simon in her arms. Her facing was beaming as though the boy was her very own. "We heard such screams coming from here and then the ambulance came and was gone in seconds. When we realised the kiddies were on their own, I came straight over." Her face distorted as she relayed the next bit of information, "Simon, here, was choking. He had some sausage in his mouth," she tenderly touched his face as she spoke, "his face was going blue, it was a whole sausage there and he couldn't chew it. Greedy little monkey, hey?" she joked, not for an instant did she think that Simon had stuffed a whole sausage into his mouth!

"I'm Suzanne, Rose's sister, Margot's aunt. Doug's messaged me to ask me to take them both to mine until he knows what's what." (*'Margot's aunt', Deb noted, not 'Margot and Simon's aunt'.*)

"I know," replied Deb, "I remember you, and I'm the neighbour that looked after this lovely little fella when poor old Steven had his accident," she replied, placing Simon down on the ground. "I'm more than happy to look after him again until they get home. If you would like us to, I mean. Alec and I love the little chappie, he's a joy and I'm sure your sister would have no hesitation leaving him with us, but of course I understand if you feel the need to take them both. They are your family, after all."

Suzanne hated the thought of taking Simon as well as Margot. She had had little to no interaction with him, nor with Steven. It would be a whole lot more favourable with just Margot!

"You are a godsend, Deb. Thank you, yes, I'm sure my sister and brother-in-law would be much happier with that arrangement. Look – here's my number, I'll keep you informed." She handed Deb her business card from several she had loose in her bag and walked away to where her niece sat waiting in the car.

"Aunty Sue, come on! Let's go to your house. What took you so long?"

Suzanne sat in the driver's seat of her black, expensive BMW, delaying turning the key to the ignition. "Why didn't you tell me that Simon was with the neighbour? She told me he was choking on a sausage, who gave him a whole sausage, Margot?"

Margot turned towards her aunt, giving her the innocent look, "I don't know, do I? He must have got it himself from off the barbecue. Can we watch Frozen again tonight and then you can tell me all about your holiday?"

"Sue, can I call u? Rose has lost the baby. I need 2 spk 2 u 2 know if Marg and Sim R ok."

She looked at the message on her phone, knowing that she should feel some sympathy. She didn't. She was watching Frozen again for the umpteenth time, wrapped under the duvet on the settee with her niece who was never bored with the repetition that was showing on the screen. *She* was bored though, having watched the damn film over and over, knew every song and every word of the damn script.

She should answer her brother-in-law's message, tell him that yes, he could call her, to reassure him that his children were ok, they were safe. But she didn't. She couldn't be arsed!

Chapter 17: Deb, Alec, and Simon

"Katy, you'll never guess what happened next door!" Deb was on the phone to her daughter for their weekend catch ups. "There's been another awful accident. Poor Rose is at the hospital now, and your dad and I are looking after young Simon – the little love. Margot has gone to that sister of Rose's, you know the one I mean, the one who writes those books."

Katy was eager to hear more, and her mother was just as eager to impart all she knew. "Your dad and I heard such a palaver and thought something dire was happening, somebody being murdered! It was Rose, seems she slipped on some water on the patio and anyway they're at the hospital now, and your dad and I are looking after Simon until they come back."

"And I can tell by the enthusiasm in your voice that you're over the moon, Mum," Katy chuckled. She knew how much her parents couldn't wait to become grandparents. Babysitting Simon, no matter the circumstances, was a blessing for her mother.

"He's a joy, I tell you, Love, an absolute joy, and as good as gold. He's looking a right Bobby Dazzler, too, now that he has a bit of a suntan. We're only too happy we didn't have that little madam to look after. I know I shouldn't speak badly of a child but there is just something about the girl that I do not like. She's a strange one but I can't put my finger on exactly what I find distrustful about her."

"Mum, you should pity her, she's only recently lost her little brother. She will seem odd, the poor girl's too young to understand, isn't she? I remember vividly when Tim was rushed to the hospital with appendicitis that time, I was really confused. You and Dad making all those trips to the hospital, taking him comics, fruit, and cards. I wished that I could have had an appendicitis too, so that I could have all that attention, all those good things that he was being treated to."

Her mother laughed out loud, "and when he had his hernia operation and was taking the Calpol and you asked to have some as well, and Tim said, 'you can't have any Calpol because you don't have a hernia!'"

"You see, Mum? I'm sure she's just been feeling a little left out. It was just her until the twins arrived. Crikey, that's understandable, she was old enough to realise. And Rose had two babies to see to as well as look after Margot, making sure she was included in everything. Poor Rose, I say! Poor Rose *and* Doug to have lost little Steven that way. And now you say she's had an accident herself and is at the hospital?"

"Yes," Deb answered soulfully, "and her baby's due in a few weeks' time. Oh, Katy, it will be dreadful if she loses this baby! They don't deserve all this bad luck."

*   *   *   *   *

"*Okay, u can call.*" Suzanne sent the text message, and within seconds her phone rang.

"Suzanne, I'm sorry," he choked on his words, "I'm, err, sorry to have to ask you but could you keep them until I can sort myself out?"

She actually felt sorry for him, his voice was faltering with emotion, "she's in a bad way, a *real* bad way. I don't feel like going through all the details right now, but we lost our little girl." He started to sob, silently, "Sue, it's breaking my heart! It's all my fault. It's all my bloody stupid fault."

Margot sat on the sofa, laughing at the scene on the TV, wrapped up in a duvet sitting next to her aunt, oblivious and uncaring.

"What is?" she asked her brother-in-law, earnestly, "what's your fault?"

"The pool! I wish I'd never bought the damn thing! I thought it was going to be a treat, for the kids. For all of us. I wanted us to create some memories. Sue, I took loads of photos and now I wish to God I hadn't. I don't want to see the photos I took; I wish I could turn the clock back."

Oooh, didn't everyone? How many people walking this planet – or all the centuries before - had said the exact same thing? Freeze-frame, pause, rewind. No such luxury, no matter your status, your bank balance, your notoriety. Time, nor history, can ever be erased. A hair's breadth, that's what it boiled down to, a miniscule of a second that could change every single thing. Tipping the balance between life or death, good or bad, happiness or regret.

She regained her composure, "Simon's with your neighbour. I've got Margot here with me. She's fine."

"Ok, yeah, ok. That's ok." He was mumbling. "I'll call Alec, make sure they're happy to have him until I get back…"

He broke down sobbing, which tugged at Suzanne's heartstrings a little. "Sue… " he was blubbering like a baby now, "Sue… " she heard him blow his snotty nose into what she hoped was a handkerchief and waited for his next words. "I gotta go. Give Margot a big kiss from me, tell her we love her and that we'll see her soon. Thanks." And with that he finished the call.

She rose from the sofa to call her sister's neighbour, Deb. Her brother-in-law's pitiful sadness unsettled her as she pictured him making the phone call from some quiet place within the hospital, checking up on his children whom he had failed to consider in those extreme minutes, his primary concern being that of his lover, his soulmate, his wife.

They'd certainly had more than their fair share of knockbacks. Two children they'd lost. Two! It was unimaginable having to bury one child and now they'd lost their unborn daughter, and Suzanne hadn't even bothered to ask about her one and only sister. The one who had held her before her own parents had the chance, thrilled she had a baby sister. The one who brought her the melting ice-cream cone while she'd been playing with her friend.

The very same doting sister who held her hand when the policemen sat them down to deliver the news of their parents' fateful accident just before Christmas, and who packed away all the unwrapped presents from under the tree and stuffed them in the attic because Christmas would never be the same ever again. The sister she had adored and looked up to her whole life until she discovered the secret she would never have known until she found those negatives, photographs, newspaper cuttings etc hidden under the floorboards of her father's garden shed when they were clearing out the house ready to sell. The Tupperware container that she was never meant to have found or known about, where inside was a photograph with a childish scribble across the image. . . 'I hate Steven'.

Chapter 18: Rose's homecoming

It didn't feel like home anymore. Home was supposed to be a refuge, salvation, a safety net. It was where you *lived*, where you grew, where you could close the doors and curtains from the outside world and breathe. You were supposed to be able to curl up under that blissful comfort of your own four walls and carry out your charade of normality, whatever normality was supposed to be.

Rose didn't feel anything normal anymore. Her grief was too raw, too intense, painful, and unfair. When she first arrived back, she wanted nothing more than to envelope herself in her children, demanding Doug bring them both to her. She needed to see they were alive and well, needing to smell and feel them but Doug wasn't sure the time was right, feeling she needed to have some space to convalesce.

Men have no clue about the maternal needs of a woman, they are so different in every way. Here he was thinking they could have a quiet, relaxing evening spent over a bottle of expensive sparkling wine to take away her pain and make her feel better! What planet was he on? His answer of the perfect get-over-it-quick was a kids-free night, a cheap take-away and an expensive bottle of bubbly, cuddled up on the settee! The fool!

She hadn't the wherewithal to express her disappointment. She needed to see her children; she couldn't bear to watch her husband's enthusiasm over his effort to appease her. Her appetite for life was diminishing as rapidly as her tolerance for his lack of understanding.

She walked out of the front door and knocked at her neighbours'. Alec stood in the threshold in his pyjama bottoms and tee-shirt and ushered her quickly inside, closing the door behind them.

"Deb, Rose is here, Love. I'm sure she's come for Simon. Come on in Rose, your little lad's here, as good as gold."

Rose neither acknowledged him nor moved from where she stood. She looked, to all intents and purposes, like she'd forgotten why she was even there. She appeared as broken, fragile, and insignificant as a fine Edwardian wineglass that, since ancient times, had been thrown into fireplaces when alcoholic beverages were considered sacred and a gift from the gods.

Deb rose from her settee and walked towards to her, hugging her with the utmost genuine sympathy she felt. "He's asleep upstairs, Rose dear. Shall we go upstairs so you can see him?" She didn't answer, merely glancing upwards and started to ascend purposefully, with Deb following behind.

She peered into the bedroom where Simon was sleeping, the door open – Deb leaving it that way, not wanting Simon to feel shut in in an unfamiliar environment. Rose tilted her head from left to right, looking confused at her son as he slept in the bed of her neighbour. "Steven," she whispered.

"No, Rose. It's Simon," Deb corrected her, sympathetically. "Look, come and see."

"Where's Steven?" she asked, searching Deb's agonising stare.

Deb felt dreadful. The poor woman. What IS she going through? She didn't know how to answer her. She looked so pathetic, and whatever answer she was going to give was going to cause her more pain.

"Rose, Love. Simon can stay here with Alec and me tonight and he'll be as right as rain. Don't you worry. I'll bring him back in the morning, you go home now and try to get some sleep, we're happy to look after the little fella for as long as you need us to. Your sister telephoned me to tell me that she's looking after Margot so you've nothing to worry about."

"Nothing to worry about," Rose echoed, mechanically. "Nothing to worry about."

She turned to walk back down the stairs and stopped midway, turning to her neighbour "I just wanted my sister."

Deb patronised her, "I'll call her, ask her to come over. Would you like me to do that? I can ask her to bring Margot, too."

Rose ignored her and continued her descent down the staircase, opened the door and strode outside, leaving Deb leaning on the door jamb watching her departure, wondering whether to call Suzanne or leave it until the morning. She decided on the latter, it was late.

Doug couldn't sleep. It was hot, he was sweating, kept pushing the bedclothes off in an endeavour to cool down. He was restless, bewildered, sad, angry. Rose wasn't the only one who was suffering the loss of their unborn daughter, he was devastated too. He had been elated at hearing the news of Rose's pregnancy and that they were expecting another daughter, a sister for Margot and Simon. Nothing was ever going to replace their precious Steven, but another baby was another life and another reason to rejoice. He had secretly wanted to name the new baby Stephanie, in memory of their lost son, but Rose had other ideas. It was going to be Grace, their 'Saving Grace', but now plans for their little Grace - who didn't even get a chance to draw her first breath - were already underway for her interment, alongside her brother.

He looked over to his wife who lay beside him and noticed her eyes open, "Rose, how are you feeling?"

She wanted to murder him! It had been the most inane question anyone could ask of her! How could anyone in their right mind, *think* of uttering those stupid words? *'How was she feeling'*? She didn't reply, his question unworthy of a civil answer. He was stupid. Stupid, stupid, stupid!!

*   *   *   *   *

Suzanne felt guilty. It had been three days now since Rose had returned home after her dreadful accident and she felt she should at least take Margot home or offer to keep her for longer. She was torn, not sure of what was the best thing to do. Doug hadn't been much help either, leaving everything in her court. She'd telephoned the neighbour to ask where Simon was, if he'd been returned. He hadn't, he was still with her and Alec, Rose seemingly sinking into a deep depression.

Grace's funeral was scheduled to take place in two weeks' time, they were burying two of their children in less than eighteen months. Eighteen months!

The swimming pool sat there, the water now green and stagnant - a haunting reminder of those few hours of happiness that summer's afternoon. The blood-stained patio that Doug had tried scrubbing was, thankfully, fading in the autumn sun. But memories could never be scrubbed away as easily as that, erased by the harsh cleansing ingredients of a bottle of bleach... If only!

Rose wanted out. She didn't want to go back to living her life as it was. She wanted a brand-new start away from everything that hurt, away from the house or horrors, the memories, the country, the past. She was going to give

Doug an ultimatum. She was going to live in Italy, with or without him!

Chapter 19: Gossip

It was supposed to be her labour day, her *birth* day, Grace's due date. But it wasn't, it was yet another cruel reminder of what she had lost – again, what they had lost as a family. Doug also had another child to mourn, Margot and Simon a sister, Suzanne another niece. What had she done to deserve this never-ending, excruciating torture? Was she being punished by a higher entity for something?

Everybody has their fair share of hardships, she readily acknowledged that, but surely they had had an elephant's bellyful?

She'd lost both parents in a horrible, unforeseen accident, Doug had lost a twin brother he'd been told, and now they had both lost two of their precious babies.

She remembered being pregnant with the twins, Doug being thrilled to bits, stating that the twin-gene must be from his side. And the boys were a dream come true. The only fly in Rose's ointment was her detachment from her sister, apart from that they assumed their lives were perfect.

It was far from perfect now though. *Since Steven's accident,* everything had turned upside down, but she thought she had seen a glimmer of light at the end of the tunnel when they discovered they were going to have another baby, their 'take-away' daughter – Grace.

She despised God for what He was putting them through. She went through the motions of looking after Margot and Simon, feeding them, washing their clothes, walking to and from school, happy to palm both off to her neighbour or her sister.

She hated Doug for getting her pregnant again so soon while she was still grieving over Steven, and she hated the feel of his body as he lay next to her in their bed, dismissing any show of affection from him no matter how small. She didn't want him spooning next to her she wanted him to sleep anywhere other than next to her. She hinted he move into one of the other bedrooms for the time being and she would put Margot and Simon together, in the same room. They were children, it would be fine. Doug could sleep in the garage for all she cared, she didn't want any intimacy, idle chitchat, a sad puppy-dog face constantly following her around the house asking if she was ok. She wanted to scream at the top of her voice that NO, she was NOT ok, and she doubted she would feel ok ever again!

*   *   *   *   *

Deb had taken Simon to the park which was located on the outskirts of the city centre, not a twenty-minute walk from their homes. The weather was still gloriously sunny and warm, even though it was late September. The park was full of young mothers with hyper-active happy toddlers, gathered together on the benches while the kiddies played on the swings, the slide, and in the sandpit. They all knew Deb and showed no signs of surprise at seeing her with Rose's little boy, inviting her to join them in their gossip.

Simon, unstrapped from his pushchair, ran happily to join the other children, Deb never taking her eyes off him.

"How is Rose?" asked one of the mums moving up on the bench to accommodate Deb. The same question asked umpteen times, receiving the same dumb answer over and over, "not too good, as one can expect. She needs more time; things are still too raw." Everyone nodding in agreement.

"What about their little girl, Margot? How's she? My Alfie's in her class at school, and he can't stand her," said one of the others.

"Really?" replied Deb in Margot's defence, "well, I suppose the poor child has suffered a great deal more than your Alfie, in her short life!" (She was thinking back to her conversation with Katy, who knew what effect it had on her?). The mother hung her head in embarrassment, "I'm sorry, I didn't mean to be dismissive, of course she will be affected, but Alfie says she's always been a bit of a rum 'en, way before Steven's accident. None of the kids like to play with her, she's too cruel."

"Cruel? What do you mean?" Deb looked at the faces of all the mothers looking at her expectant expression.

"Deb," another mother took over the conversation, "you're a good neighbour to that family, but they're nutters! The whole lot of 'em. Time you took off those rose-coloured spectacles of yours and get yerself down to SpecSavers for a proper pair, then you might be able to see more clearly. I can't believe your defending the little bitch. That Margot is bad news! Did you know that she's never invited to any of the other kids' birthday parties?"

No, Deb didn't know, how could she? Poor Margot!

The mother who just had spoken stood up, gathering all her belongings and called for her daughter, Pocahontas. (Deb inwardly cringed at the obscurity of such bizarre names, these days. Who in the right mind would name their child Pocahontas!) "That poor little mite you're desperately trying to defend, got one of the younger boys by the throat and was practically *strangling* him!"

Deb gasped.

"The recess bell rang, and the teacher saw her with her hands round his throat. The kid was gasping, he couldn't breathe. The boy told the teacher that Margot had told *him* he had a sore throat and *she* was going to make it better. Yeah, broad daylight, too. Sorry Deb, but like I said, you need to keep an eye out, that kid has a hidden agenda, even though she's only a little girl."

She was shocked to the core, she felt all of a dither. "Simon! Simon, come along now," desperate to leave, she'd heard enough, too much! What was she supposed to do now, with this new-found knowledge? Should she tell Rose? She couldn't possibly! She couldn't burden the poor woman with any more bad news, it would destroy her. And what did the other woman mean by *'they're nutters! The whole lot of 'em.'*

*   *   *   *   *

Rose had spent three blissful hours in solitude. Margot was at school and Simon was with Deb, next door. She felt extremely liberated and focused for the first time in... she didn't know how long, but whatever, those three hours all to herself had been a godsend. She'd rearranged the sleeping arrangements in the bedrooms, either she or Doug could have the room that was once the boys' room, she'd moved Simon's little bed in with Margot.

She felt greatly satisfied, she'd achieved something positive. She'd packed a lot of Steven or Simon's clothes in boxes, there was no longer the need for two identical sets of everything. The whole wardrobe was empty, plenty of space for her or Doug's clothes.

The hands of the clock were moving quickly, and it was almost time to walk to Margot's school to collect her. She didn't want to go, she panicked at the thought of leaving the safety of her fortress walls, the thought of facing those false, pitiful, sympathetic glances of parents who would never understand what she was going through, as she endeavoured to hold her head high, giving the impression of being the perfect mother, able to face any storm or whatever else life threw in her path. The palms of her hands began to sweat and tremble as she reached for the house keys, her pulse began to race rapidly, forcing her take slow, deep breaths.

She felt overwhelmingly nauseous of all a sudden and hurtled upstairs to the bathroom where she fell on her knees in front of the toilet, lifted the seat and vomited, perspiration running down her temples, and she knew there was no way she could venture out of her door and walk to the school to collect her daughter.

She curled into the foetal position under her floral bed cover, gnawing at her knuckles. She had no idea how long she'd been there, but the trill of her phone alerted her senses, startling her. On the caller display she saw 'School' and knew the reason why. She didn't care. She ignored the call, and all the following calls. Then she turned her phone off and sank into a deep, deep sleep.

Chapter 20: A Tangled Mess

Doug knocked lightly on Suzanne's front door, too lightly he wondered, she may not even hear. He half hoped she wouldn't, even though he was desperate to talk to her, to talk somebody who would spare him enough time to listen. He didn't even send a forewarning text message to tell her he was on his way over, not wanting to give her the opportunity to refuse him. He couldn't handle any more negativity or rejections.

It was eleven thirty at night. Her make-up was on a cleansing wipe laying on top of several others in the fancy wicker waste basket next to her bathroom sink; she was getting ready for bed. It was her first niece-free night she'd had in days. She'd managed to indulge in a whole bottle of not unreasonably expensive red wine without the guilt of a secret tipple behind her niece's accusatory eye.

The knocking at her door was unnerving. Who was behind there? Surely not Garth? He couldn't have been released from prison again and found where she lived now?

"Sue…" She recognised the pathetic, pleading utter of her name from the other side of the door and opened it.

Doug stared at her sheepishly then walked slowly towards her, grabbing her shoulders and kissing her neck, his hands fervently groping her body like he'd never felt the contours of a woman's body before.

She clung on to him with the same urgency, remembering the first time her legs had buckled under his touch, repeating his name over and over, then kick-slammed her door shut.

They didn't make it to her bedroom, instead they tore at each other's clothes in an attempt to reach flesh, feeling an almost forgotten passion as they fell together on the floor, writhing behind the closed front door, their satiated screams of ecstasy going unheeded by the whole universe.

They lay there for a few moments afterwards, slightly embarrassed at the tardiness of their union. He with his jeans round his knees, his socks and shoes still on, she with her wine-breath, stained tongue and cigarette stench. But it hadn't stopped them catapulting head-first into sin again, had it? Neither of them had taken a moment to consider any consequences, until the euphoria began to ebb.

What type of a person would betray a sister like this? And what kind of selfish husband would risk losing the remainder of his family for a quickie on the floor with someone other than his beloved wife, the one who was hurting so badly that no words could ever describe the pain she was going through? And what kind of heartless brother-in-law would repeat a deed that prevented someone daring to marry and have a family of her own?

Doug and Suzanne – that's who!

Doug rolled over onto his back, scrambling to pull up his jeans. Suzanne drew her dressing gown over her naked body, cringing at the inanity of trying to cover her modesty when only minutes ago she'd thrown all caution to the wind.

"Sue, I'm sorry," he uttered, feebly.

She wanted to lash out at him. Sorry! How dare he? Talk about adding insult to injury, he'd just made love to her and then announced he was sorry?! 'Made love' was *hardly* the appropriate term for what they'd just done, it was a moment of release, of lust, a despicable weakness on both sides that created yet again another reason to keep estranged.

Doug stood up, tucking his white tee-shirt inside his jeans, "I should go."

Suzanne stood up too and held the door open for him, she couldn't bring herself to say anything out loud. She slammed the door shut as he scuttled away like the guilty swine he was, and she yelled every obscenity she knew, hoping to God he'd heard every word.

She sat at her marble-topped kitchen counter for at least another half hour after Doug had left, chastising herself for leaving herself wide open for another heartbreak. Her signature half empty bottle of gin mocked her, as did the overflowing ashtray and the scribbled note she'd managed to write to remind her to get the Morning After Pill from a chemist somewhere far away where the staff wouldn't know her. She disgusted even herself.

Doug pulled up outside his house and switched off the car's ignition, sitting in contemplative silence for about ten minutes, berating himself for his gross stupidity. He wanted to cry. He should've been stronger, resisted, manned-up and been the example of which he was trying to portray himself to his children.

He tried to justify himself because of Rose's dismissiveness towards him, depriving him of his conjugal rights, it was her fault! What hot-blooded man would put up with the constant refusals, the rebuffs, and being forced to move into another bedroom?

Suzanne had always been 'up for it', according to his old mate, Stuart and the many others. Rose had been the one who was the more reticent of the two, keeping Doug at arm's length, and he was the friend who had to endure listening to Stu's X-rated escapades while he fashioned away his lies fabricating his own prowess, and it was just a month or two before his pal received the 'Dear John' text from Suzanne that Doug made his mistake.

He could hardly forget that. Stuart's old Renault Clio had a major mechanical fault, late at night. Very late at night, gone eleven thirty, and it had occurred in a very remote, dark place! It was obvious why they had been there.

Stuart called Doug to come and help him, he not being that kind of capable guy to sort out anything to do with car problems, and it transpired that the problem was even beyond anything Doug could fix. The only alternative was to call out the recovery – which was going to be at least a couple of hours.

Sue stood outside of the vehicle smoking her cigarette, showing not the slightest embarrassment at their predicament, and Stuart asked Doug if he would take Suzanne home while he stayed back to wait for the help that was coming.

That was Doug's first mistake. The *first* time he'd made a 'mistake' with his girlfriend's sister. He dropped her off at the same front door where only a couple of hours earlier he'd dropped off Rose, the woman he'd sworn undying love to, his body stinking of two different feminine scents - only one coming from a bottle's atomiser.

After he dropped Suzanne at her house, he was overcome with shame and guilt, for his girlfriend and his work mate. He was full of remorse and tortured himself relentlessly, resulting in him proposing to Rose the next evening in an endeavour to sanctimoniously absolve his debauchery, his treachery.

Chapter 21: Break-Ups

Suzanne was flabbergasted! She had assumed that Doug had, at last, seen the light, realised his true feelings, his destiny.

When she walked back into her home she leaned against the door, euphoric, her flushed face was smiling from ear to ear, elated that the night had finally brought them together. She was on Cloud Nine and glowing. She didn't even feel any antipathy for her sister because she truly felt that it was her and Doug who belonged together, it was so obvious! For years it had been poor old Stuart who was the scapegoat in the whole foursome scenario, and it was her who had commandeered all the sexual advances to the guy knowing it would eventually get back to Doug, hoping he would be jealous.

Yes, she was devastated. She had to endure her sister's blissful excitement, proudly showing off her sparkling diamond ring to all the work force at Bent and Sons, grimacing behind her fake smile at the never-ending banter of 'it will be you next Suzanne' of her colleagues.

She couldn't stand it - the humiliation and anger she felt, it made her feel sick. She *was* sick; every morning. Every damned wretched morning!

'Stu, sorry. It's over. It's not U, it's me. Going 2 Spain to join some friends. B good.'

* * * * *

Suzanne arrived at St Pancras Station, bewildered. Her old friend, Corah, was supposed to be waiting for her, as pre-arranged, but was nowhere to be seen. She should have known better than to rely on someone as dilatory and unpredictable as Corah!

She'd handed in her notice at the office, told Rose she was going to London to stay with Corah but not to tell anyone else.

Rose was genuinely shocked and pleaded with her not to go. "Sue, you can't go to London! Why would you want to go there? What am I going to do without you? Please, don't go!"

"I'm going, Rose, whether you approve or not, I want to go. I want more to life, some excitement, reality. I don't want to end up here in a dead-end job..."

"Like me, you mean?" Rose interrupted her, keenly. "Like my boring life?"

Suzanne looked at the awaiting expression on her sister's face, "No, Rose, no. Your life is far from boring, look at that expensive ring on your finger; look at that wonderful man you're going to marry and imagine everything you have to look forward to. I'll never be a million miles away, good God, Rose, you have been the best sister ever. You've not only been like a mother to me, you've been my *best* friend, practically my only friend, but I want what you have . . . "

"You *can* have what I have, Sue. Marry Stuart and we can both have it all!"

Suzanne tried hard not to laugh. Marry Stuart! When hell freezes over, she thought, nor could she ever have what Rose had – her fiancé for one thing!

*   *   *   *   *

Corah was still nowhere to be seen and Suzanne was beyond miffed. She'd called her, texted her, and waited and waited.

"Been stood up?" a voice asked her. She looked behind her to see a grinning, balding 'Grant Mitchell' look-alike stirring a cup of coffee. He had that same sexual allure as Yul Brynner, albeit a younger version, and the last thing she contemplated right now was an over-abundance of testosterone deviating her away from the sole purpose of her planned few months down the smoke.

"No," she replied assertively, leaving nothing else to warrant further conversation.

"No doubt she'll be wearing her hair in a ponytail as she's done forever, and she'll look like she's chewing a wasp," he read out loud, his phone held up in front of him. "Hmm, are you chewing a wasp?"

She ignored him again, looking around, feeling sure her friend would turn up any second. The Grant Mitchell look-alike drank the remnants of his coffee, rose from his seat and stood in front of her. "Corah has asked me to come and meet you because she's been held up." He waited for her to answer but she just stared at him, then she picked up her phone and called the number she had on redial.

"Corah! Where are…"

"Just go with Garth, Sue. Something's cropped up and I couldn't get to meet you. He'll take you to my place, he's got a key, I'll be there as soon as I can," and she hung up.

Garth waited, smiling smugly. "Follow me," he said, and didn't even offer to carry her heavy suitcase!

It didn't take that long to arrive at Corah's place on Consort Road but long enough for Suzanne to enjoy the sights of the capital. The crowds of people, hundreds of cars, buses, taxis, tall buildings with marvellous architecture, many oozing wealth and class, a far cry from the rambling countryside of her humble beginnings.

Garth was driving like a tourist guide, pointing out places of interest, she nodded now and again but added little towards engaging in conversation.

"You and Corah go back a few years, she tells me." It was more of a statement than a question, and she debated her answer, knowing that he obviously already knew far more about her than she did about him.

"We're old friends, yes."

"And what brings you all the way down here to the dulcet overtones of Dulwich?" he chuckled at his attempt to humour her.

She had to acquiesce; he had almost cracked a joke. "Same old, same old," she replied in a more uplifted response, "fancied a change of environment, that kind of thing."

Garth nodded as though he clearly understood, "Corah's a good pal of mine, too, so I'm sure I'll be seeing you around. Ah, here we are," he said, slowing down into Consort Road as he approached her house, "that one with the hanging baskets with all those dead flowers. I'll leave you to it then, here's the key – let yerself in."

She grabbed the key from him in disgust, hauled her suitcase from the car, furious he hadn't even offered to help her, and walked to Corah's front door where the white paint was flaking away. She recoiled as she stepped over the threshold, the smell knocked her back, it was like a den of iniquity!

Ten thirty p.m. and still no sign of Corah! She'd already taken herself on a tour of where she was going to be spending the next however many weeks, months, and decided the small bedroom with the single bed was obviously earmarked for her. She liked it, it was adequate, pretty, clean. Plenty of space for her large suitcase full of bits and bobs. A nice old-fashioned kidney-shaped dressing table with floral drapes, and the three mirrors on top where she could do her hair and make-up and see the back of her head when she positioned the mirrors just so.

She looked in awe around the large kitchen diner with its huge American-style fridge and Ikea table and stools, all seemingly ultra-modern compared to her and Rose's home. From the kitchen window she looked out onto a tiny overgrown garden, a tip compared to the neighbours either side. She looked up at the kitchen clock again, the hands didn't seem to have moved from the last time she'd looked.

Suzanne opened the fridge door and smiled when she saw an assortment of wine bottles. She was her own person, she wasn't under any mother's restraints or apron strings, she was adult enough to be where she was, and she took a bottle, knowing that her friend must have stocked up in anticipation of celebrating her arrival. Good old Corah.

Chapter 22: Corah and Suzanne

Suzanne would notoriously accumulate fly-by-night friends as readily as she would accumulate the latest trend of collectibles, no matter what the newest or fashionable in-thing, always trying to fit in, unlike her sister, Rose, who didn't bother to try. She would lie in bed feeling lost sometimes, a forebodingness that she couldn't shake off or explain.

When she was about nine-years old, Suzanne would often climb out of her single bed and snuggle up next to her sister, wrapping herself around her. Rose would scold her when she felt cold feet touching hers, but no amount of "get back in your own bed!" would make any difference to Suzanne; she needed to feel the physical closeness of another human body. Their mother, after coming to her wits end, decided the best option would be to provide alternative sleeping arrangements for the two of them and so she and her husband moved their own brass and iron double bed into the girls' room, swapping it for their two singles.

Corah was three years older than Suzanne and a year older than Rose. She was beautiful and she knew it. She'd been a child model since she was four years old and appeared in umpteen shopwindows on massive billboards advertising everything from food to toilet paper! Her nickname at school was 'eat it, shit it, wipe it' and that's just about the depths of cruelty kids have. They didn't care that their childish taunts would cause Corah to cry every time she saw her face on the TV commercials extolling the virtues of the ultra-soft toilet tissue, showing her smiling serenely as her 'mother' handed her a flippin' quilted loo roll! It was deathly embarrassing.

When she turned eighteen, she was offered a modelling contract for footwear – she had the most perfect feet! She remembered one of her horrid cousins proclaiming that if she chopped off her feet and stitched them onto her neck, she'd be beautiful.

She modelled shoes, stockings, and tights. Pedicure professionals falsely showed 'before and after' procedures, displaying *her* two perfect feet and calves to advertise their surgical expertise. Where Corah's bank balance was concerned, she had no scruples.

Corah moved to London because that's where she was needed, and Dulwich was smack-bang close to where it was within easy commute to her gigs, a place that was also buzzing with cool celebrities. The rental on the property, however, was another issue altogether; many paying lodgers - and some non-paying lodgers - came to and fro from her front door... until she met the lovely Garth.

Suzanne had looked up to Corah for as long as she could remember - having achieved the type of notoriety that she could only dream about – and convinced herself that one day she too would have an equally enviable, successful future. They went to the same gym, Monday and Wednesday nights, that progressed to going to the pub afterwards to undo all the good they'd slogged and sweated away at previously. Corah was a terrible influence on Suzanne, it was she who introduced her to her best friend – alcohol!

She decided to open the dusty bottle of Chateauneuf du Pape. Not one from the fridge, no, she'd put that one back. This bottle was in the cupboard underneath the sink, next to the dusters, cleaning sprays and oven cleaner, tucked right at the back, forgotten about. Heaven forbid she'd cause ructions on her first night by helping herself to the new stuff. She'd use up the old stuff first, this 2010 bottle needed drinking up before it went off, even though she shouldn't *be* drinking but what the heck, she was wanting to both drown her sorrows and celebrate her freedom. She found the corkscrew, found the glasses in the cupboard, poured herself a large measure and toasted herself.

By crikey, Corah, she uttered to herself, fancy leaving this at the back of the cupboard! It's bloody gorgeous! Her phone beeped, *'b there in 5'*. It was from Corah.

She was starving, she'd not eaten all day bar a banana she'd had before she boarded the train for London and hoped that her friend was going to bring some food back with her!

She was giggling to herself as she read her phone message, excited at the prospect of seeing her old friend again, looking forward to a reunion where they could sit and talk for hours and hours about everything and nothing. She hadn't heard the door open but looked up in surprise as her friend and Yul Brynner who had collected her from St Pancras stood in front of her, armed with a steaming, white plastic carrier bag smelling of fish and chips. Corah's shocked expression at seeing her half-empty bottle of Chateauneuf de Pape that had been a 21st birthday present from her father, mirrored Suzanne's as the smell of food sent her turning to the kitchen sink where she deposited about fifty quid's worth of vintage wine!

"But you weren't here, Corah!", she tried to justify herself the next morning, her head pounding but receiving no sympathy.

"Exactly! And I wasn't here to tell you that you couldn't drink the bloody oven cleaner either, but you didn't help yourself to that did you?"

Suzanne sat nursing her mug of coffee, feeling tender and full of remorse, promising over and over that she would replace the damn bottle, and Corah reiterating that it could never *be* replaced – it was a gift from her father! She was saving it so that she could drink it with him! A replacement bottle would never be the same.

Things hadn't started on a good footing and Suzanne knew she was 100% to blame. She felt awful, in more ways than just having a hangover and guilt at having consumed her friend's birthday gift. She was embarrassed at her stupidity, and in front of Garth too who'd been very hospitable. She'd thrown up in front of them both. What an outstanding first impression she made.

*   *   *   *   *

The door slammed as Corah left, going – assumed Suzanne - to her work. She dared to sigh with relief, she needed to reboot, get her act together, make amends, go out and source another ridiculously expensive bottle of the stuff she'd poured down her throat like it was a cheap bottle of forgotten plonk!

She poured herself another cup of coffee, was it her third or fourth, she couldn't remember. She felt rancid, she looked it too!

"Feeling a touch tender?" came the male voice emerging from the settee in the living room.

She cringed, vaguely remembering that Garth was still there, and knew she had to do the hospitable thing and offer him some coffee, or breakfast, which was two of the last things she wanted to do.

There was no hiding place, so she replied, "if you're decent you can come and get some coffee, or tea if you'd prefer."

He waltzed in wearing just his boxer shorts, "coffee, please. One sugar," which left no doubt that she was expected to make it for him.

The smell of his male body made her heave and once again she had the excruciating embarrassment of retching towards the sink, missing it by inches and her vomit running down the cupboard doors.

"Okay, actions speak louder than words. I get it, I make you sick. I have been told that before, but was there really any need to be so convincing?"

She wanted to laugh. That was the second joke he'd cracked. "Garth, I'm sorry, it's not that," she chuckled, "I'm not used to drinking. I hadn't eaten yesterday, and then I found that bottle and I just thought it was old wine, and…"

"And you pissed off Corah. And should you be drinking, in your condition?"

She was horrified! Corah must have told him? She promised she wouldn't say anything to anyone. Her expression told him that she was shocked at his revelation, "Oh stop it, Corah hasn't said a dicky bird. I have two sisters, seen it all before. That's why you're here isn't it? Same old, same old. Change of environment, that kind of thing?"

Oooh! No pulling the wool over this guy's eyes. She wanted to disappear into thin air, not having to sit and listen nor explain herself to him, yet he had an understanding quality about him that made her almost want to spill everything out in front of him, but she couldn't, she didn't know the man, he wasn't going to listen to her bare her soul.

An hour and several cups of coffee later, Garth had heard the lot! He never interrupted her once. Suzanne imagined his two sisters, wondering if they realised how lucky they were to have such an empathetic brother like him. Perhaps not, who even *did* like their brothers?

"So, you're going for a termination?" He asked.

"Yes," she answered positively, then justified herself with "I'm too young to be a mother, and I'm not even sure..."

"Yeah," he interrupted, "you said. Well, all I can say is it isn't the baby's fault. Nobody gets a requisition form approved for being born, but it's your life, your body, your choice. Have you made the arrangements yet, you know, for the abortion?"

She recoiled at the frankness of his question, the brutal, dirty, sound of 'abortion'.

"I have. It's tomorrow, half two."

Garth went back into the living room where his clothes lay in a pile at the side of the settee and quickly dressed. As he walked out the front door he shouted back to Suzanne in the kitchen, "I'll pick you up tomorrow at one o'clock" and slammed the door.

As the door slammed shut, she suddenly felt so vulnerable and alone. She nursed her cold coffee while she reflected on the conversation they'd just had. It had been a comfort talking to this man, this stranger, even though he had neither encouraged nor discouraged her in what she was preparing to do.

She checked her emails to double check her appointment time, directions to the clinic, the do's and don'ts, things to expect 'afterwards', etc, etc.

It was a despicable thing she was going to do. If her own dear mother was still alive she would have discouraged her from doing this. No doubt the initial discovery would have been shocking, there would have been curses and tears, but ultimately the prospect of becoming a grandmother would have over-ridden all those first terrible accusations.

She felt ashamed and saddened at her inability to confide in the one and only person she truly trusted – her sister.

Chapter 23: It's Done

It was five p.m. and Suzanne heard the buzzer on the front door of the clinic. She'd been sitting in a room full of silent women reading magazines – allegedly, checking their phones; faces of expressionless women who didn't talk to anyone, nobody daring to acknowledge the dastardly deed they'd all paid for to be there.

She glanced around her, counting young girls even younger than herself, and ladies in the room waiting for some guilty sperm-donor to come and collect them; tallying up the monies paid daily by each desperate woman not wanting to continue with the natural course of pregnancy. Times that by seven, and times that again by four, by twelve…

What a lucrative business, she quickly realised! People were getting rich from reducing the population of the planet. And what happened to all those aborted foetuses? Where did they go? Where had her baby gone?

The buzzer sounded again. Someone wasn't taking their finger off the doorbell and all eyes looked up, glancing at each other accusingly as if everyone was to blame, she heard the door open and close, then "I'm here to collect my wife" from the corridor, and cringed, it was Garth!

She grabbed her handbag and flew out of the room, not wanting him to pop his head round the door and everyone believing that he *was* her husband. She'd chosen London rather than The Midlands for the procedure, to eliminate any chance of bumping into someone who might recognise her and then her guilty secret being bandied around her hometown by wagging tongues and pointing fingers.

"Your wife?" she asked sharply.

"Thought it sounded better. Hey, don't worry, I'm sure there are loads in the same boat, and who cares anyway? Come on, the car's in the car park. How are you feeling?"

"I don't feel the slightest bit different, to tell you the truth. They just anesthetised me and then I woke up, got dressed, and was told to go and sit in the day room. They gave me a cup of tea."

Garth nodded. He opened the passenger door and closed it after she seated herself and buckled up.

"What are your plans now then?" he enquired.

"I'm going to stay with Corah for another week or two and then I'll decide what I'm going to do and where I'm going to go. I packed in my job you see. I fancied a new scene anyway, something different. Something better paid too! I'd like to see if I can get into journalism or the media, I've always hankered after doing that, getting the nitty-gritty and dishing the dirt to the public." She chuckled, "I'm just a nosy cow. I like writing though, always have done."

Garth looked at her and smiled, "Sounds interesting. Hmm, I'm glad you're staying on for a while. You never know, you might actually like it here and decide to stay."

Two weeks after Suzanne's termination she managed to find work via an employment agency, temping at various companies in and around Southeast London. She was having a blast. Corah was thoroughly enjoying having a friend stay, a rental income, and a drinking/party buddy; they were out every night of the week, coming back in the small hours nissed as pewts!

Corah took her to all the liveliest joints, mingling with the popular crowd, introducing her to substances that heightened the thrill and buzz of this wild exotic scene.

Garth became totally smitten with Suzanne. She was a live wire, a tigress, and he couldn't keep his eyes or hands off her, much to the envy of Corah who had always had more than a soft spot for the man.

She would bury her head under her pillow when Garth stayed overnight, put ear plugs in, bang on the wall next door to warn them to keep the noise down, wishing it was her bed he was in, making her scream out in wild abandonment.

Suzanne was getting out of control; her new-found liberation was accelerating at the speed of knots and her two closest pals were becoming a tad concerned. She had gained quite a bit of weight in the ensuing weeks but attributed it to the fact that her periods hadn't yet returned after her abortion, assuming it was normal. She didn't care now; she'd suffered none of the post-natal depression or anxiety the clinic stated she may encounter. And Garth always took care of 'protecting' her from another unwanted pregnancy.

One night as they both lay post coital, Garth stroking her stomach, he leaned backwards, studying her form.

"Sue, did you actually go ahead with that termination?" he asked earnestly.

She laughed at him, "Of course I did. You took me there, and you collected me afterwards."

"Because I would say that you're still pregnant!"

"I cannot possibly be. I paid good money to that place, contributed towards their millionaire status. Do you have any idea how much money that place makes on a daily basis? Drugs and abortions are the big money-making endeavours to be involved in, Garth. Guess how much it cost me tonight for that weed and a couple of tablets. Go on, guess?"

"I think you should go back to the doctors, Sue, or get another test 'cos I'm not convinced that you're not still pregnant!"

Chapter 24: The Body Blow

Suzanne sat there perched on the lid on the toilet seat in Corah's stark white bathroom. It was not possible. Garth had taken precautions every time, and he was ultra-careful too!

The wand had turned blue instantly, in exactly the same way it had done all those weeks previously.

She studied her nakedness in the bathroom mirror, running her hands over her bulging tummy, totally bewildered why she was in the very same predicament...again!

Who could have possibly known that she had been pregnant with twins? She was outraged. Surely the clinic should have known, done the appropriate tests and aborted the *two* foetuses instead of just one!

It was too late now, she was informed, she was far too long into her pregnancy to legally go through another termination. She would have to go full term, give birth, become a mother, and she was incensed, sad, frightened!

There was no way she could do this, be a single mum, bring up a baby, live with the black cloud hanging over her for eternity. So once again, Garth came to her rescue - like the proverbial knight in shining armour - and took her to the Adoption Agency where she was confidently assured her baby would be placed with a loving couple, desperate to be the loving and caring parents that she could never be.

And that's when the post-natal depression kicked in, after she'd given birth to her son. The tiny mite that had been subjected to copious amounts of alcohol whilst growing in her womb; pills, tobacco, and substances that contained nothing to promote its health or wellbeing. He weighed just a mere five pounds.

Suzanne sank into a deep depression, ignoring calls for work from the employment agency, ignoring both Corah's and Garth's encouragement to 'pull herself together' and 'get a grip'. How could she? It wasn't her fault. It was her hormones. It was the clinic. It was Stuart or Doug, Rose, or her stupid, stupid dad for jumping the red light and killing himself and her mum. It was the baby's. It was God's fault!

"Garth, I need some uppers."

"Sue, you don't. You just need time."

"I *said*... I need some uppers!"

"And I *said*... you need time. This is what's to be expected! You've not been able to nurse your baby, have him here with you. You'll be experiencing a loss; this is all natural."

"And how would you know, hey? Mister-bloody-know-it-all? How would you know what it feels like, hey?" She swung at him, "does this hurt? Can you feel *my* pain yet?"

She looked around the kitchen for something more substantial to hurt him with, noticing a bottle of wine on the work surface. She clenched it with both hands and hurled it at his head, it broke in parts, the red wine pouring down his cheeks, his neck, shoulders, and clothes.

The once loving and phlegmatic Garth, retaliated in a way he never dreamt he would be capable of towards any woman and lunged at Suzanne with a chunk of glass, slicing her arms in his effort to defend himself against her vicious attack, "You f***ing bitch!"

Everything went downhill from then on. Garth eventually acquiesced and went out in search of the euphoric medication Suzanne had demanded was her right to numb her pain and bring her back to life, he crossed lines that he vowed he'd never cross.

Love did that to a person, or perhaps it was obsession rather than love. Love? Obsession? The two words kinda ran parallel, and sometimes it would be good, and others… well???

Corah had felt left out. Her two friends seemed to have forgotten her now. She witnessed her dear old Garth change before her eyes. She no longer enjoyed a simple drink down at the local and coming back to hers with fish and chips and give a hug and kiss before they both left in the morning to go to their respective places of work.

It had been an almost non-committal relationship, at least on his part. A good night out with an old pal, and a satisfactory conclusion afterwards, on the old occasion. She wanted more though, a lot more. She envisioned a future with Garth, the happily-ever-after scenario. She was waiting, hopefully, for him to come to realise the same. But Suzanne was now on the scene!

Garth's meagre dealings with the heavies in the business were peanuts in comparison to what their other clients were bringing to the table, but they wanted more from him. They could see he had potential and wanted him on-board. He had that look, for one thing, that menacing, foreboding aura, a far cry from the actuality of the man.

'Spider' took him to one side whilst he discreetly passed the pre-arranged substances in exchange for cash, "the boss wants you to have this," he said, passing a large packet to him, "here's a grand's worth, plus a little something for the weekend for your good lady. See you back here next week, same time."

There was no opportunity for explanations or excuses, he knew exactly what he was meant to do. What the boss wanted, the boss got, and he cursed his stupidity and weakness at his involvement all because of some crazy bitch of a girl! He'd taken the legendary 'King's shilling' and couldn't see a way out.

However, much to Garth's surprise, he found plenty of eager customers willing to buy from him and found it an incredibly lucrative way to fill his pockets with pound notes. The first batch was gone within a week, the boss was paid in full, and he was offloading batches every day and night thereafter. Suzanne and Corah felt they were walking into a cake shop, getting high as kites more often than not.

Spider had told Garth that his boss was pleased with his progress and decided to entrust more substantial quantities with him, different variations of substances, too. It was a doddle, money for old rope he told himself, location and working hours to suit and nobody to have to report to.

For the next twelve months he was selling it to whoever asked. He had no scruples as far as his conscience and wallet was concerned. If they were foolish enough to part with their hard-earned money to relieve the boredom and monotony of their nine-to-five office jobs, who was he to refuse? Everybody justified their spending on whatever made them happy, be it alcohol, cigarettes, flash cars and expensive holidays, big houses and designer labels, drugs...

College students and teachers, nightclub revellers, tourists visiting the city, doctors and nurses, suited businessmen, and the celebs that frequented the upmarket bars. He didn't discriminate when it came to his customers.

Even the homeless fraternity managed to beg enough for a quick fix now and again. Those poor souls down on their luck, sleeping rough in shop doorways, always gave him a ready smile when he did business there.

How could he have possibly known that an under-cover drug squad officer had been on surveillance, mingling on the streets with the down-and-outs, watching him?

Chapter 25: Garth's Downfall

Garth had just collected a shedload of gear from Spider when he received a text from Corah. It was almost midnight; he was doing his rounds. One of the homeless guys had asked him to get some heroin - not such an unusual request but the guy was unusual - not the average street-bound dishevelled no-hoper. This one was a little older than himself, mixed race, good looking once you saw past his unshaved face and his filthy clothing. He obviously used to work out because Garth observed his muscular physique, the bright whites of his eyes, a contrast to other drug-induced takers. His vocabulary was cultured, too.

Garth squatted next to his torn sleeping bag, handing over the requested heroin and pocketed his fee.

"Mate, what's your story? Why are you here?" he asked sympathetically.

"Will *my* story be any different to the others?" he asked.

"I don't know, will it be? Everyone has a story. There but for the grace of God go us all."

The man reached out to shake hands, "the name's Noah, as in the Biblical sense," he chuckled. (*Grubby hands but tidy fingernails, Garth noticed*). He sat up straight and continued, "only been here for a week or two, came down from The Elephant. Didn't feel safe there after witnessing an old boy get victimised, pissed on, kicked by three imbeciles who thought they'd have a bit a fun with someone who couldn't retaliate."

Garth nodded, picturing the scene.

"Sickened me to the stomach, I tell you. I went to intervene and that's when the bloody cowards scarpered! Yeah, it was fun to pick on someone weak and incapable but feared someone with a bit of wherewithal about them. I did a bit of boxing, years ago, but then I stupidly got involved with this malarkey. Not taking them, no. Buying and selling. Just like you."

Garth inwardly cringed. Was this how he was going to end up?

"I'd turned professional, about six months. Some of the lads started taking speed but I didn't want to be involved with anything like that. Liked to think I got to where I was on my own merit, hard work, training. Didn't touch alcohol, fags, or drugs. Anyway, a mate of mine needed some gear bringing back from Amsterdam, I was over there, a boxing match. He was a good mate, so I said I would."

"You got caught?" Garth enquired.

Noah nodded. "Five years in Wormwood. Lost my championship, my reputation in the boxing world, my wife, home, the lot. This is home now," he said, spreading his sleeping bag over his legs.

"And the heroin? You take it to blot everything out?"

"Nah," replied Noah, "never touch the stuff."

Garth left Noah, pitying his sorry plight, realising how easily people could lose everything. Their lives, their dignity, their reason to live.

He read Corah's text message, *'where R U? Bring us something nice back, R pot is empty.* xx'

He wasn't surprised to find the pair of them sitting at the kitchen table, drunk as lords, empty wine bottles on the drainer. It would be a rare Friday night if they weren't. In fact, it would be a rare any night to find them *not* the worse for wear.

The three were becoming a little too familiar with each another, Garth sensing Corah's jealousy at the intimacy between him and Suzanne. Suzanne's nonchalance with Garth only made him more determined to pursue her, keep in her good books, hating himself for his weakness where she was concerned. She was a drug herself to him, and he was like a pathetic puppy-dog, always coming back for more, no matter how carefree she was to his feelings.

He gave them some gear and left, he had other customers to supply, more money to collect. They didn't even notice he'd gone.

The knocking on the front door stopped their giggles as they looked across at each other, Suzanne's half-rolled joint poised in front of her tongue.

"The silly arse has forgotten something again," laughed Corah as she rose from her seat to answer the door. "The silly arse, who's just a farce, and goes around breaking both our hearts…" Suzanne added, laughing like a drain at her feeble attempt of poetry, but her laughter ended abruptly at the sight of two men standing behind a very worried Corah.

"Ladies, I'm PC Drew Hartshorn and this is my colleague DS Noah Ambrose of the Southeast London Drug Squad. We have reason to believe you have narcotics on your premises, illegal substances supplied by a certain Mr. Garth Payne."

The two girls froze, no apology for the late intrusion, their officiousness alarming. Suzanne panicked, the cigarette in her fingers was going to land her in jail and she hadn't even had chance to celebrate her 'coming-of-age'; she was doomed, going to be raped on a daily basis by all those butch, hardened criminals she'd seen locked up on so many television documentaries. What was her sister going to think?

Neither of the girls spoke.

"We'll overlook your weed on this occasion, we just want your friend's supplier. We know he gets his supplies from Spider, but we need *his* source. The Big Boss."

Corah answered coyly, "we don't know, honestly, do we Suzanne?" she asked beseechingly, "we only do recreational partaking."

Corah wanted to die. She could imagine her modelling career plummeting rapidly once her employers got wind of this, and then what would she do to survive? It was all Suzanne's stupid fault - she'd had to nursemaid her since she first set foot in London, and now look where it had landed her - into the arms of the law!

"He's coming back later, half an hour or so he said," Suzanne blurted out pathetically. "You can wait for him here. Would you like a drink, tea, coffee? A cold beer?"

"You bitch!" Corah spat as she threw her cigarette lighter across the table in disgust, after the policemen had left, "you were flirting with them! Here's your 'Get out of jail free' card, go straight to Go, and collect your thirty pieces of silver on the way!"

Chapter 26: Running Away

Poor Garth. Suzanne had well and truly stitched him up and Corah was livid. It was all Suzanne's fault that he'd succumbed to drugs in the first place! He'd never so much as smoked a cigarette until she'd needled away at him over and over, passed him a pill on her tongue as she kissed him, encouraged him to 'get a life'.

"Oh come on, Garth," she'd taunt, "everyone does a little, it's a sociable thing nowadays. Don't be so bloody boring!" And whatever Suzanne wanted, soft lad acquiesced.

"I think it's time you left, Sue. He will know the score the second he comes back here and those cops nab him. Even a worm will turn and he's not gonna be the usual phlegmatic Garth Payne anymore. He's in BIG trouble, even more so when Spider and his boss get wind. I think you should get as far away from London as possible. Now, while you still can."

Suzanne managed to get the first train out of St. Pancras back up to Loughborough, in Leicestershire, then a taxi to Woodhouse Eaves to her family home.

She sighed with relief to find the house empty as she dumped her heaving suitcases in the hallway. Rose thankfully was at work.

It had been a long time since she sat at the familiar table in her parents' kitchen, talking with her sister over their first coffee of the day before setting out to catch the bus to work, every morning. She was invariably tardier than Rose who always had to chivvy her along, to hurry in case they missed the bus and then there'd be hell to pay with their employer. More so Rose, as she had to 'clock in' every day!

London had given her insight into a brand-new world; one full of excitement and adventure. Bright lights and pulsating music, beautiful people and beautiful places, popularity, and who-knew-what kind of opportunities. Returning home to Loughborough would seem like stepping back in time. How was she going to endure it?

Rose was stunned when she saw that her sister had returned, like the prodigal son. She flung her arms around her, smiling from ear to ear, and they chatted away non-stop for hours, Suzanne omitting more than she revealed.

Rose didn't delve too deeply, she was just over the moon to have her sister home again, but she couldn't wait to offload all her wedding plans she and Doug had been making and about wanting to sell up to buy their very own home, overjoyed that she now had her chief-bridesmaid.

They never resumed their usual nights out together either. In fact, the first reunion with Doug was excruciatingly awkward, with neither knowing whether to embrace, kiss... There were forced smiles and awkward silences, stilted laughter at inane quips and jokes, false enthusiasm over the wedding preparations and house-hunting.

Eventually Suzanne managed to secure temporary employment at The Leicester Mercury office (*the local newspaper*). She was covering maternity leave of one of the journalists that covered local crime. Most of her days were spent at the Court House in Leicester's city centre and she loved it! The Court House was a magnificent building in Every Street and the amount of times she would relish telling anyone over a drink that she knew Every Street in Leicester never failed to amuse her.

"Corah, I'm loving this job. I'm actually getting paid to write about everyone's misdemeanours and crimes. I can spread the gossip like a cheap margarine and our readers love it! I've only been back a few months and I know Every Street in Leicester!"

She failed to patronise her enthusiasm, "Garth's in the nick, he sent me a letter, good of you to ask about him!"

"Look, Corah, nobody forced him to become a dealer. Why are you still blaming me? Garth did it for the money, he got greedy, the bonehead!"

Corah recoiled at her belittling description of their once-dear friend, remembering the happy times, the laughs, until it all went tits up.

Alan Botters was the Editorial Manager at *The Leicester Mercury* and he'd been scrutinising the new stand-in's flourished pieces of crime reporting. Isobel Rock had taken her sabbatical maternity leave with the set-in-stone promise to return once her time was up. That was often the case in most instances but, more often than not, the mother's priorities changed once they experienced the overwhelming bliss of motherhood, and then made that humble call to say they wouldn't be returning after all, ultimately submitting their notice to terminate their employment.

'Big Al' as he was referred to, the big boss at *The Mercury*. Big by name, big by stature, big by personality, and respected by every single employee.

He would often peruse the case stories Suzanne produced from the courts and find himself amused. In his editorial mind, she managed to paint a picture, portray a story beyond the case. *The Mercury*'s followers had increased. He wanted to keep her on, hoping that Isobel Rock would decide her best career would err to motherhood.

He got his wish. Six months after Isobel had walked out of *The Leicester Mercury* front doors, heavily pregnant, armed with bouquets of flowers, cards and baby clothes, he received a phone call telling him she would not be returning to work. He grinned like a Cheshire cat.

And Suzanne preened. She was actually looking forward to going to work, rising early, GHD hair done, bobbi brown make-up done, suited in the finest Austin Reed suits and Michael Kors' stilettos. She sat in the court room knowing her favourite *Agui Di* perfume would bounce off the walls, permeating the nostrils of accusers and accused.

Rose finally received an offer on their family home, almost the asking price. Now she had to discuss and agree it with Suzanne.

Although it was an inevitable course, it saddened both sisters. This was their family home. It held a million memories of happier days of living with their mum and dad, their childhood, and beyond. The pantry still had shelves of pickled onions, beetroot, red cabbage that their mum and dad had spent hours peeling all the shallots, boiling beetroots and red cabbage, their hands stained red for days afterwards.

They even found a Tupperware box of margarine wrappers that their mother would use to grease tins when baking. "Who still did this?" they asked each other as they laughed over the things their mother could never throw away.

Since their parents' accident, both Rose and Suzanne had lived as it was, neither wanting to get rid of anything. It seemed sacrilege to part with their belongings, their clothes, their memories. The garden shed remained as their dad had left it; a floorboard with a screw loose he intended replacing (*just like yer dad, their mother laughed, a screw loose.*) Gardening tools, saws, drills, boxes and tins of nails, hooks, spanners.

Was one supposed to dump it all into a metal skip? Their clothes too? Were they expected to consider everything good in their lives, as unwanted as a nasty smell? It was painful, but nevertheless, it needed to be done.

Rose and Suzanne pledged to clear the house together. Doug had found a nice three bed semi-detached in an area he felt would be the ideal place to start married life. Suzanne found her perfect bungalow just a couple of miles away to be close to her sister, a couple of miles away to be further from her brother-in-law to be. All was tickety boo.

Chapter 27: I Hate Steven

Woodhouse Eaves was a prestigious area in Leicestershire and thus much sought after. Beautiful countryside, fabulous walks, wonderful pubs to sit outside on a glorious summer's evening. An easy commute into either Loughborough or Leicester. Train station, good schools, it ticked everyone's wish list.

Their three bedroomed, detached - albeit dated - with off-road parking, commanded a decent sale price, enough for each sister to procure their own new home. Doug was rubbing his hands together, they'd need only a minimal mortgage considering the major lump sum that was coming from Rose's inheritance.

Suzanne's more modest bungalow she managed to buy outright. Every penny she earned was spent on herself, indulging in expensive wines, cigarettes, designer labels, and – because old habits die hard – the odd pill or two!

They both had their reasons to be excited, embarking on new beginnings. Together they'd emptied bedrooms, cupboards, distributing photograph albums their parents fanatically kept up to date. The sisters huddled together turning the pages of albums, reminiscing and laughing at seeing their younger selves from babies to teenagers.

They poked fun at each other at their old school photographs, the annual ones that all parents felt compelled to buy. Rose had begged her mum not to buy the one she'd had taken when she was fourteen because she had a huge zit on her forehead and as she always wore her hair tied back, it was now immortalised forever.

As the memories tugged at their heartstrings, they sobbed, almost hearing the familiar banter of their mum and dad as if they were still there in the same room.

"You're just like mum, Rose." Suzanne said whilst turning the pages of one of the photograph albums, "I think I'm more like dad."

"I am not!", she replied indignantly, "you are!"

"No, YOU are. You're the home maker, like mum. You keep everything sweet. I'm like dad, don't give a toss."

There was half a bottle of wine that sat precariously between them, and Rose reached over to fill her empty glass, "You're so wrong! It was the other way round. Yes, mum was the home maker, but dad was like her negative.

He was like an obedient puppy dog, did everything she said and asked for. If mum had asked for…"

"A bit like Doug, then? Is that what you're saying?" Suzanne laughed out loud at her bravado.

Rose frowned at her, "Sue, is that what you think? That I'm manipulating Doug, like our mum did to our dad?"

"Rose! I never even considered our mum did manipulate our dad. YOU said it, you said our dad was like an obedient puppy dog. What are you talking about?"

"But you said 'a bit like Doug then', insinuating that he's as weak as our dad."

"I never said our dad was weak! Flippin' heck, Rose, how did our conversation end up like this?"

Rose stormed off upstairs to bed, whether she realised she'd knocked over her glass of wine or not, she paid no heed.

She lay underneath her favourite Egyptian cotton sheets with the hand-crocheted edging that had a been a favourite of her mother's. She'd been silently fuming over the conversation with her sister when previously they'd enjoyed the rare chance to be together and talk about the past.

After a couple of glasses of wine, she was just entering that dream-like state. Rose found herself walking towards her mother who was lying in her beautiful brass bed, smiling at her. She was just a baby herself, but she felt so much older in her dream. She saw a baby in her mother's arms, her father standing proudly beside her smiling and beckoning her forward. The midwife was holding another, it was bloodied, grey and wailing. She was confused. Two babies?

"This is your baby sister, Rose," the lady in the nurse's uniform told her, "would you like to hold her?"

She held up her little arms and drew her close. She sniffed at the newness of her newly born sister and felt an overwhelming sense of love. She glanced at her mother, her father, the midwife, and ran out of the bedroom.

* * * * *

"Get your bloody cold feet away from me!" Rose slurred.

Suzanne ignored her, like she did always. It had always been a bone of contention, their sleeping arrangements.

Suzanne had always felt the need for bodily contact, to be near her sister. Rose only had herself to blame, commandeering her sister from the very day of her birth, and the very reason their parents had swapped their beds.

Everything had been cleared out. Their personal stuff moved into their respective new abodes and they were happily anticipating their new lives (well, with trepidation.)

The new owners were due to arrive imminently, and Suzanne had volunteered to be there to hand over the keys. She sat in her dad's shed at his workbench wanting to feel and smell him for the last time before these memories became too distant to recall. That stupid loose screw in the shed floor that he never got round to fixing. *'Your dad's always had a screw loose'* she remembered her mother saying.

"And she was right, Pa," she chuckled as she dug her fingers into the loose plank, surprised it had come up so easily!

An old Tupperware container. That's what it was, just a small one but Suzanne looked around furtively like she remembered Garth stashing secrets away in similar hiding places!

She opened it cautiously, hoping and praying it wasn't going to be anything as incriminating as the life she'd just left behind her. Was it worse? Could anything be?

It contained several strips of negatives, difficult to make out the images. Why would her dad hide a packet of negatives in his shed? Several photographs too, including one single black and white photograph scratched out so the face couldn't be clearly seen, a childish scrawl written over it, "I hate Steven."

Suzanne sat back, scrutinising the eeriness of the black and white images, realising she may be more like her mother after all, because her dad – evidently - DID give a toss.

Who the hell was Steven?

Chapter 28: Distancing

'I hate Steven' -- Suzanne looked at the scratched, unrecognisable photograph over and over. What did those words mean? Who hated Steven and why did someone feel the need to deface it?

She shuddered, suddenly feeling an inexplicable horror, a loss that she had no comprehension she should feel, but then realised she *did*.

A vague recollection of euphoria, serenity, and… she couldn't describe beyond that, just that – it wasn't, it wasn't anything! It was gone. She reached out to a nothingness that she had no comprehension of. Her right arm was missing, herself alien, she felt her soul have been severed.

She continued to look at the other photographs; there were several. There was Rose sitting in a big chair with a baby in her arms, some sort of nurse standing over her. It looked as if it could have been the day she was born. There was another of her mum with two babies, sitting up in her brass bed and smiling at the camera. One of her and another toddler, sitting in highchairs with birthday cakes in front of them, each with a single candle alight.

Suddenly the penny dropped and she gasped. She must have been a twin; she had had a brother! She flicked through the remainder of papers and pictures and found a birth certificate folded in half, the confirmation of years of feeling like something was missing. A newspaper cutting reporting the woeful story of how four-year old Rose Smythe found her two-year old brother, Steven, dead in his cot. She read on... 'death by misadventure' the coroner ruled.

She sat in her old dad's shed, a throbbing in her ears, wondering what the connotations of her find meant and why her dad had hidden them in such an obscure place?

Why was Steven never talked about, and why had no one ever told her she was a twin? Poor Rose, she said out loud. How awful for her to have found her own baby brother dead in his cot. But would Rose even remember, she was after all only a child herself.

She thanked God she had gone into the shed to sit and reflect about her dad for a while, otherwise she would never have found the plastic container and she would have never known about this Steven.

She couldn't grasp the situation though. It was unfathomable that her brother's death had been swept under the carpet all those years and kept such a huge secret. It was as though she was forgetting something important, lost or misplaced a treasured piece of jewellery because nothing made any sense! It was irritating. She would need to talk to Rose and get some answers to her questions.

It was Saturday morning, for which Suzanne was glad. She didn't think she could have faced going to work after finding and opening Pandora's Box. After she'd handed the keys over to the new owners, she was desperate to go to her own new home and open a bottle of something... anything!

The people seemed nice, an Asian couple late forties, kids flown the nest, they'd been looking to move somewhere quiet, more upmarket from their last home.

So, I'm one of two, she thought, and that's why I was pregnant with twins! That blew her mind because she had assumed the twin gene came from Doug. It could be that Stuart had been the one to impregnate her after all. Either way it didn't matter, she never wanted to be lumbered with a child – or children.

Who did she really take after? Could it be her entire family were experts at keeping secrets? and what a terrible secret it was too. She had a right to know! It was a cruel thing their parents did.

She decided she would go out sometime over the weekend to buy some magnolia paint for her living room to brighten it up, brighten herself up because she felt very downhearted. The cottage was lovely as it was but, naturally, she intended putting her own stamp on it. She wanted a gold and cream colour scheme after watching Love Actually umpteen times. There was a particular scene with Julia Roberts being interviewed in a room that was adorned with luxurious gold furniture and furnishings, and she'd fallen in love with the idea that once she had her own place, if it was good enough for Julia Roberts, it was going to be good enough for Suzanne Smythe. She was going to source a second-hand bed settee and upcycle it with some sculptured gold fabric and make curtains to match.

Her cottage had only one bedroom so the bed settee would be perfect for any overnight visitors. Excluding overnight male visitors who would obviously share her own bed!

She also wanted to get in the car and drive the two miles to Rose's new house to see how she was settling in and show her the Tupperware Pandora Box. Surely she would be as surprised as herself?

She loved her new home, she knew that Corah would be green with envy, her in a rented place. London was fabulous but there was no way either of them would have been able to afford to buy anything there in a million years, not even a garage!

It was a bittersweet feeling to know that she and Rose had been able to buy their own homes so easily but purely because they had their parents' home to sell, otherwise it would have been the same for them as it was for everyone else trying to step onto the property ladder, a whacking deposit and a lifetime of hefty mortgage repayments.

She did get in her car and get some paint, and she also dropped in at Rose's house. Doug was up the ladder trying to replace five light bulbs in the 80s chandelier that Rose was adamant was staying put. The atmosphere was a tad tense as he felt it looked too old-fashioned, he liked modern, could never understand the sisters' preference for past eras. They couldn't understand his yearning for the banality of grey and whites, chrome and leather.

Suzanne was more than happy for Rose to take as much from their parents' home as she wanted, whilst she 'bagged' their brass bed. Doug didn't want the bed anyway, he wanted a brand new one, not negotiating starting *his* marital life on a mattress where his in-laws conceived his wife!

"Oh Sue, thank goodness you're here," said Rose. "We could both do with the distraction. Mr.Grumpy-drawers here is getting on my nerves. Tell me, what is wrong with this light fixture?"

Suzanne looked up at the ceiling. "Nothing, it's fabulous. I'd love it in my place."

"I do, too. He wants to rip everything out and start from scratch. The reason we bought this house was because we thought it was perfect to move straight into. It's in good decorative order, the garden's good, there's a brand-new combi-boiler upstairs, we don't HAVE to spend a penny! But 'he who must be obeyed' has different ideas to me. We have a wedding to pay for too, so I do not want to be wasting money unnecessarily when things don't need to be changed or altered just for the sake of it. I'm not out to impress the neighbours!"

Suzanne chuckled, she sounded just like their mother.

"Me neither, Rose. I adore my little pad, it's perfect. Just enough for me to manage. No mortgage, no major restoration works. All my wages for little old me. I'm even thinking of buying myself a nice BMW because I can! No, not right now, but in a few months' time I'm gonna get rid of my Yaris and get a newish Beemer. Having said that I do like my Yaris, never given me the slightest problem."

Doug climbed down the ladder. "When you two crones have quit slagging me off, can one of you put the kettle on so I can have a cup of tea. Or a beer, that would be nicer."

The two sisters sat together round the kitchen table whilst Doug went outside to the garden, talking to his new neighbours.

"Rose," Suzanne began tentatively, "I wanted to come over last night to talk to you, but I didn't. I think I was in shock, and I honestly don't know what to think."

"What do you mean?" Rose asked.

Suzanne reached into her handbag for the Tupperware container and pushed it towards her, "I found this underneath the floorboards in dad's shed. I kinda went in there to say my last goodbye to him." She studied her face, waiting to see any reaction.

Rose opened it and picked up the negatives, the photographs, the folded birth certificate, the newspaper cutting, her face deadpan. She took her time, looking at the front and back of each picture, laying one on top of the other.

She looked into the expectant, hopeful face of her sister, "I have no idea, Sue."

"Look, Rose," she pointed to the birth certificate, "Steven Smythe, same date-of-birth as me! He must have been my twin brother! And here's a picture of mum holding two babies, and this one of you holding me. Is it me? This newspaper clip says Steven died at two years old, you found him. Do you remember? Is Steven our brother? Look at this one here, it's a birthday party or something 'cos we have cakes with one candle in the middle. Rose, do you remember anything? Why would our dad hide all of this under the floorboards of his shed? I would never have found this had I not gone in there to have my last five minutes with him."

Rose never gave away a thing and Suzanne couldn't determine whether she was hiding what she knew, protecting their parents, or if the whole thing was as big a shock to Rose, as it was to her.

"What do you think, Rose? Did mum and dad keep Steven's death from us both? I can't remember him at all, can you?"

Rose looked at the newspaper cutting, the date; she would have been nearer to five than the stated four-year old they portrayed her as. She did remember seeing Steven's lifeless little body in his cot, his skin a greyish, dull white, his lips a shade of purple, his eyes shut. She'd gone at the behest of her mother to see if the babies were awake so she could bring them downstairs for breakfast. Her adorable, darling sister was standing up in her cot, arms outstretched, smiling towards her. In fact, she remembered seeing Steven in the middle of the night when she heard Suzanne crying, she saw him with his head between the bars on his cot, struggling to free himself.

"No, I can't Sue. I'm as confused as you are. I didn't know we had a brother, and I didn't know you were a twin. But we were so young, and if Steven was never talked about then I guess it's understandable that neither of us ever knew about him."

Suzanne nodded, packing away the remnants of Steven's short life back into the greying Tupperware, disappointed that Rose had been unable to recall a single memory of him.

"I want to find out more, Rose. I'd like to see the autopsy report, find out if he was buried or cremated because if he was buried then we can go and see him, take some flowers. I wonder if our mum and dad ever did that? Do you think our Aunty Pat would know? She must do. I know she and dad didn't see each other for years but she did come to their funeral. Do you have her address, is it amongst mum's things?"

"Oh, Sue, I wouldn't know where to look! Doug took everything up to the attic when we moved in, I'd have to look. I can barely remember her myself so I'm sure you can't, but I do remember dad telling me that they didn't get on, though I can't recall why. Perhaps because brothers and sisters are often like that. I'm glad we didn't have any brothers, remember poor old Judy next door with her vile brother?"

Suzanne gasped, "Rose, we must have had a brother! Don't you remember *anything* about him?"

"No," Rose answered matter-of-factly, "I only remember just me and you."

Chapter 29: On a Mission

The following weeks passed in a blur for Suzanne as her mind tried to grasp the reality of her newly found knowledge. She was desperate to know the truth, why she and her sister were never told anything about their brother. She tried to recall if there was an anniversary of Steven's death that was celebrated in any way, but she couldn't. There were no boyish toys anywhere in the house they lived in, no photographs in frames on the mantlepiece aside hers and Rose's, forgotten about as if he had never existed.

How sad, Suzanne thought, and how strange. She imagined her dad would have been thrilled to have had a son and heir, someone to share his passion of golf with, a buddy to teach DIY and go for a beer with as he got older, instead he was surrounded by females, dolls and prams, periods and mood swings, loud music of boy bands and then the dread of any inappropriate boyfriend turning up.

He was a great dad. The quiet, dependable type. She could never recall him losing his temper with either her or Rose, unlike their mother. Sometimes she would feel quite sorry for him as their mum corrected him mercilessly on his was's and were's. "Was you, Suzanne?" he'd ask, and their mum would never fail to chime in with "WERE you Suzanne? Not WAS you!" It was a standard joke in their household. He was a slow learner, allegedly. The sisters often wondered if he did it deliberately, to wind her up, because he'd chuckle and give them a wink.

Perhaps their Aunty Pat would be able to enlighten them more – once they managed to locate her, of course.

That's always the problem when generations have passed. The horse has bolted, and you have no way of getting answers to questions; they take all the knowledge and secrets to their graves. Suzanne knew very little of their lineage, rarely meeting up with any family members. She wasn't even sure if they had cousins, certainly none had ever been to a birthday party at their house, nor had she or Rose been to any of theirs.

She was told that both sets of grandparents had died and therefore had no reason to miss them. Some of her friends would talk about their respective grandmothers or grandfathers and she would consider herself lucky she didn't have them after hearing one of her friends telling how she'd gone to visit her grandmother in the old people's home that stunk of wee! Everyone thought it was disgusting, some declaring ardently that theirs didn't, whilst others laughed and agreed.

Hash Mistry never laughed, he loved his grandparents, he lived with them, and it was his own dearest grandmother who made his favourite vegetable samosas because his mother didn't always have the time with her being out at work all day long. Hash Mistry loved his grandfather equally as much as his grandmother because he relayed stories of being a boy himself, living in Pakistan. How he would make the most amazing kites and have kite races where all the villages participated.

Hash Mistry *did* know all about his family history, he had many siblings, cousins, aunts and uncles, and many exciting stories to tell.

Young Hash Mistry also had a huge secret that he would never, ever reveal to his school chums, and that was his Christian name - Hashmuk. Nobody was going to nickname him 'horse muck'.

Suzanne hero-worshipped him. She envied him, admired him. As a seven-year-old growing up with no large family like Hash and all his exciting stories, his grandmother's delicious vegetable samosas, she wanted to marry him.

She sat with her laptop open and Googled Steven Smythe, surprised to find so many hits. Suzanne narrowed her search and almost knocked over the half empty bottle of wine at her elbow as she read the headlines. It stated that Steven was two years old, but that was incorrect, he would have been *nearly* two years old, according to the tabloid dates. And Rose, "four-year-old Rose Smythe…" Wrong again, Rose would have been almost five!

She preened herself in a congratulatory way; she would never make these blunders when reporting court cases.

'*Death by misadventure*' was the concluding evidence. In layman's terms 'cot death' or 'Sudden Infant Death Syndrome' (SIDS). She hit Wikipedia and read on… '*Sudden infant death syndrome (SIDS), also known as cot death – or crib death, is the sudden unexplained death of a child of less than one year of age*'.

But Steven wasn't less than a year old, he was almost two! Perhaps he had underlying health issues? What if she had something wrong, too? Perhaps they both had. She had no idea. Apart from her pregnancy termination and then the birth later, she'd never been hospitalised.

She was none the wiser after her internet search, but that did not deter her from wanting to learn more, determined to ascertain what had happened to his body, was he buried or cremated? There were ways to find out and places to visit that would confirm all her unanswered questions.

*　　*　　*　　*　　*

"Suzanne," it was Big Al. "Monday morning you're in Court 2 on that perverted grandfather case, the rape of his two granddaughters that were entrusted into his care. Get as much as you can while you can and transmit back to me. I'd like to get this one out tonight."

"What time?" she asked.

"Ten. Reckon it's gonna take a while, the bastard's trying to say the girls lured him. What a crock of shite, they were minors for God's sake. And he's an ugly brute if ever there was one. Looks just like Fred Flintstone. Wish I could get my hands on the dirty perv, I'd have his bloody guts for garters, so I would. And they walk amongst us, you know. His work colleagues didn't have an inkling. Thought he was a real decent chap, taking his grandkids under his wing after the parents were proclaimed unfit to look after them, being the druggies they are."

Suzanne cringed, knowing how easy it was to take that path of destruction, the cop out to reality and hardships.

He continued. "The kiddies were going to be placed in care, foster care, but the grandparents offered to look after them. Well, how lovely. Poor kids would have fared better in foster care if you ask me. I tell ya, Sue, what kinda sick guy would do that to his own grandkids, hey?"

"I don't know, boss. You tell me. You said 'what kinda *guy*?' presuming all rapists, child molesters and perverts are male. That's not always the case."

"You're getting too deep now, Sue. Most cases are, wouldn't you say? Of course, there are always exceptions to the rule. Anyway, like I said, get down there for ten o'clock and report back as much as you can. I want to make it tonight's headlines."

"Al, you know you can't. We have to protect those girls, their identities. They . . "

"I know. God, do you think I'm stupid, woman? Of course we can't print names etc but get the nitty gritty and leave the rest to me." Her phone went dead.

Woman!?! How dare he!

Suzanne stared at the suited and shaved Fred Flintstone look-alike in the dock, trying to portray a decorum of respectability to the courtroom, and her stomach shuddered in disgust, picturing him with his thirteen-year-old and eleven-year-old granddaughters. A paid 'lady of the night' would have difficulty earning her money with this guy, this brute who had taken away the innocence of his very own kin, destroying their childhood.

A grandad was supposed to the ultimate family member of trust, like Hash's amazing grandfather. A *grand* dad, a more knowledgeable and loving version of one's own father.

What horrors was she going to hear? How could these girls have ever comprehended how their adolescent lives would begin? Suzanne would never know. She remembered how she and Rose used to share the same bath as youngsters, each one bagging the plug end because it was deeper. Their dad coming in to wash their long hair and rinsing it with the shower head, neither of them embarrassed because there was no need. Until the day she remembered Rose throwing her head forward, her hair falling in front of her and saying "look Dad, I can wash my own hair now," and dad leaving, quietly saying, "I'll get your mum to come in."

Suzanne was too young to understand Rose's sudden reluctance to have their dad in the bathroom with them. Mum took over from then on. Rose was coming into puberty.

The court was adjourned after Fred Flintstone reported it was one of his work colleagues that had Googled *'Grandfathers abusing granddaughters'*, not him! Incriminating evidence the police found on his phone.

She'd sent all her notes over to Al while she sat in Crusty's having a chip butty and a glass of wine. An unusual lunch yes, but it was where everybody congregated during lunchtimes, the daily shoppers and scores of office staff. You could also get the peace and obscurity of unwanted attention – sometimes.

Doug plonked himself in front of her, startling her from her perusal of Google as she shovelled the last remaining chips into her mouth.

"Didn't quite think of you as a chip butty bird," he smirked.

"You've no need to think of me at all," she replied.

He dismissed her sarcasm, "another?" he asked.

She contemplated whether she should accept, knowing the right answer would be no. But she was a bordering addict, be it drugs, alcohol, or him.

She waved her empty glass high. "Why not?"

Chapter 30: Rose

Rose watched her daughter, Margot, sleeping. She was developing into a beautiful girl, inheriting the same dark hair of her and Doug, the button nose she had sprinkled with light freckles, and that perfect shaped face of her husband. She glanced over then to the sleeping Simon, totally different personalities. Simon's arms were splayed either side of his sleeping head, hopefully - Rose thought - dreaming beautiful dreams.

She sat cross-legged on the floor between her two children and took out her packet of pills from her jeans' pocket, the same type the doctor prescribed *when Steven passed away* to help her endure another day, the same ones she took now to blot out the pain of her recent loss, she popped two and swallowed them. She didn't want to leave the room, or her babies.

Doug was sitting downstairs watching some DIY video on his iPad. He'd talked about dismantling the pool and building an extension to the kitchen, but Rose didn't want to listen or talk about home improvements or getting rid of the pool. She didn't want to remain in the same house, or even the same country. Every day things gnawed away at her, making her resentful of even the rising sun in the mornings.

She lay on her back for another ten minutes, the tablets beginning to take effect until she felt more calm, more focused.

It was a monumental descent, every step felt heavier and more painful. She cursed her pitiful existence, the four walls barricading her inside, sound-proofing her internal screams, keeping her a prisoner in her own sanctuary.

"Come and sit with me, Honey," he said as Rose walked into the living room. "This is what I'd like to do with the kitchen, extend it out on the garden, we've plenty of room."

His words went over the top of her head, she was bored with his big ideas, exhausted at his plans, tired at pretending everything was ok because everything was not ok, because nothing would ever be ok ever again, how could he not understand that?

What was it with men that they were able to switch off so easily? Did all men have this ability, or was it just hers? Rose doubted she would ever feel normal again and yet here was her husband talking about stupid kitchen extensions! It must have been purely a ruse to stimulate Rose, to excite her enough to take her mind off the traumas she'd been through. He'd even had the audacity to have an exceedingly large gin and tonic ready for her so that he could paint the pretty picture. The plans of a nice new kitchen to look at whilst sipping on strong G&T, and hey presto, the magic ingredient for a night of passion. Not!

The last thing on Rose's mind for the last however many months was sex, contrary to Doug's which was all the time. Whilst he was perusing modern, state-of-the-art kitchens from B&Q on the internet she was drooling over idyllic Italian stone buildings with river frontages and tens of olive trees, guaranteed sunshine practically all year round. She could sell the house, she'd contributed the majority of money towards, she could easily afford to do it. She'd take the children, they'd love it! What a future they'd have. They'd be bi-lingual, they would have amazing opportunities, and Doug could come and visit as often as he wanted.

"Look, Rose, this one. I like this and I think it wouldn't take a lot to construct."

"I'm not interested, Doug. I've told you before, I don't want to be here. I want a divorce. I want to go to Italy."

He stifled a snigger, he'd heard it a few times now but Rose would never leave the UK and take the children. She had the security of the schools, the NHS. She'd have to learn to speak Italian, deal with the legalities, she'd be alone in a foreign country without having a car — she couldn't even drive!

He knew she was still in mourning and was taking anti-depressants. He worried about that, feeling she needed to get a grip and get over it, she had Margot and Simon to look after. He wasn't happy with her taking the tablets. How could she be a proper mother to their children whilst depending on chemicals? Even little Simon had said an odd thing or two lately about mummy getting angry with him and being in bed all the time. Margot was oblivious.

He certainly couldn't take time off work to stay at home and look after everyone, there was too much to do at the factory. Besides, that's what her role in life was. And it was only during the week, Suzanne had Margot most weekends.

She had it easy in one way, compared to families years ago with several children to look after. They had no money worries, unlike most of his work colleagues with young families and only the one income. His plans to extend their home was going to increase its value.

"Do what you want, Doug. I've told you how I feel but you never listen. All *I'm* here for is to keep home for you three because if I was single, like Suzanne, I wouldn't have to bother cooking every day, washing and ironing, cleaning and pretending to be the perfect mother when evidently I'm anything but. I wish I could just sit at a laptop all hours God sends and write fantasy like she does or go back to work from nine to five, come home to find my clothes miraculously washed and ironed, hung on coat hangers in the wardrobe, dinner on the table, house sparklin' clean, but I CAN'T because of you!"

"Me? Because of ME? Well, forgive me my darling wife, but I was always under the impression everything had been a joint decision. I thought you wanted to be a stay-at-home-mum. If you want to go back to work we can get Simon into a nursery, we can afford it. Rose, if it will make you feel better, do it. Look for something that suits you. Loads of mothers do it."

"I'm going to bed, and I don't want a bigger kitchen. If you want to spend money on something to make me happier, book me some driving lessons."

She opened the bedroom door as quietly as she could muster, without waking Margot and Simon. They were both fast asleep. She didn't view them in the same awe she had done in the past, she saw them as an encumbrance, envying the freedom her sister enjoyed, responsible to and for no one.

As she turned to leave the room she stood on the packet of pills she'd taken just an hour ago. They must have slipped out of her jeans' pocket. It was empty, though she thought she'd only taken two and it had been a full packet of twenty bright red pills.

Chapter 31: Everything Changed

Suzanne was busily hammering away at her keyboard, desperately trying to make sense of what was going on in her mind, getting it down in black and white on her Word document.

It had been over eighteen months since her last book had been published and she'd procrastinated for months getting back in the saddle after the last family tragedy, rather *Rose's* last tragedy.

The neighbours had gossiped, the tabloids had been cruel and unforgiving, even good old Al had become distant. Mud sticks in a small community and Suzanne's former work at *The Leicester Mercury* and her court days were testament to that. She was no stranger to curtain twitchers or wagging tongues, but she tried to take no heed.

She resigned from her journalist job, the court room too clinically stark a place in which to sit, considering everything that happened almost two years ago at the inquest of Simon, her nephew with whom she'd barely had any interaction.

'*Pity my Sister*' was the title of her new book and Adam, her publisher, had warned her not to let it be personal. "Be careful, Sue," he said, "revisiting old memories could become very painful."

But it wasn't painful, it was a release. It almost felt therapeutic as night after night she sat until the small hours, reading, researching, learning, and writing.

She rarely heard from Doug anymore after he sold the house and moved to another county. Margot had been taken into care which was, she felt, just like being incarcerated into a prison for children!

She didn't feel able to offer her a home after the things she'd learned, even though she had always had a special bond with Margot, loved her more than anything or anyone in the whole world.

At first, she tried to dismiss those feelings that Margot knew exactly what she was doing, and then chastised herself for daring to contemplate that her niece had the slightest idea! She was a ten-year-old girl who was only doing what any doting sister would do, give those sweets to her little brother. How could she have possibly known they were harmful tablets?

But she had sat with her, talked with her, and in her gut… she felt uneasy. Margot was totally carefree, almost excited at being the centre of attention again.

"He liked the sweeties, Aunty Sue, he'd never had them before. Mummy told me I could give him them."

"Margot, what do you mean 'your mummy told you to give him some'?"

"She had some first and then said she'd leave the rest for me to give to Simon! If I was a good girl and did that, she would buy me a new Pandora charm for my bracelet, the next morning."

"She asked Simon if he wanted to go and see Steven and Simon said yes, he did."

Suzanne doubted that Simon would have been able to understand what that meant, he was only two when Steven had his accident and he'd never, as far as she was aware, even asked about him. Margot certainly hadn't mentioned anything.

"Can I come and live with you now, Aunty Sue?"

* * * * *

Rose had been admitted into a clinic for the manically depressed and Doug had been informed it was going to be a very lengthy road to recovery. She'd lost three babies in a short spell of time but the therapists analysing her had ascertained much more than depression; she was schizophrenic!

Suzanne was furious with the diagnosis of her sister, it was preposterous! This was Rose they were talking about, her sister. Rose who practically raised her, mothered her from the moment she had been born. These so-called medical experts knew bugger all as far as families were concerned.

The Chief Medical Officer at the sanatorium tried to explain things to her and Doug in layman's terms. "Rose has managed to conceal her condition for a long time, or more probably she has been totally unaware! The tablets she had been prescribed for her depression are not ones we would have been happy for her to take; it exacerbates her condition. She would have been living in a different dimension, almost like a parallel universe."

Suzanne and Doug risked a sidewards glance at each other, ashamedly.

"Your daughter, Mr.Foster... Margot? I believe she's been taken into care."

Doug nodded.

"I don't believe we have any of her medical reports here. And there's no family member she can stay with until a suitable foster family is found for her?"

Doug looked at Suzanne, a pitiful pleading look in his eyes. "No," said Suzanne firmly, "we're a small family and unfortunately my job takes me all over at a moment's notice. I can't offer Margot the stability she needs right now. Besides, if her own father can't pack in his work and become a stay-at-home-dad..."

(Corah's words tickled irritatingly at the back of her mind, *"You bitch. Here's your 'Get out of jail free' card, go straight to Go, and collect your thirty pieces of silver on the way!"*)

She knew her words would hurt; they were intended to. She was disgusted with him at how quickly he'd decided to sell up and move away, abandoning what was left of his broken family.

*   *   *   *   *

She'd gone through the autopsy report on her brother, Steven, wondering what had prompted Rose to name her son after him when she claimed she couldn't remember anything about him. Coincidentally both Stevens had been around the same age when they died in tragic circumstances.

Or it was it a coincidence? Steven and Suzanne, Steven and Simon. She didn't believe in coincidences, she always maintained that everything was meant to be. But toddlers dying in unusual circumstances *wasn't* meant to be. Neither was Rose's slip on the wet floor that caused her to lose her unborn daughter, and then Simon, poor little Simon who had somehow managed to fatally ingest harmful pills. It was no wonder Rose had lost her mind. She'd lost everything. Her home, her family, her life.

Rose's belongings were piled high in wooden crates and cardboard boxes in Suzanne's garage where they would remain until, hopefully, she recovered and could start all over again; apart from the one box that Doug brought down from their attic.

"Could you keep this one inside, Sue, rather than in the garage? Rose was always steadfast this one be kept safe. I think it contains a lot of your family's history. You know, birth certificates, death certificates, photographs, that kind of thing. You might as well hang on to it now."

PART TWO

Chapter 32: Aaron, the Spotty Teenager

He was a bit miffed he never had a reply from Suzanne Barsby over the email he'd sent regarding *In Sickness, Not in Health*. He'd found not the just one error, but three! Okay, nothing major but even so, what was she paying her editor for if someone as inexperienced as he could find them? She should pay *him* for consulting services instead, guaranteed no mistakes!

She called Jo in Bali to wish him a happy New Year. "Apa kabir, manis? selamat tahun baru. It's almost midnight here so I guess it's seven a.m. over there."

No, it was not, it was EIGHT o'clock in the morning! She should have done her research, Googled Bali times vs GMT, taken into account the clocks going back. How careless of her.

He doubted anyone else would realise, but that's where his forte lay, finding the little details that went unnoticed to the lesser discerning eye.

And the other ones. Oh, Miss Barsby, how could you? Haven't you yet realised the fundamental differences between blond and blonde? Alright and all right?

And yet she hadn't acknowledged his email or written to thank him! That was rather rude, Aaron thought.

He didn't always hear back from his emails immediately. Authors are busy people, writing, marketing their books, but most did and that's when he printed off their replies and kept them in his many folders. Some, from the more prestigious authors, he'd laminated.

He wouldn't take slight at Ms Barsby's lack of decency, instead he decided to give her another chance, and wrote again. This time, she did reply:

"Dear Mr.Penfold, or may I address you less formerly and call you Aaron?

Many thanks for taking the time to not only to read my books, but for highlighting the errors contained therein. Please forgive my late response but circumstances out of my control have prohibited an earlier reply.

I am thrilled you enjoyed In Sickness, Not In Health and felt empathy for the dilemma of my character, Simone.

In answer to your question... haha, no, my characters are all fictitious people, conducive to the ramblings of my weird imagination, like most authors, I presume.

May I take this opportunity to thank you again for pointing out the errors you highlighted and trust you will continue to be one of my most treasured fans.

I remain yours sincerely,

Suzanne Barsby"

Now that's better, Ms Barsby, much better. That's the more decent thing to do! But once again you've blotted your copy book. It's *'formally'*, not *'formerly'*. I will have to write and correct you yet again... now that we're on first-name terms!

246

Chapter 33: More from Aaron

Suzanne had written over forty thousand words for *Pity my Sister* and was storming away. She was loving the satisfactory feeling of writing distant and obscure memoirs whilst hiding behind the façade of her *nom de plume*. Hoodwinking her followers and devout fans into thinking she had this incredible ability to write titillating fantasies.

If only they knew she was inwardly saddened to learn her whole formative years had been a charade. She could hide from her demons behind her laptop screen, paint a totally different picture from her keyboard. Tap tap tap and behold, she'd created a brand-new scenario, but ultimately, she would always face the true, familiar image in her bathroom mirror every morning.

The delete key was invaluable in her writings. If only the human body had that same ability to delete or rewind. How many prisoners on Death Row had wished the very same thing?

A split-second, life-changing decision in some cases, but not for all. Some managed to waltz blissfully through life without so much as a backward glance, or an ounce of remorse for their guilty actions. The lucky ones. Those like Rose, herself, Margot, and even her own mother and father. The millions of other non-innocents walking the very earth they should be buried under.

Evil had many faces of disguise in this so-called idyllic world; it had been that way from the year dot. One only had to pick up a history book from the library to read of man's inhumanity to man throughout the decades. The genocides, the wars, the massacres. It still went on, the human-being is such a grotesque excuse for mankind because KIND is supposed to be the definitive word!

She was halfway through another chapter when her Messenger pinged. It was from Aaron Penfold, and she sighed.

'Hi Suzanne, many thanks for your reply. I'm happy to oblige you with any future editing needs. I'm a stickler for perfection, in the literary sense, so if you ever need an expert eye to glance over your WIP I'd be happy to do so, for an agreed fee, of course. You will have no reason to question my integrity or discretion and I am more than happy to furnish you with references from more prolific and esteemed writers, should you deem this necessary."

The cheek! *'More prolific and esteemed writers,'* indeed, how very dare he? He was taunting her, seemingly knowing exactly what he was doing. She pictured him standing in front of his PC mock-launching his fishing line, complete with a carrot dangling from the hook, hoping to reel her in. The cocky little bar-steward.

Well, he had another thing coming. She already had a fabulous trio of editors and readers who did an incredible job of correcting her word blindness to those she'd missed.

But damn him, he *had* found errors that they'd all missed! He was right, and she despised those people who were notoriously right!

* * * * *

Aaron was approaching his eighteenth birthday. He considered celebrating it in some way, with someone, but he had no friend in the real life apart from Isaac. He had been tagged in on a book launch by this new author, Mernie Carmichael, who was appearing at the Elephant and Castle next month. It wasn't his thing, short stories. He wanted to get involved from the very beginning and Mernie hadn't enabled him to do that as she'd already enlisted the help of an editor, but he clicked to confirm his attendance anyway, it would be something to do, another chance to meet like-minded authors.

Anyway, Suzanne had a new title buzzing around in her mind, it was going to be *Secrets, Sins, and Siblings* when she realised how the letter S had been significant throughout her life. The names of her and her brother Steven, Rose's boys, Steven and Simon. The titles of her books.

"Rose's psychiatrist needs to examine me, too," she thought. Mississippi, how many S's in that? She and Rose used to do the little hand clapping routine as they spelt it out. All the kids at school did.

The mind is a peculiar thing, she acknowledged. Her dad used to say, "there's a hair's breadth difference between the sane and the insane."

And he was so right! The mind can be incredibly fragile in some whilst frighteningly powerful in others. It was impossible to know what people were thinking when they committed heinous crimes. How is it that people can murder without showing any empathy or guilt? How could one terminate a pregnancy and give another baby away to complete strangers without feeling remorse or sadness? And how could any normal little girl fail to cry at the end of Bambi?

Saints or sinners? Saviours or Sociopaths? Those S words again. Psychos, too, that counted because the P was silent. Storytellers, sadists... which category would siblings come under?

She sent a text message to Doug to tell him that she was planning on visiting both Rose and Margot over the weekend.

She'd reluctantly succumbed and emailed five chapters of *Pity my Sister* over to Aaron who now was going to be privy to reading everything she wrote prior to sending to her editor. He was good, she had to acquiesce. Nothing passed his scrutiny. She felt miffed that this once spotty teenager was indeed the real thing but had to concede in paying him the fee he asked because he'd saved her hours of research, and he was always exceptionally quick with his responses.

Doug replied that he, too, was planning his regular weekend visit, but to Margot only. He would be going on the Sunday morning because there was a car boot sale on a farmer's field a couple of miles away from the care facility and Margot had suggested they take a trip there.

Suzanne was envious, she adored the car boot sales! She often frequented one on the A47 towards Hinckley and it was like a weekend drug to her, never knowing what she was going to find. Her little bungalow was practically bulging at the seams with possessions that she simply could not resist for the odd fifty-pence or pound.

She had a figurine of Little Red Riding Hood that was hallmarked from Harrods, she didn't even try to knock the guys down when they asked for a fiver. Bed linen was her weakness; she had mountains of the stuff that she would need another lifetime to use. Only the handmade stuff she collected, though, the same as her mother did. Sheets and pillowcases that were embroidered and edged with crocheted work, bolster cases that nobody ever used any more but were perfect for her old brass bed. She could never understand why folk wanted to part with this beautiful old stuff in preference to the modern bed linen that never looked or felt as elegant or classy. But that was in her favour as she never paid more than a couple of quid for something that some poor old Victorian lady probably spent weeks making. And books, dozens and dozens of books, usually paying peanuts for a bagful! She was dreading the day that she actually came across one of her own books being downgraded to 'car-boot-fodder'.

Why wasn't Doug going to visit Rose, she wondered? Had he forsaken those promises he made to her all those years ago? Again? Had he moved on, gotten someone else?

She remembered the night Rose came home after their first date, the time he offered her a lift and took her for a drink, the day *she'd* gone for an interview for another job. What if it had been the other way around and it had been she who had been standing at the bus stop in the rain instead of Rose? Would he have stopped and asked her to get in the car, instead?

What ifs?? It was all hypothetical anyway. Rose had been so excited that night, and it was Rose he had married after all.

No, she would not be joining them to go to the car boot sale, she would visit on Saturday. She would, once again, sit with her spaced-out sister, drugged up on her antipsychotic medication and read to her, as she occasionally did, depending on Rose's mood.

Suzanne drove her dusty black BMW into the car park of the sanatorium and parked up. She knew she ought to have cleaned the damn car, but she was notoriously dilatory. Besides, did anyone ever suffer drastically from driving a dirty car?

The facility encouraged its patients to venture out, go sightseeing, for a coffee with their visiting families, and Suzanne would sometimes take Rose to a homely little café inside an historical medieval house that was reputedly listed in the Domesday Book. It had been sympathetically restored several years earlier to replicate the era of its day. They served cream teas and sandwiches to eat either inside or out. A huge bookcase and little knick-knacks were in an adjoining room where visitors could bring and buy.

Rose was sitting in her room, dressed and waiting for her sister's visit. She offered a slight smile when Suzanne gently knocked at her door and walked in. She was painfully thin, Suzanne noticed, drawn and wan, looking much older than her thirty-eight years.

"Hey there, beautiful," said Suzanne at her best attempt to act cheerful. She felt duty-bound to do this visiting façade seeing the predicament Rose was now in. She'd seen more of her whilst she'd been so-called 'incarcerated' than she had when she lived a stone's throw away! But what else could she do? Blood's thicker than water etcetera, etcetera!

She felt sorry for her, and who in *their* right mind, wouldn't? As children, Rose had always been the best sister anyone could have asked for growing up, so she felt she should at least repay her in her hour of need.

Rose watched Suzanne, then burst into tears.

"Hey, Rose. Don't cry, sweetie." She hated that word, sweetie, but it escaped her mouth before she had time to think about it.

"Shall we go to the café and have some cream cakes? Go through the books and choose a couple?"

"I'd like to read some of your books, Sue," she said, brushing her tears away. "You've never let me read anything you've written. Why not?"

Suzanne was suddenly taken aback! Rose was correct, she'd never read one.

"Are they about us? You know, our lives. With Mum and Dad, Steven, and me? Are they?"

"Rose," Suzanne tried to diffuse her sister's anxiety, feeling uncomfortable under her watchful stare, anticipating her answer, "I write novels, you know that. I write fictional stuff but of course I recall on my memories as all authors do. You berated me years ago, if you remember, telling me not to disrespect our parents, and I've never done that, nor will I ever do. I'd never do that to you either, Rose. But . . . yes, in a way my books do include passages of our lives, but not in a derogatory way. I paint a picture in the same way an artist will paint from memory, and Rose, some of those famous painters have created masterpieces which sell for stupid amounts of money. In every book I've written I've never mentioned actual names to my readers, it's purely make-believe."

"What are the titles of all your books, Sue? I'd like to ask Closet Walrus to get them for me."

"Closet Walrus? Ha-ha, Rose, who or what is Closet Walrus?"

Rose turned away from Suzanne to look out of her window, "Remember Judy who lived next door to us? We hated her brother, Clive. Clive Walden. We called him Closet Walrus because he was frightening, and we felt so sorry for Judy for having such a horrible brother."

Suzanne felt a faint memory of being a child and Clive brandishing his airgun, chasing them; her, Rose, and Judy. They were petrified!

"This guy reminds me of him. The same red hair, freckles all over his face, but he's nice now, he brings me books to read. I'm actually enjoying reading too, Suzie, and I'd like to read your books, I've told him all about you."

(Suzie? Rose had *never* called her Suzie! Oddly, she never spoke about Doug or asked about Margot or Simon, or Steven. It was almost as if she was living in her past life, before her parents' untimely departure from the world, before she met Doug, married, and had her own family.)

"I'd like you to leave now Suzanne. My brothers have said they don't want you to be here when they come to see me. They want to talk with me, not you."

Suzanne looked at her pathetic, fragile sister who thought she was going to be visited by brothers!

"Rose, we don't have brothers, you and me. It's just us two. It was mum and dad, me and you."

Rose stood up and started shrieking, wailing like a banshee, "You liar, liar, pants on fire. Liar, liar, pants on fire. Daddy, Mummy, tell her... *tell her!*"

An orderly or somebody in a white uniform heard Rose's screams and rushed into her room looking totally alarmed. They pacified her in seconds with their reassuring words, a full syringe, and tenderness while Suzanne looked on in bewilderment. Where had her sister disappeared to?

Chapter 34: Visiting Margot

Suzanne sat inside her BMW. She couldn't be bothered to turn the ignition key because it felt like a failure, to rev the engine, switch the gear into reverse and drive away. That simple operation of distancing oneself from family ties that sometimes bound like painful shackles, like a cojoined twin. She felt that tie, that guilt, and wished she could have been an only child.

Is this how Margot felt? She'd never considered that for a moment but then she dared to. Margot had been her parents' Princess, their first born, their whole world, and hers, too! Rose's second pregnancy had been but a formality with twin boys. How disappointing!

Doug was excited though. Over the moon! In fact, because he'd been a twin himself, he always declared, he was ecstatic about becoming a father to twins.

She drove to Greenlawns, where Margot was living. No one would know that Greenlawns was home to twenty-plus children from the outside. It appeared like any other very large house in a nice, secluded area with immaculate gardens and lots of trees. The staff and children lived as one big family, cooking and eating together, helping with laundry and light gardening chores.

Most of the children had to share a bedroom with another of similar age and abilities. Margot shared with Kerry, a quiet girl who rarely spoke a word to anyone, her head always hidden behind a book. Suzanne wasn't altogether sure of why she was at Greenlawns but heard a whisper that Kerry's mother had left her home alone whilst she went away for a week, partying with her friends in Ibiza. Kerry had been six years old and had had to fend and feed herself for the whole seven days. A teacher had become suspicious after Kerry hadn't brought any lunch and was stealing food from her classmates and she had worn the same smelly clothes for four days.

Suzanne waited in the foyer while someone went upstairs to Margot's room to tell her she had a visitor. She was surprised at her niece's unusual lack of enthusiasm to see her.

"Hey, maggot!" She risked using a former term of endearment.

"Don't call me that!" Margot snapped. "I've told you before, my name is Margot! Like the prima donna ballerina."

Suzanne felt the day was going from bad to worse. First her sister, now her niece, who was acting the very 'prima donna' of her namesake. Talk about walking on eggshells around one's own family!

"Sorry, Margot. I was just trying to make you smile. You look a bit off today."

Margot shrugged. "Have you brought me anything?"

"Yes, of course. I got you some of these magazines, there are some great…"

Margot snatched the magazines from her hand, "I don't *need* magazines, I *need* tampons. I told you to get me some!"

("Told," thought Suzanne, not "asked!")

"I thought all your toiletries were provided by Greenlawns. No, Margot, you didn't *tell* me to get you some tampons."

Margot rolled her eyes, "God, I'm just surrounded by idiots. Why don't you listen to me, Aunty Sue? I *told* you that I wasn't going to use those disgusting pads they make us wear here. I want proper tampons. The boys here make fun of us."

"How do the boys know? They can't see. Margot, what are you talking about 'the boys make fun', what boys?"

Suzanne was flabbergasted, and quite alarmed. That must be mortifying for the girls if the boys did – as Margot proclaimed – make fun!

Margot quickly altered her demeanour, "I'm kidding. I don't think they actually do *know*, but they like to have a joke about it and come out with their stupid comments and Kerry's mum got her some proper tampons last time she visited, so I want some, too. Those pads are revolting."

"Ok, I'll bring some next time. I'm putting your bad attitude down to the fact that you're on your period."

"And what's your excuse? Got yours too?"

Suzanne was furious. The little madam was turning into a very precocious young woman, and she was quite shocked.

"I tell you what, Margot, I think I must've called at an inconvenient time. Best I go and come back another day when you're more amiable. I feel I've wasted a perfectly good day visiting you and your mother when neither of you appear to be the slightest bit grateful. I hope your father gets a better reception when he comes tomorrow. Ask *him* to bring you some tampons."

She turned heel and walked away, the outside sunshine a welcome reprieve from the cold altercation she'd just had with her niece.

Margot watched her get into her car, from the doorway, and drive away, she tossed the magazines into the bin and walked back upstairs to her room.

Suzanne drove away in a fury, driving a little faster than she ought to have been. Angry at the expectations of Margot when she felt certain she'd never mentioned anything about buying her the damn tampons! And then she felt guilty at feeling angry because of course Margot was going to be angsty and irritable, it was par for the course when coming into puberty. Not that she or Rose had ever been like that, the perfect daughters they were!

She hadn't noticed the blue flashing light behind her at first. She did hear the sirens, though!

Chapter 35: Breaking the Law

She was so angry with herself! She'd never been pulled over by the police for driving too fast. She'd never so much as had a parking ticket – ever! The only encounter with the police she had during her lifetime was in London with that dishy cop, Noah somebody-or-other, who had come after Garth!

Oh dear! She hoped they weren't going to be too brutal; she had her career and reputation to protect. She needed to save herself and thanked God she'd worn a buttoned blouse. After she'd pulled over, she undid several buttons and sat bolt upright in her seat, partially exposing her 34D attributes and at the same time yanking out her ponytail clip so that her hair fell provocatively across her shoulders, inwardly smirking that she could sweet talk her way out of an inevitable speeding fine by flirting with the policemen who were now approaching her vehicle. Dismayed beyond belief when she realised that one of them was a policeWOMAN!

No, she admonished, she didn't know she was doing sixty in a forty limit, she'd had a very stressful day. The

Policewoman was very condescending, patronising almost. She'd heard and seen it all before and then she noticed her name on her drivers' licence.

"Oh, Suzanne Smythe!" she exclaimed excitedly. "You used to go out with Stuart, Stuart Duffey from Ferwell Engineering. You're the writer."

Was this a good thing or another nail in her coffin?

She rebuttoned her blouse and tied her hair back. "Guilty on both accounts, I'm afraid."

The police lady smiled the most gratifying smile, "Ms. Smythe, I owe you so much... if my Stuart hadn't dumped you when he did, he would never have met me."

Suzanne studied her cautiously, wanting to make sure if she was hearing correctly.

"I've got all your books too, you're a terrific writer! I know you as Suzanne Barsby in print... Hey, tell me, all that stuff in *Finding the Negative* and Lizzie's realisation that she'd adopted, and *In Sickness, Not In Health*, where the brothers found out about their sick demented parents, where do you get all your ideas from?"

The spineless sleazeball! He had the audacity to say *he* had dumped *her*! Ah well, at least it prevented her from receiving a speeding ticket. A signed copy of her new book was the agreed bribe. A bittersweet agreement surrounding circumstances that even she couldn't have thought up!

*   *   *   *   *

She walked into the familiar warmth of her hallway. The comfort one feels when coming home after tumultuous episodes leave you feeling drained and a great desire to throw in the towel. How quickly everything changes, she thought. Life really was so short! Everybody said so, but the older she got the more she acknowledged that everybody was right!

There was no time to sit about regretting things done or not done. No point in reprisals or retributions. She couldn't undo any wrongs she'd done years ago nor would she, even if she had the chance to do it all over again.

She walked into her kitchen and opened up the screen to her laptop. She saw messages from Doug, Aaron, Corah.

She slammed it down and sat there, her hand on top, thinking back on her dismal and unproductive day.

She needed a drink, a good drink, and went straight to the cupboard where her bottles of Lidl gin beckoned like the perverted tinkling of the Pied Piper's flute. She drank a small glass down in one. It invigorated her... so she poured another and read through the messages.

Doug: *"What did you do to piss off Margot today? Couldn't you be a little more sympathetic? Christ, Sue, what's wrong with you?"*

Aaron: *"Good morning, Suzanne Barsby, hope you're well. VERY intrigued with Secrets, Sins, and Siblings! Oooh err! However, the dates are all wrong. I'll fix that, and by the way, yes Laburnum can be a poisonous tree, but fatality is rare in most cases, unless ingested by minors – if this is the way you're going . . . You might want to consider researching* Tetrahydrozoline *eye drops!!"*

Corah: *"Garth's dead. Call me when you get this message."*

Chapter 36: Aaron's Work Experience

Greenlawns was going to have a new, temporary, member of staff join their team, some young man from Brighton who had recently qualified in his first year of Clinical Psychology and this was going to be his first actual working experience.

Aaron had been as pleased as Punch at finally being accepted at an establishment that recognised his qualifications. Six whole months to learn through involvement.

He'd always had this niggling fascination for psychology, what made people tick. What made people do what they did, what their thoughts were. When he was about five years old, he'd asked his foster parents if they would get him a chicken from the butchers they used. When they asked why he wanted it (*presuming he wanted to cook it!*) he replied that he wanted to somehow connect the brains to the Hubble satellite to see if he could make the chicken come alive again. Thus, he found himself in the unfortunate situation of being shipped from pillar to post in many unloving foster homes.

He was a stickler for perfection, in exacting the truth. He was unique in a strange but old-fashioned way, even down to way the dressed.

He stood in front of Greenlawns with his laptop folded in front of his arms, his suitcase and a couple of boxes being unloaded by the taxi driver, envisioning the next few months he would be working here. He looked up at the windows and saw a pretty young girl with dark hair staring down at him, the net curtains draped around her head as if trying to hide behind a bridal veil.

"Mr. Penfold! Welcome to Greenlawns," Mrs. Ratchet enthused. "I see you managed to find us ok. Here, leave those, I'll get one of the boys to bring your luggage in. Come, come. We'll sort the taxi out and get you settled in asap." She actually said 'asap'!

Aaron thanked the taxi driver with whom he'd enjoyed an interesting conversation along their journey, then followed Mrs. Ratchet inside the open doors of Greenlawns, hoping her unfortunate surname wasn't indicative of the infamous Nurse Ratched!

So far, so good. His room couldn't have been more perfect! It was a far cry from his more humble accommodation in Brighton! Everything was spot on. It was clean, spacious, and had a glorious view of the back garden. He would have no bills to pay, he had accommodation, food, Wi-Fi, AND a weekly allowance of fifty pounds! It almost made him want to weep. He'd done it. He was going to be assisting those who work at evaluating people, looking into their minds and finding out what was going wrong.

He was well aware that it could be many years before any patient was totally entrusted under his jurisdiction, but he was a quick learner, besides which, he had plenty of time, and patience.

Mrs. Ratchet had left him to become familiar with his new surroundings, inviting him to join her in the Staff Room in half an hour's time so that she could introduce him to the rest of the members of staff, have some lunch, show him around the facility and go through his Job Description. He'd emailed his character references ahead of his arrival and posted a signed copy of his Contract of Employment.

He sat down on the corner of his single bed, gazing around his four magnolia painted walls, then looked for a power socket to charge up his laptop.

He knocked tentatively on the Staff Room door and waited until someone called for him to 'come in', surprised to see only half a dozen others, besides Mrs. Ratchet.

"It's Saturday afternoon, Aaron. Many of our young people are collected by their families and taken out for a few hours, so the staff have a relaxing day themselves. Oh, don't you worry, by tomorrow night we'll have a full ship again. A full crew too."

His eyes wandered over the enormous bookcase, wondering if all the books were medical encyclopaedias.

"We have all sorts of books, Aaron. Please feel free to take whatever interests you. I take it you are a reader?"

"I am indeed. I love all books. I read everything I can get my hands on. Books are food for the soul."

Mrs. Ratchet chuckled, "I've always said the very same thing. Now then, let me introduce you to everyone."

The dining room was huge with enormous patio windows - floor to ceiling - and which was full of sunlight. In the middle of the room was the dining table set out in place settings with cutlery, condiments, jugs of cold water, paper napkins. A serving hatch was in view, the shutters raised so that trays and trays of hot and cold food could be displayed.

Aaron was starving. He'd eaten the last of his food from Brighton the night before, trying to make everything last so that he wouldn't have to go out and buy any more, and this food smelt divine.

"Just go the hatch and help yourself, Aaron. It's chicken fricassee or fish and chips today. Or if you're vegetarian we have that option too. And salads, of course, always plenty of salads."

Aaron nodded politely, hoping she would leave him to get some food, and then apologised profusely as his stomach started to rumble.

"Oh dear me," she laughed out loud, "I'd better leave you to it. When you've finished your lunch, come and find me and I'll give you the conducted tour and show you your itinerary. You'll be working with Stefan and Jean to begin with. But hark at me, rabbiting on while your stomach thinks your throat's been cut. Go," she shooed, "we'll talk later."

Aaron liked her, she seemed such a jolly character. He hoped the rest of the staff members were as friendly and accommodating.

Chapter 37: Aaron Meeting Everyone at Greenlawns

It was Monday morning and, as Mrs. Ratchet rightly stated, Greenlawns was buzzing with people. Aaron was unsure how to address the youngers in their care. Were they inmates, patients, custodians, prisoners?

"They're our guests, Aaron," Mrs. Ratchet confirmed sweetly.

"So, they can leave at any time?" he queried.

"Some can, if the courts and their families agree, but unfortunately most are here because they need our tender loving care to get them back into society so that they can live a normal, happy life. Stefan and Jean will prep you on the ones you will be involved with."

"Are there any dangerous *guests* here?"

"Well, don't you think we're all capable of being dangerous, Aaron?"

"Oh, Mrs. Ratchet, I'm sorry, I didn't mean to imply..."

She brushed his apology away. "No offence taken. I understand your question. I believe that each and every one of us has the capability to do harm as we're equally capable of doing good. Circumstances influence our behaviour. Some of our younger guests have endured traumatic childhoods, experienced things they should never have to, and this will undoubtedly impact on the way they handle things, how they behave. At Greenlawns, we like to think we're offering them some breathing space, time to reflect. We talk to them, we listen to them, and we work with them."

"You're a lovely lady, Mrs. Ratchet. I bet your children were glad to have such an understanding mother as yourself. Oh, I'm sorry, I'm being presumptuous, do you have children?"

She howled with laughing, "I had three utter horrors, I tell you. Threw a huge party when the last one left to join the Royal Navy."

She walked away shaking her head and laughing all the way back to the Staff Room.

On the following Monday, Stefan, Jean and Aaron met in the Gloucester Room. Each 'consulting' room was named after a county or a Shire. All clinical references were taboo. Greenlawns was an alternative to home.

The room had the same floor-to-ceiling patio doors that revealed the beautifully manicured lawns and gardens beyond. A Persian-type carpet partially covered the oak flooring. Aaron looked at the pretty dark-haired girl lounging in a dusky-green dralon armchair, the two others sitting in seats placed haphazardly around her.

Stefan introduced Aaron to Margot and explained that they had their weekly chat at different times and in different rooms. The only thing that was regimental was the day.

"Aaron," Stefan turned to look at him, "would you like to talk to Margot? Tell her about yourself, ask about her."

Aaron looked at Margot who looked at him with a smirk on her face, goading him to ask a question.

"Margot, hey? Beautiful name. And am I to presume you are just as infamous as your namesake?"

She didn't answer.

"I personally love the ballet. A ballerina must have amazing strength, not just physical strength but of character too. A ballerina is disciplined, commanding, passionate. Margot Fonteyn was the best of the best, wouldn't you agree? I'm sure you will know who she is."

Well, of course she knew who she was! Was this man a fool? But she did like the way he described the attributes of Ms Fonteyn, likening them to herself.

She was giving nothing away. Stefan and Jean sat listening and watching.

"Everyone's heard of Swan Lake. It's the most famous ballet in the world, I believe. The music, the dance, the story. It's very poignant, wouldn't you agree, Margot?"

Margot's condescending smirk disappeared. No, she didn't know the story of Swan Lake. Why had no one explained it to her, or taken her to watch it? She moved herself on the armchair, sitting back slightly.

"I take it that you don't know the story. Never seen it, Margot?"

"Tell me then. What is it about?"

"That would be easy wouldn't it, for me to give you all the answers? Find a book about it, get a DVD, Google it. It's about love and betrayal. That's all I'm giving you."

"Margot, I think that would be a positive thing for you to do," Jean chimed in. "Aaron's right. Swan Lake is the most beautiful ballet and portrays a magical story. I think you'd really enjoy it."

She still declined to offer anything towards the conversation.

"How did the visit go with your dad, yesterday? Did you go to the car boot sale?" Stefan asked.

"Yeah, he was late though, so a lot of people were packing up by the time we got there. I hate him, he's always late!"

"Hate him, Margot? You hate him because he's late?" Stefan prompted her.

"I hate him because he's my dad and he's always late, ok? I hate him because he sold my house and moved away. Why do you want to know why I hate him? Because *I DO*, that's why!"

Aaron dared to add his two pennyworths, wondering whether he was entitled to do so or not, so decided on the softly-softly approach, "love and hate are very similar emotions you know, Margot - sometimes impossible to differentiate between them. I'm reading this book at the moment which is awful, I hate it and yet I'm loving it. Like Monday mornings, getting up out of bed and hating the fact that I'm having to leave the comfort of my bed but then realising I love that I'm alive and living a new day. You understand?"

He noticed his two colleagues smiling at his attempt to humour her and didn't feel so bad for his forthrightness.

"It's ok to hate, Margot," said Jean, passively. "You're entitled to speak how you feel. Do you think your dad hates you?"

Margot felt very frustrated. "My dad does hate me! My mum hates me, and now even my aunty hates me."

"And apart from your dad, your mum, and your aunt who you say you hate, who else do you hate, Margot?" asked Stefan.

She flopped back in her chair, debating her answer. She looked at Stefan who had just asked the question, across to Jean who was watching appraisingly, and then at Aaron.

"Him!" she spat. "I hate *him*."

Chapter 38: Kerry

Aaron was apologising profusely for his intervention with Margot, but Stefan and Jean dismissed him, laughing and praising him for his contribution towards her therapy.

"No need for any apologies here, Aaron, that was great! We don't pussyfoot round them when asking how they feel. I loved how you drew on her name and then introduced the ballet theme to her. It gave her something to think about. And that love/hate thing too, spot on. It's always a bonus to see a situation through new eyes and Margot has stormed off with a bee in her bonnet, but you've given her food for thought."

Jean agreed with Stefan, "Margot's experienced many tragedies in her young life. She's angry, I think that was evident just now. She probably feels rejected, as many of our guests here do. It was quite a revelation for her to show any feeling, she's not usually so forthcoming. Don't take it to heart when she said she hated you too, it's normal. We're told that all the time, aren't we Stef?"

"About twenty times a day. Anyway, tomorrow we will be talking to our next young lady, Kerry, Margot's roommate. Don't be surprised if we don't get a single word from her. She's extremely introverted and prefers books to people."

The next day Kerry walked into the Gloucester room, hardly daring to make eye contact with anyone. She had a book in her hands.

Aaron winced at her presence. She was painfully thin, her arms were covered in bruises, her blonde hair was greasy, lank, and in dire need of a good trim. She sat on the edge of the same green armchair that Margot had sat in, looking worried.

Jean began. "Hi there, Kerry. We have someone else with us today. This is Aaron. He'll be with us from now on. He's lovely, and I'm sure you gonna like him as much as we do."

Kerry nervously risked a peak at Aaron, and then looked away.

"Did you do anything over the weekend? Go out? Did your mum come over or get in touch?"

Kerry squirmed at the mention of her mother and shook her head.

"Kerry loves her books, Aaron. What are you reading right now, Kerry?" asked Stefan.

She turned the book over to reveal the front cover and Aaron leaned forward in his chair in excitement.

"Oh, you have a copy of *Finding the Negative*! So do I! Do you have her next one, *In Sickness, Not In Health*?"

Kerry almost broke into a nervous smile.

"I know the author, personally," he went on. "I met her when she came to Brighton, doing her book launch. I got her to sign my copy and now I help her with her editing. I like to think we're very good friends."

Everyone looked at him, confused about his sudden effervescent enthusiasm.

"Sorry, Kerry," he laughed, "I just got a bit carried away there. Carry on."

"You know the author of this book?" she whispered.

"I do, yes. I know a lot of authors. I like to admit my claim to fame is helping many writers with their works. I have this idiosyncrasy for perfecting the written word, it's my OCD."

Kerry's pale face lit up with relief. "You have OCD, but... but you're a doctor?"

Aaron laughed, and so did Stefan and Jean. "I'm not a doctor, Kerry, and yes I have my own form of OCD. Most people I know have some form of OCD. One of my former foster mothers had a most bizarre case. She had this thing where she always..."

Kerry interrupted, "You... you were in foster care?"

"Yes, Kerry. I was."

Kerry started to cry, silent pathetic tears running down her scrawny face. Jean moved towards her and put a comforting arm around her, "I was in foster care too, Kerry. That's what determined me to go into this profession because I know what it's like. We're all here to help you."

"Kerry," Stefan probed. "Those bruises on your arms, I didn't notice them before. How did you get them?"

Kerry dismissed his obvious question, wanting to know more about Aaron's OCD and Jean's declaration of being in foster care, but couldn't bring herself to ask direct questions, so the silence continued for a couple of uncomfortable minutes.

"Lizzie was lucky," she eventually said, looking at Aaron with her hands clasped around her book. "At least she knew she was loved, that's got to be good, right?"

Aaron nodded in agreement, remembering how Lizzie had been devastated upon learning about being adopted. She would never have known until she found those negatives...

"But it didn't form who she ended up being, Kerry. Lizzie became a phoenix, against all the odds stacked against her. I think that is what the author meant to portray, that we're all in control of our own destiny. You can either sit on your laurels for evermore, feeling sorry for yourself, or you can decide to reinvent yourself."

Aaron let that sit with her. No one spoke for a while as they all contemplated what had just gone on. Kerry *never* contributed towards their weekly talks, she was always withdrawn, fragile, introvert. Stefan and Jean were pleasantly surprised at this little interlude, which they would categorise in their notes as progress.

"Bloody hell, Aaron! We were told that this was your very first work experience. You know you can get sacked on the spot for falsifying your CV."

"Stefan, I'm so sorry. I feel I've overstepped the mark, but I couldn't help myself! I just found both girls really intriguing. They're like polar opposites of each other, like yin and yang but then again, the same in many ways. Please remind me to keep my big mouth shut and sit in the background as I'm supposed to be doing and talk only when asked to."

Stefan laughed, "Aaron, Jean and I have enjoyed your interaction with the girls. It's enabled us to see them in a different light. And that's what this whole establishment is about, learning about them. The more we learn about them the more we can help them move on. They've both been positive reactions, thanks to you. You seem to have made some kind of connection with each of them. Jean and I are looking forward to working with you. Can't wait to see how you fare with the boys."

Aaron was feeling mighty chuffed with that praise from Stefan. It was actual productive interaction and he too felt immensely positive.

The dining room was filling up with boys and girls as lunch was being served. The boys kept to the left-hand side, the girls the right. That was the rule. Aaron, however, hadn't been told this rule and as he placed his tray on the table at the far end of the girls' table on the right-hand side, fifteen-year-old Bobby Harkins stood up and screamed. "Oi, pervert! Watcha doing down there on the girls' table, hey? Nurse Ratchet, how come he gets to sit with the girls, and we can't?"

Aaron was confused, he'd frequented the dining area before and never encountered a problem, but then he looked round and could see his mistake.

Mrs. Ratchet stood up in an effort to calm the boys down. "Oh, for goodness sake, Bobby, he who is without sin cast the first stone, I dare you! Mr. Penfold is a newcomer to Greenlawns, is this the way you go about welcoming our newbies? Forgive me if I'm wrong Bobby Harkins, but wasn't it you who took a pee outside on my strawberry plants when you first arrived because you claimed you couldn't find the toilets, killing my beautiful patch of strawberries? I wouldn't have mentioned it had you not so indignantly belittled our new member of staff in front of everyone. You see, nobody is infallible, Mr. Harkins, we all make mistakes. Mr. Penfold, do come over here and join us, I've no doubt you may have lost a little of your appetite, but please let it be temporary. You will need your strength to deal with the likes of some of our ruder guests."

The boys at the boys' table were tittering collusively. They'd all peed on her strawberries, and her rhubarb and beetroot!

Chapter 39: Suzanne

Ok, Suzanne thought dismissively, Doug's message was half to be expected. Margot had obviously given him the old sob story again of nobody loved or understood her, which was a total load of bunkum. She was realising more and more that she was just a spoilt little bitch who was making demands on her, and her tolerance was declining faster than the melting icebergs of the Antarctic! How dare she speak to her in that tone of voice?

And the next message from Aaron, that was great. He was doing exactly what she was paying him to do. He was a good tick on her list.

Corah's message. *"Garth's dead, call me when you get this message."* That was a shock. She'd delayed making the call and felt ashamed of her procrastination. Garth. The lovely Garth who was once such a profound and valued person in her life, in both their lives. If it hadn't been for her, she had no doubt that Garth would be alive, living happily with Corah.

Young people and their misgivings, their mistakes. Are they to suffer for evermore? Is every young person who makes a big mistake going to have to feel the guilt hereinafter? When does it all go away? Is there some amazing device on Amazon to buy that can wipe away all one's unwanted memories? Why hasn't anyone invented it yet? It would undoubtedly be a best seller. A bad-memory eraser. If they can make a microchip to implant into animals to find out where they are if lost, or make robots to look and sound human, why can't they make a chip or pill for anyone needing an escape? Surely that's not beyond the realms of possibilities these days? There would be no need for a lot of these so-called healing facilities for people who are struggling to cope with depression. One could simply pop along to a chemist a buy a happy pill. Loads of people bought happy pills! They should be on prescription, or in machines like chocolate bars or fizzy drinks. Insert a fifty-pence coin and have a great night! Instead, they resort to secrecy and lies to escape the tedium of their everyday existence.

"Corah, pick up, damn you. Do you want me to come down? I will do. I want to. I know you're there, Corah, I know you're listening to this call. Look... I can imagine how you're feeling right now because I'm with you. I'm coming over so we can both sit together and you can tell me what happened. I'm sorry for your loss, Corah."

Corah sat on her settee listening to her old friend's rehearsed words of sympathy. *'I'm sorry for your loss, Corah'*. No, she wasn't! She was only saying the words she was expected to say. The same words spoken a million times over and contained the same lack of everything but real sorrow!

The words were meaningless. They offered nothing of genuine comfort. 'I'm sorry for your loss', like she'd mislaid something, lost something, not 'I'm devasted to hear about Garth's passing, I'm saddened beyond belief, and I will truly miss him'.

But people didn't say those words, they just said, 'I'm sorry to hear about your loss'. Stark and unfeeling. Distant and non-committal, and then brushed to one side, not giving any further consideration.

She was half-heartedly contemplating making the journey up to London to be with Corah, to talk about Garth and the fun times they once shared, pay her last respects at his funeral, whenever it was going to take place, but she knew she wouldn't. It would be a total farce for her to show her face and offer profound sympathies when truly she felt nothing but a weight lifted off her shoulders. Ever since their last unfortunate reunion she had felt like looking over her shoulder wherever she went, wondering if someone was following her, watching her. Now she felt less of a need to be so paranoid.

She felt her demons would be interred along with Garth's big body, the past buried with him, no matter what Corah felt. Besides, she was far too busy with her writing, Adam was keen to get *Secrets, Sins, and Siblings* published so that he could acquire enough money to send his poor unsuspecting wife, Beth away for a couple of weeks' respite so that he and his mistress could jet over to Tenerife to enjoy some much needed sun, sea, and… well… satisfaction!

Suzanne was close to concluding the book and Adam was already excited about it, having read the chapters she'd already forwarded to him. He considered it quite a dangerous subject to tackle, worried about whether or not it would affect her, delving too deeply into dark family histories, airing one's dirty linen for the world to see. She was brave, he thought, because even though Suzanne had never disclosed details of her private life, he was astute enough to be able to read between her lines, and her lies, hiding behind her nom de plume.

He often wondered how she managed to write so proficiently about children when she had none of her own. How she managed to weave scenarios about children's behaviour, their ability to hide from reality and avoid truths. Children weren't born with the capacity to tell lies, everything in life was black and white to them. It wasn't until they started growing up that they learned how to tell the odd fib or two, keep secrets, and do bad things.

But he was no expert on child behaviour either, so he was just happy to go with her flow and produce her work because he reaped the benefits of her growing fan club.

On her last book, *Pity My Sister*, he was surprised to read her acknowledgement to Aaron Penfold for his *'invaluable editorial help and eye to detail, without which my book would be filled with many calendarial errors'*. He'd seen the name before, Aaron Penfold, in other authors' acknowledgements. His name had kept popping up and he wondered who he was and how Suzanne had found such a treasure. He'd certainly made a positive contribution to many of his authors' works of late and made a note to ask about him when he met with her in the near future. Authors were always on the hunt for a good editor.

Suzanne's Messenger beeped: it was from Corah.

There's going to be an inquest as Garth was found dead in his cell yesterday morning. I don't know any more details yet. Only received notification from a sister of his yesterday, she's devastated. No need to come down, nothing you can do here. I've got quite a bit of work on too, at the mo. My plates of meat are in high demand, who would have thought so many people had foot fetishes, hey? Just kidding, it's shoe wear and foot jewellery, and I've managed to bag a few gorjus ankle bracelets! Spk soon. C. x

"Perfect," thought Suzanne.

Chapter 40: The Guests

Kerry had returned to her room, a slight skip in her step after her meeting and talk with the counsellors, the creases in her forehead dissipating as she dared to feel a little more optimistic about herself, learning that even those who appeared to have it all, the confidence, a good job or career, had been in similar circumstances to herself once upon a time.

She'd never considered that fact for a second, assuming they all came from loving stable homes, nurtured along the way by adoring affluent parents, having the glorious opportunity to further their education by attending universities and then going out into the big wide world to help others.

That new guy, Aaron, and then Jean. They'd both admitted they'd been in foster care! They must have had the same uncaring mothers such as she and yet they had both seemingly overcome their abandonments and were trying to help *her* overcome her own insecurities. It was a revelation and she felt that her OCD was another thing that wasn't the be-all that was defining her as a person.

Aaron said he *knew* the author of the very book she was reading, and he'd actually *met* her! She'd never met anyone famous and yet this guy, this Aaron, evidently was because he'd told her that he knew lots of authors.

Kerry was tentatively walking on cloud nine, feeling she had a one-upmanship on her roommate, Margot. She almost felt she would be able to defend herself against her when the teasing started because her mother had decided to go off partying, leaving her to her own defences all those years ago.

She was now considering that it wasn't her fault after all. She had been a child who rightly depended on her mother to look after her. Kerry was always under the impression that she was destined for the scrap heap because she had been made to feel unworthy of even her own mother's love and attention. But if this guy, Aaron, and Jean, had walked her walk when they were young, then there was hope, a light at the end of her tunnel.

She wanted some more answers and decided she would go and have a talk with Mrs. Ratchet who was like mother hen to them all, she would ask if she could confide in her. She'd always told her that if ever she needed to know anything, anything at all, she only had to ask, and she'd try her best to help.

Bobby Harkins was one of the next guests to sit with Stefan, Jean and Aaron. He knocked on the door and walked straight in, considering himself too important to wait to be invited, pausing for a second or two upon seeing Aaron sitting down.

"I didn't know the pervert was going to be here," he said cockily.

Bobby was thirteen and a proper pain in the proverbial arse! Always the first to instigate trouble wherever the occasion afforded him, loving the attention and admiration of his peers. He wasn't the brightest lamp in the street, but he did have a great love for dogs, all breeds, and it was his ambition to one day become a police dog handler. He had no time or respect for anyone who didn't share his passion of animals and would threaten to kill any person who had tortured a dog.

He had long dark hair which he tied back in a little ponytail, and dismissed anyone who ridiculed him over it, and a little scar on his top lip, the result of a stand-up confrontation against his brute of a child-molesting stepfather. 'Harky' knew all about perverts!

"Bobby, do come in and take a seat, and you will never refer to Aaron as a pervert again, do you understand?"

Bobby refused to answer.

"Name-calling is not acceptable here at Greenlawns, as you well know, and I'm surprised that you felt inclined to draw the subject of perversion to yourself. Did it make you feel clever in front of everybody? I didn't feel it made you look clever. I actually felt quite sorry for you; it made you look a fool, Bobby. Your so-called pals might laugh at your bravado and wit for a second or two but then it's forgotten about, like old news. Hardly worth all the drama wouldn't you agree?"

Bobby had the good grace to look uncomfortable, not daring to make eye contact with anyone.

"Anyway, thank you again for joining us; now, would you like to talk about your weekend? I believe you went to stay with your grandparents. Did your mother come to see you while you there?"

"No, she didn't. My grandad said she had the flu and so she couldn't get over." He shrugged his shoulders dismissively as if it was no big deal.

"So, how did you spend your time at your grandparents'?" Stefan continued.

His face lit up. "We went to watch the sheep dog trials in the big farmer's field near the Roman ruins. It was fantastic. It's amazing to watch how they manage to round up the sheep so quickly, reacting to the shepherd's whistle. We got there before anyone else turned up, so we stood right at the front, and then afterwards my grandad took me to meet one of his friends. He's a farmer, see, and he let me fuss his dog. It was a girl dog. Her name was Elsa and he said he named her Elsa after that lioness in Born Free. Born Free is a film, my grandad said, I've never seen it but I'm sure I would like it."

Stefan, Jean and Aaron sat smiling at hearing Bobby's enthusiasm over his weekend visit.

"You really do love dogs, don't you, Bobby?" Jean said, more of a statement than a question, it was always the main topic of his conversations.

"I love them more than I like any person. They're loyal and never let you down. Everybody should have a dog. Well, not everybody because some people don't deserve them, those who treat them badly."

"What's your favourite breed of dog?" Aaron asked.

Bobby looked at him, studiously, "I don't really have a favourite, as such. To me, they're all good, but I suppose I'm more interested in larger breeds like the German Shepherds. I would like to be able to work with them one day, train them... you know."

"Have you ever owned one?" Aaron continued.

"No," he replied bluntly.

The bell eventually rang for lunch and Bobby leapt out of his chair making his way towards the door. "By the way, Bobby, if you can get hold of a dictionary here, perhaps there's one in the library, you might want to look up the definition of the word 'pervert'. It doesn't always mean what you think it means."

Bobby looked at Aaron, he didn't know that. He had always assumed there was just the one meaning.

"He wasn't telling the whole truth just then, Aaron," Stefan confided, "there was a dog in the house before he came here, but his stepfather killed it. Bobby was manic and attacked him with a knife. If his grandfather hadn't turned up at the house when he did, God knows what would've happened. He's very close to his grandad and his grandparents adore him. The stepfather's in prison now, you can read his case file later, and once Bobby's on the mend, he will be going to live with them. He doesn't want to return to live with his mother."

"Lunch time, guys," Jean sang, "I'll type up the Activity Logs this afternoon. You can help me if you like, Aaron, and you can tell me how you feel the sessions are going."

Instead, Aaron went up to his room. He would have lunch later when the dining room was less busy, he needed to get to his laptop and make a few notes about the morning's discussions. He was looking forward to the afternoon when he could look through the case files Stefan had promised and really get some insight.

"Hmm," he thought pensively. *"So far, so good!"*

Chapter 41: Doug

Doug's new house was much smaller than the marital home he had bought with Rose when love's young dream was all he thought about. It was a two-bedroomed terrace with a nice little conservatory at the back of the kitchen, extended on to the postage-stamp back garden, totally adequate for him.

Parking was limited in the street, so he'd sold his car and replaced it with a motorbike, an old Yamaha Virago he found in mint condition for its age, one previous lady owner. It looked sedentary with its high handlebars and sloping seat, similar to the style of a Harley Davidson, and it was a doddle to run.

His new girlfriend liked it too, she loved to wrap her arms around his waist as they wove around the country lanes, going faster than the main roads allowed, the exhilarating thrill of speed.

Eve was twenty, almost half Doug's age, and he cared not a jot what people said or thought. Let them pass their snide remarks about hanging on to his youth, it was pure jealousy, he was the one with the young bit of skirt hanging on to his arm and his every word.

He was a free man now. His wife was never going to be the woman she once was, he would be divorced in a few months, single. The world was his oyster again. He'd lost so much in the past and concluded that life is for the living, it was not a rehearsal. Of course, there would always be Margot to think of and he paid his dutiful visits, taking her out, calling her, sending her little gifts in the post. He wasn't being a bad father, but his world had shifted on its axis, and he had no alternative but to move with it. Hence his new lifestyle.

He never considered himself to be a bad father or a bad husband. On the contrary, he had been the perfect provider for his family. He, too, had been a victim of circumstance and if his wife had been more forthcoming with her marital duties it wouldn't have entered his head to have had those little interludes with the others, or his own sister-in-law. And goodness, she had been just as willing!

Anyway, he told himself, it didn't matter now, he had Eve, and she never refused him anything. They'd only been dating for a few months and Doug wanted to keep things casual, commitment-free. No point lumbering himself with another clingy woman at this stage in his life when the vast ocean was full of different fish to fry.

He had been expecting a barrage of expletives from Suzanne after he sent her the message, berating her for upsetting his perfect little prima donna. But she was his daughter's aunty, it was her duty to make sure she got everything she needed. She had to step into Rose's shoes now and take on the maternal role, that's what families are supposed to do, look after one another.

Her silence, however, baffled him. He was not used to hearing nothing from Suzanne, she always gave him feedback after a visit. He considered whether he had been too brutal and perhaps a more apologetic approach would soften her up. He would send an email later that evening after Eve had gone home.

Suzanne had deliberately held off from answering Doug's message, imagining Margot's dramatic story telling of her visit, her own 'oh woe is me' version and how nobody understands or loves her. She was developing rapidly into a mardy teenager, too soon by half!

Margot was a very clever and cunning girl who seemed to have developed an uncanny knack of twisting everything so that she was made to look the victim. It was Rose's fault that Simon had thought the pills he'd taken were sweets, she said that Rose had bribed her to give them to him. Suzanne thought it odd Margot hadn't eaten a single one herself.

It was Rose's own stupid fault that she'd slipped on the wet patch that day of her accident, even though Margot had wee'd in the very same spot after standing there dripping with water, having just got out of the pool.

It was Suzanne's fault that Doris, the golden retriever puppy, had escaped from the garden and was run over because she should have ensured the gate couldn't be opened.

It was Doug and Rose's fault that she felt angry at not being allowed to see Steven in his coffin because she wanted to see what he looked like, dead.

Lilo, the doll she received when she was five years old, had been thrown in the dustbin because she'd gouged her eyes out with a knife she'd got from the cutlery drawer, and then proceeded to slice off all her fingers, toes, and hair. That wasn't her fault, she just wanted to know if Lilo felt any pain like Simon did when she stuck pins in his leg.

Suzanne was adamant she wasn't going to resort to replying to his message. She wanted to, but - no, she needed to - have a talk with Doug, a sit-down, cards-on-the-table chat with him. She was hoping to receive some reassurance that her suspicions were just a figment of her over-active imagination and that she was totally wrong, remembering all the lovely weekends she'd spent with her niece, snuggled up on her big sofa, painting finger and toenails, watching childish DVDs as they tucked into slices of pizza.

She parked her BMW a little way from his house, all the car parking spaces occupied. She got out and locked the door then heard a familiar laugh and panicked, hoping no one had seen her.

The swine, she thought. The filthy rotten swine! There was Doug kissing some blonde floozy at the front door, his hands all over her like a bad rash. She crouched down at the side of the passenger door, watching – she wasn't sure out of envy or disgust – as the two slobbered over each other like a couple of love-sick teenagers. She held her breath whilst clutching her car keys, praying she wouldn't be seen or heard, and was relieved when the young woman eventually left, on foot she noted, so presumably lived close by.

She was shaking but wasn't sure what had attributed her to feel so upset. Poor Rose. Her poor deluded sister had been dumped like a sack of rotting potatoes through no fault of her own and Suzanne felt murderous.

She watched Doug watching the young woman walk away, both of them waving and blowing silly kisses until she vanished round the corner. She caught her breath and opened the car door, slinking guiltily into the driver's seat, and lit up a cigarette. She wouldn't be having the conversation she needed to have with him after all. He wouldn't be pleased to know that she knew about his latest conquest. He could continue to portray the injured party for as long as he liked but she now knew better, and she would keep this little snippet of valuable information to herself... for now.

It was well past midnight when she arrived back at her cottage, feeling agitated at the show she'd just unwittingly witnessed, saddened that her family was in tatters. She looked around at her neighbours' houses, noticing some still had their downstairs lights on whilst others were in darkness, presumably fast asleep or, she wondered, making love with their better halves. She never considered hers a dysfunctional family, growing up. Their house was full of fun and laughter, happy school days and holidays, normal, she had presumed. But it had been far from normal, as she had found out the day she found the evidence in her dad's garden shed.

She opened her front door and walked inside. She had a faint memory of Doris the dog running up to greet her when she walked through her front door, her little tail wagging ten to the dozen, running round and round in circles. Someone actually pleased to see her.

She went to her favourite cupboard that housed her gin and decided it was the perfect night to drown her sorrows. Gin was good for that, the most satisfying thing she had in her life, that and her escapism with writing. Gin was helpful with that too.

She sat at her kitchen table and opened up her laptop, dismayed to see a load of junk mail in her inbox, a message from Aaron, and another from Adam. She deleted the junk mail and decided to read Adam's message first.

Who's your new editor, this Aaron Penfold? Been seeing his name in a couple of clients' books lately. Is he freelance? If so, can we talk? May have a lot more work if he's interested. Call me.

She'd ask Aaron, he'd be chuffed.

Good evening Suzanne. Hope you are well. In your book, Pity my Sister, can you tell me what led you to discover the diagnosis of Margaret? I mean, I know the medical name for her condition but what made you come to research it and find out? What founded your journey? I ask because it's usually something a crime thriller writer would write about and have a vast amount of knowledge of the subject, not your usual modus operandi. Margaret's hidden killings were undertaken by such a young girl with an incredibly high IQ and, because of her tender years, no one could quite believe it. I understand all of that and find it quite fascinating, like you!

She lowered the lid of her laptop, couldn't be bothered to answer back. Why was he trying to dissect every little thing she wrote? He was being paid to do her editing only, not analysing the whys or wherefores.

"Because I'm a writer, you stupid boy, that's what I do and I can write exactly what I want without having to justify anything to the likes of a jumped up wannabe like you!"

And what was that extra bit, *like you*, supposed to mean? Was he saying he found it as fascinating as she did, or – because of that comma – did he mean he found *her* fascinating?

No. He definitely meant that he found *her* fascinating, *hence* that comma. If he had meant he found the writing fascinating he would have written it differently, he was the OCD expert on punctuation after all. He could have written *I understand all of that and, like you, find it quite fascinating* if he hadn't meant it the other way.

He knew exactly what he was implying, and it unsettled her. Would he know that she would know, or would he assume she didn't?

"Is this your real name?" he asked, pointing to Suzanne Barsby. The words suddenly echoed from the past.

"Do I look like I'm not real?" she answered coolly. He laughed, "it's been 'surreal' to meet you, Miss Suzanne Barsby. Can't wait to read this one," he said, tapping his new acquisition. "I'll send you a personal review on your website. Bye, now."

She sat back in her chair trying to think back to that day at her book launch in Brighton. The young gawky, spotty teenager who she seemed to recall feeling slightly sorry for as she watched him walk away with her book under his arm, his familiar ten-to-two lilt, reminiscent of sailor who'd been at sea for months at a time.

Chapter 42: Greenlawns

Jean was typing up the last of her notes and was dying to finish off so that she could walk outside and enjoy the last few hours of sunshine before the evening sessions began, when Aaron joined her holding two large mugs of black coffee.

"I was being presumptuous and brought you a black coffee, I hope that's ok?" he asked jovially.

Jean was probably old enough to be Aaron's mother, it was difficult to tell. She was petite with long, red, frizzy hair and a face full of sepia freckles. If one was to view her from behind she could easily be mistaken for one of the young guests at Greenlawns, and Aaron found this intriguing. It was easy to make assumptions about people based on their appearance, first impressions et al. Who didn't? It was human nature that one's eyes took in the scene, sent the messages to the brain to conjure up the picture and judge a fellow human being accordingly. That's what people did, every single one, it was love, hate, or indifference at first sight. Animals were different though, perception was totally different for them, they judged on smell, body language and behaviour. The human species could learn such a lot from animals.

"You didn't bring me any sugar, Aaron, and I have a very sweet tooth. Be a love and fetch me a couple of sachets."

Hmph, his work colleagues were already trying to take advantage of his good nature and treat him like the underdog he was expected to be. He'd need to nip this in the bud before they had him acting like an obedient puppy, performing to their every beck and call.

"Black is better for you. They say once you've had black you never look back. Sugar's so bad for you, rots your teeth, and if I may be so forward in saying your teeth are wonderful, so try and enjoy the coffee without the additives of poisonous substances."

Jean laughed. "Poisonous substances? Sugar?"

"Most probably saccharin. Did you know that saccharin can cause allergic reactions? Its sulphonamide compound can cause allergic reactions in people who are unable to tolerate sulpha drugs. The most common allergic reactions are breathing difficulties, headaches, skin irritations, and diarrhoea."

Jean looked at him with her coffee cup barely touching her lips, "Flipping heck, Aaron, how did you know about all that?"

"I was a hyper-child, or so I believe. I don't know for sure, but I do remember learning about saccharin and its adverse effects. Coffee is a great stimulant on its own. It doesn't need anything else. Drink your coffee and learn to appreciate it; it will take time to get used to without sweeteners but I think you'll come round to my way of thinking eventually and appreciate how it's meant to be. I'm sure you'll let me know if I'm wrong."

Jean shoved some of her frizzy red hair behind her ear as she studied the young man sitting in front of her and laughed at his audacity to feel completely confident in his matter-of-fact ability to enlighten her about her drinking habits. It was daring, considering they had spent so little time together, and yet Aaron sat there feeling it was his mere duty to pass on his knowledge to a fellow work colleague. It was nothing really, it was all there on the internet, should anyone feel the necessity to look. You could find anything and everything... the how to, the needs, the reasons why and the reasons why not to. Obviously, the

Jeans of the world, Aaron concluded, had opted for the ostrich option, to bury her head in the sand. He was going to love working alongside Jean.

Chapter 43: Aunty Pat

Suzanne had been trying to locate their dad's sister, their Aunty Pat, who neither she nor Rose had hardly any knowledge about or interaction with for years. Ever since her discovery of being a twin she had exhausted every avenue in her endeavour to find their aunt. It appeared she'd disappeared off the face of the earth; the home of her last known address had been demolished years ago to make way for a new affordable housing estate.

It had been by pure coincidence that she bumped into Deb - Rose's old next-door neighbour - in the supermarket one afternoon and they got chatting, with Deb asking about Rose and Doug, proffering her heartfelt condolences for Simon, the little boy she and Alec had adored. She was genuinely upset.

Deb then graciously asked about Margot, a question Suzanne realised only too well was dutiful, but acquiesced, nevertheless.

"A great-aunt of mine came to visit me a few months ago and she was talking about your family. She remembered your father and his younger sister, Pat, your aunt. They lived in the same street in Loughborough. My great-aunt went to school with your grandfather. Isn't it a small world?"

Suzanne was almost hyper-ventilating. This was the very lead she'd been hoping for.

"Deb!" she exclaimed, "by any chance would your great-aunt know where my Aunty Pat is now? I've been trying to locate her for years. Rose and I wanted to get in touch with her to get a bit of background on our family history because Mum and Dad didn't tell us much and we grew up not having that big family thing. We don't even know if we have any cousins."

"Well, I know that Pat didn't have any children, so you won't have any cousins on your dad's side as far as I'm aware, there was just him and Pat. Pat never married, see, she remained a spinster all her life but she's not even that old. In her fifties, I think my great-aunt said. Look, Love, I still have your business card, I'll give my great-aunt a call to see if she knows anything else about your aunt, and I'll get back to you. Don't hold your breath though, the old dear is in her eighties now and although she can usually easily recall the most minute details of her childhood, she can barely remember what she walked into the pantry for."

Suzanne laughed out loud as the pair stood in the aisle of baked beans and packets of pasta. Good old Deb, she had been like a breath of fresh air, she would have loved to have neighbours like her and Alec instead of the miserable, boring old fogies she had, who never so much as passed a courteous 'good morning'.

And true to her word, only two days later, Suzanne received a phone call from Deb which left her downing the tools and cleaning substances she was using to scrub the sides of her microwave and drove the two miles to where Rose and Doug used to live, a bottle of expensive Chardonnay on the back seat of her car as a huge thank you for all her efforts.

*　*　*　*　*

Barrow-on-soar was a picturesque village located not too far away from Loughborough's city centre and Aunty Pat's house was a much sought-after terraced cottage whose garden backed onto the River Soar. It was idyllic. Narrowboats and cruisers could be seen daily, leisurely making their trips up and down the waterways, the canals, a stone's throw away from the historical Navigation Pub that was always a hive of activity during the summer months.

Suzanne knocked hesitantly on the lime-green front door, using the antique horseshoe knocker. She held her breath and gasped in disbelief when the door opened and a smiley older version of her sister, Rose, stood before her.

Chapter 44: Kerry

Kerry had had a very satisfying talk with Mrs. Ratchet. She'd told her all about the therapy session she'd had with Stefan, Jean and Aaron and claimed she had felt it had been beneficial in that she no longer felt the guilt she'd carried over the years.

"Mrs. Ratchet," she said "I always assumed that I was to blame for everything that happened to me. Food was always taboo in my understanding because I felt I wasn't worthy to eat it. My mother made cooking and feeding me a chore, something she was forced to do when she'd rather be doing more exciting things. I remember her getting angry at her attempts to get me to eat the burnt offerings she put on my plate and I'd gag and cry, I didn't want to eat it."

Mrs. Ratchet held Kerry's hand as she sat in front of her, pouring out her feelings.

"A bit like some of the food they serve up in our dining room, Kerry?" she joked.

Kerry had to laugh. "I don't know if I'll ever get a real appetite for food again, Mrs. Ratchet, but after talking with the therapists yesterday morning and hearing Jean and Aaron say that they were in foster care too, and they've done okay for themselves, it led me to believe that if they've done it, so can I!"

"Kerry, you dear girl, you can do absolutely anything you set your heart on. You could become the Prime Minister of England if that's what you want to do. What would you like to do, Kerry, when you leave here?"

All of a sudden, Kerry looked startled at the suggestion of leaving the safety and security of Greenlawns.

"I... I don't know, Mrs. Ratchet. I hadn't thought about leaving here."

"But you will leave here, missy. I personally think you'd fare well with foster parents, join a family who will encourage you and love you the way you deserve to be loved. I know of a young couple who are very keen to foster a young girl like you. They're musicians and have been on the fostering list for ages; they're looking for someone who is interested in learning about music and song-writing."

Kerry struggled to comprehend what Mrs. Ratchet was suggesting. She always assumed she'd be going back to her mother one day, never contemplating living with another family. And Mrs. Ratchet had said 'a couple', that meant a man and a woman!

"You read a million books every week, Kerry. You write the most amazing poetry, too. I think you would like this young couple I'm talking about and they're coming here tomorrow night to talk to me some more. Would you like to meet them?"

Kerry looked horror-stricken at Mrs. Ratchet. The suggestion was overwhelming. She was skinny, her arms were covered in bruises, her hair was disgustingly lank and she felt so ugly. How could anyone want to have *her* as a foster-daughter?

"No!" she squealed frantically, "they'll hate me, I'm repulsive, Margot tells me I smell like a pig. That's why she has to squeeze the pig shit out of my arms and my body..."

Mrs. Ratchet was horrified at what she had just learned. "Let's go up to your room, Kerry, and collect your belongings. Would you like your very own room, all to yourself? Just you, no one else. You can have all your books on the shelf, there's a television in the room too. It's all for you, no sharing. What do you say? Actually, it's not a question... it's an instruction. Come along now, let's go and see your new room."

Margot glared at Kerry the entire time she was packing away her few possessions to go to a room all by herself! It hadn't yet dawned on her that she, too, would have the whole room to herself, but the fact that Mrs. Ratchet was instigating the whole event bugged her. Margot would have no one in the immediate vicinity to persecute, and this vexed her beyond her comprehension. She'd always had someone near to poke at, prod, stick pins in, kick, choke, jump on, push, shove, strangle, scream at! Mrs. Ratchet was surely punishing her, and she didn't like it; she had no understanding of why this was happening to her.

It was *his* fault, this Aaron guy, she sensed he was bad news the minute she set eyes on him. He'd been the one to suggest moving Kerry away from her, he was the one who needed to repent.

Chapter 45: Greenlawns Tragedy

Kerry was excited being in her new room surrounded by all her very own possessions, liberated from the taunts and frightening acts of cruelty she'd endured whilst sharing a room with Margot. She lay on the bed trying to imagine a worry-free night knowing she could close both eyes until it was time to wake up for breakfast.

She was so happy to have felt brave enough to seek out Mrs. Ratchet and have that chat. And then the talk about the foster couple, the musicians who were coming the next night to have further discussions about fostering her! She wasn't too sure what it all entailed because surely her mother's permission was needed? Five years was a long time to spend in a care facility. She would love to experience normal family life, attend a normal school, make some friends, a best friend who could come over for a girly night and have sleepovers.

She just needed to nip down the corridor to the bathroom to do her night-time ablutions then she was going to continue reading another couple of chapters in her book before switching off the light and luxuriating in the peace and quiet of her *own* room.

She tiptoed to the bathroom and began to fill the bath, she wanted to look and feel respectable for tomorrow, wash her greasy hair, scrub her fingernails. The mirror was covered in condensation from the steam of the hot water as the bath filled, so she wiped it with her dressing gown belt, and smiled at her reflection.

Eventually she took off her robe and stepped into the hot water. She scrubbed at her skin, her feet, under her arms with scented soap that had been part of a gift set she'd received for her birthday, then lay down flat with her head in the water so that she could wet her hair and apply shampoo.

Kerry hadn't heard the door open and close. She hadn't realised someone had walked in, nor would she suspect anyone would do as she'd switched the VACANT lever over to ENGAGED. Bathrooms were never locked at Greenlawns in case anyone got in trouble whilst taking a bath. If anyone flouted the rules and walked in whilst the ENGAGED sign was showing, they were in big trouble! Visits suspended, banished to their rooms after evening meals, loss of privileges for however long Mrs. Ratchet deemed appropriate.

Kerry quickly tried to sit up, seeing Margot standing over her, a dark and sinister expression on her face.

"Margot! Get out, get out before I tell Mrs. Ratchet."

Margot didn't reply, she had Kerry's towel in her hands, a utility white bath towel with the word *'Greenlawns'* on the bottom. She threw it on top of Kerry and pushed it over her face then shoved her backwards into the water, causing splashes on the floor and bathmat. Kerry was frantically trying to grab hold of the towel to pull it from her face, but the water had soaked through making it heavy and Margot already had a firm grip. She held on tightly while Kerry kicked her legs in an effort to make a purchase to lever herself up or turn around in the bathtub, but she was unable. Her gargled screams were silenced by the water entering her mouth and she was gagging, gulping, scratching Margot's hands as she desperately fought to draw breath, and for her life.

It didn't take long, a few minutes, four, maybe five before the thrashing ceased and Kerry's hands fell each side of her naked young body.

Margot continued holding the towel over Kerry's face until she was satisfied there was no way she was ever going to tell Mrs. Ratchet another thing. She removed the towel and studied Kerry's distorted face, her eyes wide open in horror, and just as she was placing it back, she started to feel the most incredible sensation she had ever experienced. A massive surge of power began to pulsate between her legs, and she found herself doubling over trying to better enjoy the thrill her body was going through, her heart pounded whilst flashes of lightning darted behind her closed eyelids, silently gasping in the explosive ecstasy. She shuddered for a few more seconds holding on to the side of the bathtub, noticing goosebumps on her arms, the hairs standing up, and wondered what on earth had just happened to her.

Realising she must leave and return to her room before anyone came along and start banging on the door asking how long they were going to be, she collected herself, peeped right and left along the corridor, and – after blowing a kiss to the unmoving form of Kerry - nonchalantly walked out, closing the door, leaving the ENGAGED sign in view.

It was Mrs. Ratchet who had been called to open the bathroom door and found Kerry lying in the bath, covered over with her bath towel. Zoey had been pacing the corridor for the last hour, banging and telling whoever was in there to hurry up because they'd been in there for ages and she needed the shower to rinse of the hair remover on her legs, it had been on half an hour too long as it was!

Zoey wasn't renowned for her patience, either, and so after receiving no answer from the other side, in a fit of temper she stormed off to yell at Mrs. Ratchet to intervene and tell the person who was taking far too long, to finish off so that somebody else could use the facilities.

Mrs. Ratchet had tried to calm Zoey down, reminding her that there was more than the one bathroom she could use, but Zoey had argued that whoever was in there was taking the mickey, and no one was answering her.

"Okay, Zoey, I'll come with you and rally them along. We'll have them out in no time."

Greenlawns was no stranger to the presence of the police force, ambulances, or fire crews. It was par for the course running an establishment for youngsters from broken homes, young offenders, or simply children in need of protection from their respective families.

Each and every guest had different demons to deal with. The lucky ones leaving Greenlawns had learnt and gained from their experiences, moved on with a positive attitude, whilst the unlucky ones would often find themselves in juvenile detention centres, and then ultimately, prison.

Mrs. Ratchet, and indeed all the staff, were heartbroken at the awful tragedy of Kerry's death. Zoey had taken it particularly badly; she'd been the one standing outside hurling expletives, telling them to hurry up and all the time the poor girl had been dead, committed suicide perhaps at the dread of having to leave Greenlawns. But Mrs. Ratchet couldn't get her head round that notion. She'd met many a suicidal youngster in her time but had never considered Kerry one of them. On the contrary, she had been brave enough to come and have that talk with her, revealing how positive she felt after the discussion with the therapists. It *had* been a brave step because Kerry was the type of girl who would go with the flow and accept whatever was thrown in her path, including being bullied.

And then there was that reference to her room companion, Margot. She remembered something along the lines of *"Margot tells me that I smell like a pig and that's why she has to squeeze the pig shit out of my arms and my body..."*

She'd have a meeting with Stefan and Jean - she needed to review their assessment report - and then she'd have a little chat with Margot and to see how she felt she was getting along ask her if she had noticed anything untoward with Kerry. They'd been roommates, they must have had some kind of friendship.

*   *   *   *   *

Margot was in a thoroughly exuberant mood. She had thoroughly enjoyed the thrill of the kill, plus she now had the whole twin room to herself with two beds to choose from. She decided she would sleep in Kerry's former bed, and as she pulled the duvet up to her chin she chuckled, looked across to her empty bed, switched off the light and slept in blissful slumber until she found herself being woken by the clanging of the 7.30 a.m. call to breakfast.

* * * * *

Jean and Stefan sat in Mrs. Ratchet's office tentatively waiting for her to join them, they had all their notes on Kerry - and Margot. Aaron was conspicuously absent.

When Mrs. Ratchet arrived, she was accompanied by a Police Sergeant who had been in attendance upon the discovery of Kerry's lifeless body.

"Stefan, Jean, thank you both for joining me. Police Sergeant Cummins here has informed me that Kerry's accident *was* no accident, nor does it appear to be suicide as was first suggested in view of the fact that I had discussed the possibility of her going to live with a foster family. It may have been daunting to her as she always assumed she would eventually return to live with her mother. Their first assessment suggested a struggle, so that led us to the obvious conclusion that she was not alone in the bathroom, but who was in there with her and who would want to kill her?"

Mrs. Ratchet continued, "We all know that Kerry felt insecure with herself and she never appeared to be surrounded by many friends, if any! Police Sergeant Cummins has told me that he's awaiting the results of DNA tests, but I'll let him take over and explain everything to you. If you would oblige, Police Sergeant Cummins."

Cummins was a weathered character who had witnessed many harrowing death scenes during his forty years in the force. Old or young, it was always distressing; a reason why many nights he would get out of bed and go downstairs to review his pages and pages of notes.

He'd seen everything from a nipper caught stealing a packet of fireworks from Tesco to an old boy of ninety who'd been terrorising his neighbours for years by breeding mice and then releasing them into their garage, all because they'd complained at the forever growing height of his Leylandii trees at the front of the two properties.

But young scallywags and neighbourly disputes were not the only problems he'd had to deal with. They were the simple, niggly things, the everyday disputes. The death of a young girl, or any child, was unforgiving and would take months and months of legwork, paperwork, expert opinions on this and that, forensic analyses, DNA diagnostics, and truths were sometimes just as hard to accept as the lies they hid behind.

His balding head was perspiring under the glaring brightness of the overhead fluorescent lighting in Mrs. Ratchet's office.

"There's definitely evidence of a struggle, skin tissue was found underneath Kerry's fingernails. The lass was fighting for her life, so the lab techs are hoping to give us something by the end of tomorrow but unfortunately for you guys that means we have to take swabs from everybody who was here yesterday. And that means everybody; guests and staff."

The three Greenlawn employees sat nodding, accepting and understanding the ways and procedures of the law, dismayed to realise there was potentially a killer living amongst them.

* * * * *

Aaron was sitting at the dining table eating his cornflakes and drinking his morning black coffee when Jean placed her tray next to him and sat down. She looked at him as he scrolled through his phone seemingly unconcerned at the previous night's events.

"Aaron, what are your thoughts? I know you only met Kerry very briefly, but would you have thought she showed any signs of suicide?"

He stopped chewing and turned to her, "Jean, what are you talking about? Has Kerry done something to hurt herself?"

"You haven't heard?" she exclaimed in utter astonishment, "Aaron, Kerry was found dead last night, in the bath."

He gulped down his mouthful of cornflakes and milk and took a big swig from his coffee mug, staring at Jean in disbelief.

"No, I haven't. Jean. What happened? What time was this? She seemed quite optimistic when she left us the other morning, I don't know what she's been like during your other meetings with her, but I thought the meeting went well. She seemed genuinely interested in the session. Was it something I said, did wrong? Jean, did I say anything to upset her?"

Aaron was frantic. He knew he wasn't supposed to interact fully on the sessions, he was merely there to observe and learn with the occasional intervention if he deemed his input was going to be beneficial. If Kerry had been upset by anything he'd said, he would be out on a limb, his dreams crumbling down around him.

"You didn't do or say anything out of place, Aaron. In fact, both Stef and I are united on that. There's going to be an inquest, obviously. The police have already been here and just now spoke with Mrs. Ratchet, Stef and me. They're going to go over the session's Activity Log and the Police Sergeant says they're going to need DNA samples of everybody who was here at Greenlawns last night."

"DNA samples? Why?" he asked.

"Because the police aren't convinced it's suicide. Look, I can't say much more but I'm sure Mrs. Ratchet will fill you in. Don't worry, taking a DNA sample just means a swab in the mouth, one of those ear cleaning thingamajigs under our tongue, or something. They're gonna test everyone this afternoon... Our interview sessions are postponed for the time being."

Aaron was uncomfortable, he didn't want his DNA to be tested. He'd come so far, why was this happening now? What could he do to avoid it? He knew all about DNA. It was supposed to be fool proof and it had resulted in hundreds of criminals being brought to justice. Rarely could a guilty party slip through the loop with a positive matching DNA result.

There were isolated cases though, he'd read about a least two cases where the DNA results were proven wrong, as a result of extensive scientific research. The one case that had intrigued him the most was that of a young American woman who, after applying to claim family benefits, was informed that her children were not hers and was taken to court for fraud. DNA had to be ascertained in cases such as hers whereby the claimant is seeking state benefits. She, and the children's father, were happy to go along with the procedure, as they considered it a formality.

The father's DNA was matched to her children but hers wasn't, and that's when the authorities decided to delve further and accuse her of fraud by either claiming benefits for other people's children or taking part in a surrogacy scam. It was only due to the fact that she was pregnant again at the time of the court proceedings that immense concentration was placed on her next birth. Immediately after the child was born, DNA samples were taken from her and her new-born, thus enabling any interference or dispute. Ironically, the results came back identical - she was NOT the mother!

It was simply not possible! The hospital team had not left the delivery room, neither had mother or child. In layman's terms, the mothers 'parasitic twin' inside her body, birthed her own children! In scientific terms, it's called chimerism, and happens once in a billion occasions.

Aaron's own DNA wasn't one of those billion-in-one chances at being matched, his had been very straight forward, easy-peasy – just like his mother. He'd never had the slightest inclination at finding out who his father is, just his mum, wondering what she looked like, who and where she was. Why he had been forsaken when he'd read so many books about how mothers bonded and felt an overwhelming love for their babies the second they were born.

It fascinated Aaron, all this science and technology. The internet was a better source of nourishment than food and water. Anything anyone needed to know could be found by a simple click on the mouse; books would eventually become obsolete because everyone could read a whole library on their iPads, phones, or PCs, if they so desired. And yet nothing could ever beat the feel of an actual book in their hands, turning a new page to read the next chapter, seeing one's own name in the acknowledgements, or a dedication on the front page, signed by the author himself.

He was angry at Kerry for piling this unnecessary worry at his feet, and yet at the same time felt guilty for being angry at her when seemingly it wasn't her fault. Someone else needed to shoulder that blame and he had a pretty good idea who.

He'd only just managed to secure this position here at Greenlawns. He was hoping to stay for at least his contracted six months! That old dilemma 'should I stay or should I go?' tormented his thoughts as Jean sat across from him, talking without him hearing a sound.

PART THREE

Chapter 46: Home Truths

Suzanne's family history lesson with her Aunty Pat had left her feeling like a kaleidoscope, sharp and unrealistic images swimming before her eyes, changing before she had time to grasp the last sentence her aunt had uttered. It was as though she'd ingested some of the incredibly expensive substances Garth used to sell in Leicester Square and other prestigious areas down 'the smoke'.

How had she never known? Why had she or Rose never been told?

She sat in her car, trembling as she tried to turn the key in the ignition, desperate to get away from anything resembling family. She felt sick. Sick at her sick family, angry at her parents, wishing they were both alive so that she could lash out and give them a severe piece of her mind.

She withdrew all the sorrow she had harboured over the loss of her mum and dad and felt that if ever there was a God, this Almighty, all-seeing Deity, he would never allow them eternal peace alongside himself in Heaven.

She drove to the Navigation Pub, a stone's throw from her aunt's house and asked the kindly landlady for a white-wine spritzer, which she nursed at the bar and lit up a cigarette.

"Aww, sorry love, no smoking inside," Ann, the landlady, reminded her, "but we can always go outside for a crafty one, if you fancy a bit of company?"

Suzanne looked up at the smiley face of the well-groomed, petite, attractive and knowing, Ann.

"Milky!" she shouted, tilting her head backwards, "take over the bar, I'm off for a ciggie."

Within seconds, a middle-aged man with blond hair and thick milk-bottle-lenses-glasses appeared behind the bar, a dead-ringer for the kid from the Milky Bar adverts decades ago.

"I'm gasping for a fag," Ann said, "haven't had the opportunity to have one this morning. Sometimes I just wish I didn't have a single customer to serve. Come on, let's go outside and I'll have Milky bring our drinks out to us."

They were alone except for a couple of cruisers moored up on the opposite side of the river. Suzanne seated herself on the wooden seat opposite Ann. "My dad used to live in this area, when he was a boy."

"Want one of my fags or are you one of those fussy types that only smokes your own particular brand?" Ann asked, offering her open packet of Marlboro Lights.

Suzanne managed to raise a smile, "only menthol, anything else makes me feel sick. Christ knows what I'm going to do when they ban the sale of menthols. I've already started stockpiling."

Ann spat out the mouthful of wine she'd just sipped, in laughter, "Oh, good grief, girl! I totally get you! I went for hypnotherapy to give up smoking a couple of years back, cost me a ruddy fortune. It was brilliant for two months, the money I spent on the hypnotherapist paid for all those cigarettes I was determined to never buy again, until I lost my little dog and what's the thing you reach for when you need comfort?"

"Gin and tonic?" asked Suzanne.

"That of course - and a fag! She was thirteen years old, my Lulu. Mad as a March Hare and a nasty little bitch, but she was my bitch and I adored her. Cancer. How can animals get cancer? Anyway, sorry, I interrupted you. You say your dad was from around here?"

"Hmm," Suzanne continued, "for a few years, lived just over the back there with the Dilkes' family, but he used to come and fish here as a child and my aunt's just been telling me about the time he fell off the bridge and went under the water. Seems he was lucky…"

Ann looked at her new friend with great surprise and interrupted, "Billy Smythe? He was indeed lucky, gal! Everybody here in Barrow-on-Soar knows that story. That was your dad? Well, what a small world, hey? My parents told me the story many times, they ran this place before I took it over. It's true, your dad was fishing from that bridge, see it over there? He was incredibly lucky because many have gone under the water here and the flow of the river has taken them away, only their lifeless bodies ever being recovered. Some guy had been watching the young lads fishing and when he saw one topple over, he jumped in and managed to pull him out. My mother said your dad was more mortified at being stripped down to his underwear because everyone could see him, before putting a towel around him."

Suzanne was thoroughly enjoying hearing this version. She'd never heard her dad tell this story, in fact he rarely told stories of his childhood.

"Hang on a sec," Ann studied Suzanne, taking a large drag of her cigarette at the same time as sipping on her glass of wine, "you say your dad lived around here, but his sister still does. She lives just down the road, there. Patricia. They're both a little younger than me, but Pat comes here very occasionally with her daughter, you know, high days and holidays. You can tell you're all related, you look so much alike."

Suzanne couldn't assess how she was feeling. She'd sat with her aunt - her dad's sister - and learned things she never was expected to know. Things that her beloved father should have told her and Rose. It explained a lot but told her nothing.

She realised her whole family, including herself, was dysfunctional far beyond her comprehension. Her poor sister and niece were cooped up in facilities through no fault of their doing. If anyone needed to be locked away for their misgivings, it was surely her. She'd been the rebellious one, the one dishing out the hurt and pain to the innocents.

She should be carrying the weight of guilt she'd inflicted on her nearest and dearest. But it was so much easier to pass it on, bury one's head in the sand and pass the blame away. Exactly like her aunt!

As she parked her car outside her pretty bungalow, she dismally surveyed her front door and the emptiness behind it, realising the worthlessness of her accomplishments. There would be no one coming to visit or accompany her in a glass of wine and celebrate her successes or offer consolation for her losses. She hadn't a single human being to totally confide in, to laugh and have fun with, discuss her sex life with - or lack of. She would always return to an empty house and engage with a blank screen, to which she would pour out her heart in an endeavour to gain admiration from cyber 'friends'.

She walked into her unlit kitchen, deciding not to switch on the light. She opened up the screen to her laptop and poured her usual tipple whilst listening to the messages beeping in her InMail box.

Chapter 47: Back at Greenlawns

Aaron was worried. He felt that everything was going to go down the pan and he was bitterly anxious. Everything he'd been working towards was about to fall flat around his heels after all those agonising months and months of planning, dotting the i's and crossing the t's. Never for an instant had he taken into consideration the enormity of what had happened so early in his schedule was about to undo the whole caboodle.

He knew he had limited time to put his plans into action before he lost his opportunity, *and* his nerve. He debated postponing everything, bide his time and wait another week or more, perhaps no one would suspect anything, and the DNA results would be inconclusive; he knew it happened. His reasons for being at Greenlawns were personal and the timing had been structured with precision.

He knew he should try to act unperturbed, to carry on as usual and to ignore the discombobulation he felt sure was going to be obvious to all and sundry.

His foster brother, Isaac, back at the Trust Foundation, had excelled himself in producing the false certification and letters of recommendation he needed to submit with his application for the work experience position at Greenlawns. Even down to the part of including a telephone number which Mrs. Ratchet had called to speak to the Professor at the said University to verify everything. Isaac was good, he was very good.

In the grand scheme of things, did it matter that the documentation wasn't legitimate? If he had been lucky enough to have the love and support of a *real* family, he would certainly have gone to university and been the success he professed to be. It was just the luck of the draw, and luck was something that Aaron never had an abundance of, like most kids in care homes, broken families. Like most of the guests in Greenlawns. They'd had to fight for every little thing and the road had been long and certainly not straight: the less strong fell by the wayside, never having the wherewithal or inclination to pick themselves up and make anything of themselves. Aaron and Isaac were not weak like those other unfortunates. They were astute, clever, and sought the retribution they rightly deserved.

Aaron had his name printed in authors' acknowledgements. He had helped them to become successful via his interaction and eye for detail. His own book would doubtless be a best seller, perhaps even turned into a film. He imagined himself playing the role of himself alongside famous actors and actresses. His mother would be so proud. She would declare her undying love for him and beg his forgiveness for giving him up for adoption, claiming there hadn't been a day go by without her thinking of him. He'd seen it happen so often on the internet.

He had a family like everybody else, but he hadn't had the same opportunity to get to know them, love them, spend holidays and Christmas with, like a normal, regular family. He didn't own a photograph album full of smiling pictures of him growing up, no little boxes of first haircuts or fallen teeth. No grandmother cuddles or bedtime stories read to him before the lights went out and he tried to sleep. All Aaron ever had was a yearning, a desire to know his roots, his family. What was abnormal about that?

He was fourteen when he found his original birth certificate, and thus his obsession began.

All staff members had been made aware that the DNA testing was going to take place at three p.m. the next afternoon, and as such, all parents and guardians who currently supported the guests had been telephoned and invited to attend.

Kerry's mother had been visited by the Family Liaison Officer from Greenlawns, accompanied by Police Sergeant Cummins. She wasn't at home upon their arrival, eventually returning from an all-nighter at around two thirty p.m. that afternoon, staggering out of her taxi and struggling to get the key in her door. It would be several hours after the effects of the alcohol had worn off before the realisation hit her; by then it was time for a repeat performance of the previous night in order to seek sympathy from so-called 'friends' and join her in drowning her sorrows.

The sombre atmosphere was depressing. None of the Greenlawns guests felt like conversing above whispered discussions. It felt alien, they felt vulnerable, afraid, trapped. The fourteen and fifteen-year-olds huddled together outside in circles trying to dissect the previous night's events, finger-pointing and blaming, daring to make macabre bets as to who would be the next victim.

Suzanne had also received the obligatory telephone call and was one of the first relatives to arrive, stalling her car as she raced to the front entrance where she almost collided into Mrs. Ratchet, who was talking to Aaron.

"Oh, Mrs. Ratchet, I'm sorry, I am so sorry, please forgive me. Where's Margot? How is she, can I see her?"

"Dear Ms Smythe, how lovely to see you, and yes of course you can see Margot, but not right now if you understand, all the guests are in the day room awaiting their call to take the relevant tests. Why don't you allow our Aaron, here, to take you to the dining room where you can get yourself a cup of coffee, or tea if you'd prefer."

"Thank you, yes, that would be lovely. Is my niece all right? Kerry is her roommate, right? Was, sorry, *was* her roommate. She must be terrified!"

"Aaron, be a love and accompany Ms. Smythe. Look after her until Margot can be released."

Released? Thought Suzanne, what did she mean by that?

She walked behind Aaron to the dining room, the smell hit her first off. That smell reminiscent of canteens, stale food and cleaning fluids associated with care homes, almost making her want to gag.

She sat down at the end of the long table, leaving Aaron to wait on her. He brought over two cups of black coffee and placed one before her, "I haven't added any milk but if you need any, there's some right here."

She took her coffee and studied the face looking at her. "Do I know you?" she asked, curiously.

Aaron threw his head back, laughing. "Oh, Ms Barsby, you write from your memories and yet you forget those who have helped pave your way to making your books a big success. I should feel aggrieved, and yet I forgive you, as I have not the capacity to bare grudges, unlike Lizzy."

The penny dropped! "Aaron!" she exclaimed jumping out of her seat and rushing over to him, giving him a big hug. "Oh, good grief, what a surprise! What are you doing here? Why didn't you let me know? I have so much to thank you for. I can't believe this!"

He closed his eyes, swimming in the glorious feeling of having her arms around him, "I throw that question back at you, Suzanne. What brings you to Greenlawns, today of all days?"

She was totally flummoxed. "Well… well, my niece is here. Oh God, I can't begin to explain everything just now because I got a call from Mrs. Ratchet this morning asking me to come over. I gather Margot's roommate killed herself last night, so naturally the police are going to be asking a lot of questions. Poor Margot's been through so much in her young years, I dread to think what long-term affect this is going to have on her. She loved Kerry." Aaron nodded, though not in agreement.

"Ah, Ms. Smythe, here you are. I do apologise for interrupting you, but could you come with me to my office? Aaron, whenever you're ready, they're all waiting."

Suzanne gave a last heartfelt smile at Aaron before leaving with Mrs. Ratchet, "I have much to thank you for, Aaron," she said nodding. "Thanks for the coffee, and for everything."

Sitting in Mrs. Ratchet's office, Suzanne was feeling on edge as she studied the concerned expression before her. "We have grave concerns for Margot, Ms. Smythe…"

"Suzanne, please."

"Thank you," Mrs. Ratchet continued, "Suzanne. Please forgive me but we seem to have reason to believe Margot may have more information regarding Kerry's unfortunate demise than was initially thought."

"I'm not with you. What do mean, Mrs. Ratchet, by grave concerns? Margot and Kerry were roommates, they're friends. Were friends. Margot was telling me how supportive Kerry's mum has been. Is Margot in some kind of danger too? Oh no, I'll take her home with me, today. Let's go and tell her now, she'll want to come with me. Have you notified her father? He'll totally agree to let her come to me."

Mrs. Ratchet felt a pang of sympathy for both Margot and Suzanne, as she did the majority of her guests. If only it was that easy to release one of her young people back into family life.

She chose her next words carefully, "Margot has some scratches on her hands and upper arms, Suzanne. Deep scratches that she hasn't been able to successfully clarify how she obtained them."

Suzanne stared at Mrs. Ratchet, her quizzical expression waiting for her to continue.

"And?"

"And until all DNA testing has been completed, all our guests and staff members are to remain here at Greenlawns. Mr. Foster, Margot's father, has been notified and I believe he's coming over this very evening. You can see Margot for a few minutes if you like, I believe she's back upstairs in her room."

Suzanne fled the room and ran upstairs to Margot's room, pushing open the door without knocking or waiting to be acknowledged, almost falling on Margot as she flung both arms around her shoulders, "Maggot! Oh my God I'm so relieved to see that you're ok."

Margot pushed her away, "Stop calling me Maggot. How many times do I have to remind you? My name is Margot! I hate you when you call me Maggot. How would you feel if I called you Aunty Poo, hey?"

Suzanne laughed, trying to inject some humour into their union. "I think Aunty Poo suits me down to the ground actually. Anyway, sorry Margot, I won't call you Maggot again, promise. So, tell me how you've been holding up. You must feel gutted about Kerry's suicide? Poor thing, did she ever talk to you about her insecurities? I bet she felt lucky having a friend like you to talk to."

Margot couldn't have cared a jot about Kerry's so-called insecurities, or her aunt and her ramblings, and wished she would go away so that she could concentrate on that thing that made her body vibrate like receiving an electric shock when she'd held Kerry underneath the water, watching and feeling all signs of life ebb away. It had been exhilarating. The thrill of the kill had been indescribable, and how could anything that felt so good be labelled as bad? It made no sense at all, and she was already plotting how she was going to accomplish a second attempt.

"I'm ready for you to go now, Aunty Poo. Oh, sorry, Aunty Sue," she smirked. "Dad's coming later, another boring visitor, so I need to get ready. Oh, did you remember to bring me some tampons like I asked you for last time?"

Suzanne felt deflated, and at the same time furious with her niece, but ashamed at the depth her feelings of resentment were plundering, and wondered where all her previous love and concern had gone, evaporating within seconds as she realised that not once had she asked about her own mother.

As she reversed her car from the car park she glanced back, looking upwards and glimpsed what she assumed was her niece, her outline just visible behind a lace curtain. A motorbike passed her as she was leaving, a Yamaha Virago she immediately recognised as being her brother-in-law's, a leather-clad biker looking totally cool cruising into Greenlawns. The boys would love it. Doug would be made to feel quite prolific for a few glorious moments, proudly displaying the attributes of its mono-shock rear suspension and its pristine exhausts, its tear-drop shaped gas tank; until he took off his crash helmet. He was early, too. Well, no change there then, Doug notoriously came too early! Suzanne almost giggled out loud at her unconscious double entendre.

Chapter 48: Mrs. Ratchet

Mrs. Ratchet had distracted herself of the surrounding mayhem by reading Bobby Harkin's case notes for the last half hour. He'd always been one of those to tug at her heartstrings, the cheeky monkey that he was. She was half chuckling to herself recalling humiliating him in the canteen, reminding him and everyone how he'd urinated over her strawberry patch the day he arrived, proclaiming he couldn't remember where the toilets were so decided to go and wee outside!

She remembered them all over the years, seeing their worried expressions and demeanours upon their arrival at Greenlawns, empathising with their loss as they were thrown into an abyss of unfamiliarity and uncertainty.

Some were most definitely easier than others, but what child wasn't? Her own three were all so different and yet came from the two same parents. She'd never classed herself as a perfect mother, far from it, and yet she felt she'd done her best for them – under the circumstances.

She sat back in her chair; Bobby Harkin's notes spread out in front of her, looking around her office walls, remembering buying the dilapidated house and vaguely knowing what she was going to do with it, with her life.

"Mummy, will you tuck me up tonight, I don't want Daddy to."

"Douglas, where is all your underwear? It's Monday, washday. Bring it all down so I can put it in the washing machine."

"Mom, can I go and stay at Grandma's house?"

"Christ woman, get these blasted kids out of my sight, and where's my f***ing dinner?"

Muriel Ratchet knew everything there was to know about broken homes. She also knew how it felt when you reached your lowest ebb and all one's maternal instincts kicked in to protect your children from the vulgar and unthinkable behaviour of an abusive husband and father.

Everybody has their breaking point, the time when the worm turns and one knows when to pack it all in, to preserve what little dignity remains and protect those too young to fend for themselves.

Nobody, but nobody, would ever lay another disgusting finger on her children ever again. No living human-being would harm them, degrade or defile them as long as she was still able to draw breath.

She had seen Greenlawns up for sale months earlier and fell in love with it. She could envision herself and her children living here, even though it was in dire need of a massive restoration input. It didn't matter, there were bedrooms and bathrooms, a huge kitchen, gardens to die for, and a yearn for freedom.

Through the innocent declarations of her own offspring, she decided to put her thoughts into action. The way to her husband's despicable heart was through his stomach, which she was all too happy to oblige.

She'd taken the children out to collect mushrooms from the fields where wild mushrooms grew in abundance. They collected baskets full of them.

It was there in the hedgerow she spotted one more, standing proud, as if waving to her, mockingly. As she bent over to pick it she knew instinctively what it was, The Destroying Angel! She had only ever seen them in encyclopaedias but there was no mistaking it. You could almost laugh at it, imagining its caricatured persona.

She recalled that night they all had their own individual pies. The big one was their daddy's, and the biggest tumbler of whiskey to wash it down, too. She was well aware that some fungi will react differently when combined with alcohol. Even the most harmless inkcap can cause adversity if ingested with alcohol.

The insurance company paid out, seemingly surprised as only recently, they declared, it was her husband who had taken out an insurance policy on her!

She cancelled her own life policy, sold their little two up, two down, and purchased Greenlawns where she and her children lived stress-free, even amongst the debris of builders as it was being sympathetically restored.

She would often look out of the huge patio doors to admire the gardens, vaguely hearing her husband's groans and gasping breaths, whilst never forgetting her daughter's pleas of *Mummy, will you tuck me up tonight, I don't want Daddy to*, and eventually finding her son's underwear he'd tried to burn at the back of the fireplace.

Yes, she knew exactly what these children at Greenlawns had been through, and she also knew the lengths some people go to protect themselves.

She checked the ledgers. There was enough in the profit account to buy what she needed. Bobby wasn't leaving for another five weeks. It was going to be the perfect leaving present. His grandfather had been a godsend helping her chose the perfect breed.

"Ah, hello, is this Mrs. Kent? I'm Muriel Ratchet from Greenlawns, I'm calling about the German Shepherd puppies you have for sale. Do you still have any bitches available?"

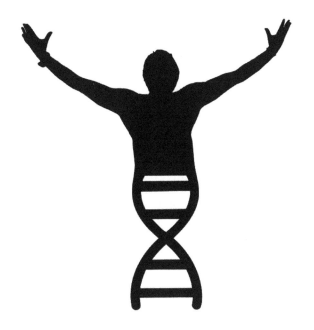

Chapter 49: Aaron

There was a knocking at Mrs. Ratchet's office door. "Come in," she shouted cheerfully.

"Mrs. Ratchet," Aaron said breathlessly, fidgeting with his phone, "I'm terribly sorry but I have to take leave, immediately. I've just received a call from my father to tell me that my mother has been taken into hospital. She's been involved in a car accident and she's already in surgery. I have to go, now."

"Oh dear, Aaron, yes of course you must! I do hope your mother will be ok. How are you going to get to the station, shall I call you a taxi?"

"I've already done it," he replied, "it's here, waiting outside. Don't worry, I've provided my DNA and you have my contact details so call me any time. But I feel I must go, my father's insisting I get back as quickly as possible. I'll update you as soon as I can."

They said their goodbyes and Mrs. Ratchet reassured him that it was the right thing to do and that she'd await his call. A huge relief washed over him as he hurried outside to the awaiting taxi.

Sitting at the window seat on the train to Brighton, everything tumbled over and over in his mind. He'd been so close, yet so far, and now he was having to go back and think of Plan B. It was galling, but how could anyone have anticipated that drawback? When was he going to get another opportunity to meet Suzanne again or find out more about Margot? He called Isaac and explained the whole depressing situation.

"It's nothing more than a slight hiccup, mate," Isaac reassured him, "at least you managed to accomplish a little of what you set out to achieve. I'll get us a pizza for tonight and we'll get our heads together for your Plan B. You didn't really submit your DNA, did you?"

"Of course not. I even brought the spoon I used for my cereals this morning with me. I left nothing there to match the two of us."

"Good, good. Well, at least you managed to get the address of Suzanne and even if Greenlawns asks her for your email address etc, it's untraceable, as is your mobile."

"Thanks, bro. You're the best. See you in about four hours' time."

They disconnected their call and Aaron sat back in his seat. He'd bide his time, as he had done for more years than he cared to remember, considering the adage, 'revenge is a dish best served cold'. He was undecided if revenge actually was what he was aiming for. After all, the definition of 'revenge' was *the act of hurting someone in return for a wrongdoing by someone else*. He didn't want revenge per se, more an acknowledgement, acceptance, perhaps even an apology - it was his due.

It was a basic human right to know one's roots, where you came from, who gave birth to you. Isaac was the closest to being classed as family, they were foster brothers: blood isn't always thicker than water!

*   *   *   *   *

'Hello Suzanne, I hope you are in good spirits, despite the circumstances of our brief encounter at Greenlawns. What a coincidence we should meet there of all places. The world is such a small place indeed.

I would have liked the opportunity to talk with you some more but unfortunately an unexpected crisis prevented me from doing so and I have had to take temporary leave. Anyway, back to your book.

*I think the scene with Violet and Margaret in chapter 24 needs a **lot** more explanation, if you don't mind me saying so. Violet's own mother had been well aware of her multiple personalities since she was a child, if I've read that right? Therefore, why don't you portray one of her many personalities here in this chapter, and hint that possibly Margaret might have inherited her mother's genes? It may give your reader a hint as to why Margaret is acting the way she is doing without giving too much away.*

Have a good evening, I'll be in touch again as soon as you send over the next batch.

Oh, p.s. thanks for the recommendation to Adam! Got two more authors to work with."

* * * * *

"So, what was she like?" asked Isaac.

"Who? Margot or Suzanne?"

"Both, I suppose."

Aaron took another bite of his slice of pizza, "Margot is a vile bitch who already hates me. She's beautiful though, Suzanne," he answered, smiling. "She hugged me, and I could smell her perfume, it smelt divine, like flowers on a warm spring day. I swear, Isaac, I could have kissed her, told her everything in that moment, but I didn't." Isaac nodded as if trying to concede his understanding.

"Anyway, I feel a little deceitful leaving the way I did. Mrs. Ratchet is a lovely lady, she's warm and caring and didn't deserve to be lied to like that."

"Aaron, if that girl hadn't killed herself there would have been no need for you to leave just yet and everything would have slotted into place. But don't you think it's a bit odd that the police needed everyone's DNA if it was just a case of suicide? Do you reckon there's more to the story than they're letting on?"

"My thoughts exactly, Bro! That Kerry gave no signs of wanting to end her life. Agreed, she wasn't the happy-go-lucky type, kinda shy and reserved really, didn't display any confidence either, but certainly not what you'd call 'depressed'. Hmm, she was either a very good little actress or the staff were keeping everything *schtum*. We'll see if we can find anything out on the internet, later. But, Isaac, if they did need DNA samples from everyone, that implies someone else was involved, wouldn't you say?"

"It could imply she either asked for someone to assist her in her act of suicide, or she didn't plan to die. Perhaps someone had a grudge against her? Nevertheless, it's all hypothetical now, and as I just said, your mobile phone has been rendered inactive. Sorted it as soon as we ended the call from the train. I've left the email for now because you'll need that for your communication with your authors, but I intend creating a new account sometime this week. You can notify them when it's up and running and they can still pay you via Western Union. We'll alter the collection points periodically."

Suzanne had been greatly surprised to find Aaron at Greenlawns and regretted not having more time to be able to chat, to talk about his involvement with her work. She hardly recognised him until he made that comment about him helping her. He had looked familiar but hadn't the slightest clue how she came to that conclusion. He had certainly matured since the last time she encountered him; that cheeky, spotty young lad who claimed to have read all her books all those years ago. And then the next memory followed of her stopover at Corah's and the dreadful, frightening experience with Garth. Poor Garth, perhaps he would still be alive if it wasn't for her, possibly happily married to Corah with a couple of children to boot.

She concluded she must be a hard nut because she felt incapable of feeling true love. Passionate love. She used people, all the time to her own advantage. Even withstanding her feelings towards her one and only niece, the one to whom she'd devoted hours of attention and money. Now it boiled down to money alone. Time, attention, and warm feelings were vanishing into the ether where Margot was concerned. Duty, too, felt a burden too heavy to want to carry.

She had most certainly made the right decision where her pregnancy was concerned, all those years ago. Rose had always been the maternal one, the homemaker, like her mother.

She thought about Doug riding into Greenlawns, looking the part of 'old-man-playing-young-man' on his Yamaha motorcycle, wondering when the last time he paid a visit to her sister in the institution, remembering how few personal effects she had surrounding her.

Rose's former marital home was once full of memorabilia, photographs hung the entire length of her staircase of her children, her wedding pictures, their parents, her and Rose posing next to the Christmas tree, each of them pointing to the little birds their dad had made for them. Happier times.

Her visit to her dad's sister, Aunty Pat, had floored her but she hadn't had the time to digest everything she'd been told because she ended up needing a stiff drink and found herself talking to the lovely landlady at the Navigation and it had been just hours later when she received the phone call from Mrs. Ratchet asking her to go to Greenlawns.

Now back inside the security of her own four walls, she could make an attempt to process everything.

She remembered Doug bringing boxes of Rose's personal belongings to her house when he decided to move away and find some new young woman to have hanging on to his every word as if he was God's gift!

There was that one particular box he'd asked her to keep inside - the one containing the decoupaged suitcase - rather than the garage because Rose had always insisted it be kept safe. She hadn't considered opening it until after her visit to Aunty Pat and her conversation with Ann, from The Navigation, and what a treasure it had proved to be, too! A whole Pandora's Box of sad truths secreted away like a bad smell, a shedload of royalties to be earned from – not necessarily disrespecting her parents and sister from making a darn good book from everything she found, but at least giving her a better understanding of her father and realising how she'd never spoken a false word to Rose when she'd said, *'you're just like Mum.'*

* * * * *

Rose was sitting on her bed wearing a long, red, sleeveless dress. Her hair had been cut short. It suited her, accentuated her high cheekbones and button-nose. She was reading a book and Suzanne knew immediately which one it was.

Rose turned to look at Suzanne who was standing in the doorway, and beckoned her in.

"I did tell you that you're more like mum, even though you said it was me. But we are still alike, me and you. Like peas in a pod everyone used to say, didn't they? Do you remember?"

Suzanne nodded. Yes, she remembered. Everyone said the same thing.

Rose turned back to her book, "and we hated boys, didn't we? That pig who lived next door, he was vile. Poor Judy. We were lucky we didn't have brothers. I used to tell Margot how we used to hate boys and brothers, how cruel they were. Margot didn't like boys either, she didn't want her brothers. Just like me and you, Suzy."

Suzanne walked over to the bed where Rose sat in front of her. She wanted to embrace her but felt apprehensive of displaying any physical contact. Rose was lost to her.

"Oh, but I loved *my* boys, Sue, *my* Steven and Simon. I loved them… so much. Margot hurt them, though. Did she tell you?"

Suzanne shook her head, no, Margot hadn't said a thing.

"Do you remember the day you born, and I got to hold you before Mum and Dad? Do you? There's that photograph somewhere where I'm sitting in a chair and you're in my arms and then I think there's another one with Steven and Mum. I didn't like Steven, I didn't want a brother, only you – my little sister."

Suzanne's eyes filled with tears at hearing her words, knowing the guilt Rose had carried from being such a small child.

"Rose, I'm *not* your sister. I'm your cousin. Aunty Pat is your real mum. She's told me everything."

Rose looked at Suzanne in utter confusion, "Aunty Pat? She... she's told you? She promised me she wouldn't. Don't tell Dad, Sue, please don't tell him, he'll be terribly upset. He'll be disappointed with her you see, she's only eighteen."

"It's ok, Rose. Mum and Dad both knew. They'd been married for ages and had many problems trying to have a baby of their own, and then when Aunty Pat got pregnant at such a young age... well, they offered to take you as their own daughter. They couldn't bear to think of you being adopted. Our grandparents disowned her, Aunty Pat, they never had anything to do with our parents either because they felt they'd intervened and were very angry. How sad is that, hey, Rose? Our own grandparents missed out on having us - their very own grandchildren - and we missed out having a grandma and grandad."

"Rose," Suzanne continued, handing her an old faded coloured photograph, "keep this picture at the side of your bed. It's you as a baby, with your mum; Aunty Pat. I think you must only be a week or two."

Rose rocked back and forth, squinting at Suzanne, studying her, trying to analyse her words.

"Mum eventually did get pregnant, thanks to you, Rose. It happens all the time. That's when Steven and I arrived."

"Steven? I'm sorry, Sue, I didn't want Steven. I loved you, though. I loved having my sister."

Suzanne's eyes welled up, the tears she'd been holding inside for an eternity, spilled down her cheeks. How long had Rose known about all of this? What other secrets had she buried inside?

"And I love you too, Rose."

Chapter 50: The Accident

The whole damned last God-knows-how-many-weeks and months, she'd lost count, had felt like a lifetime of being on a death-defying roller-coaster!

There had been the additional crushing blow upon discovery of her once true love wrapped around a young slip of a girl who had taken the place of her poor sister who had not only lost her three children, her husband, home, and reason for living alongside everything she loved, but also her mind.

Her niece, her sister's daughter – or was that her cousin's daughter if one was to split hairs and draw a fine line underneath everything – had somehow become embroiled in a sinister case of suicide / murder. She had been informed that Margot's DNA matched that of the skin tissue found underneath Kerry's fingernails and was going to be taken away to a prison-like faculty for the next however many decades. It was incomprehensible that her niece could have had anything to do with it… and yet something nagged at the back of Suzanne's mind.

Flashes of memories erupted into her subconsciousness.

"You have to take Doris, Sue. She's becoming a nervous wreck."

"Why are you crying just because Bambi's mother died, Aunty Sue?"

"Don't worry love, Simon's here with us. The greedy little monkey was trying to eat a whole sausage, his face was turning blue."

"Mum said if I gave those sweets to Simon, she'd buy me a new charm for my Pandora bracelet."

"I liked cutting Lilo's fingers and toes off, but she didn't cry like Simon cried when I stuck pins in him."

Love is blind, the saying goes, and it most definitely is. We don't interfere with the things we are scared to hear the truths of. We bury our heads in the sand like the proverbial ostrich, acknowledging nothing that is going to rock our boats or cause us grief. We are all pathetic, spineless cowards.

Even though Rose wasn't the biological daughter of their parents, Suzanne knew that at least *she* was definitely her father's daughter. He'd never had the guts to tell his daughters the truth about their lineage, instead he'd buried it underneath a floorboard in his garden shed. Like him, she'd buried her own secrets away, hoping they'd never see the light of day. She could hide behind her pseudonym, writing her fancy stories, and no one would ever be the wiser. She felt protected by the veil of shame and secrecy she'd created.

She was angry. No, that was a gross underestimation, she was furious! She was lost, desolate, and her guttural screams got louder and louder as she banged on her steering wheel in an attempt to calm herself down, realising the futility at anyone's ability to turn the clocks back and start all over again.

She began to go over the conversation she'd had with her aunt, Rose's birth mother, her father's sister, and Ann from The Navigation. She'd learned a lot in the hours she'd been there. In fact, she'd learned more about her parents and her past in those few hours than she'd known in the thirty-six years of her entire life! She wondered if she and Rose had inadvertently been swapped over at birth somehow because Rose was definitely more like their mother and Suzanne was a carbon copy of her aunt! The circle of coincidence was unbelievably astounding.

Pat had been pregnant at eighteen - so had Suzanne. Pat had given away her baby without so much as a backward glance; so had she.

Pat never married; neither had Suzanne. Pat smoked like a chimney – Rose had never attempted to try a cigarette. Suzanne, on the other hand, would never be without at least a couple of packets in her kitchen cupboard.

Pat had always been the rebellious, difficult daughter, lacked all signs of empathy and therefore never developed any lasting friendships. She had a spell in prison for growing marijuana and supplying many of her so-called acquaintances. There but for the grace of God go I, thought Suzanne.

Aunty Pat and their dad had had two brothers. Two much younger brothers, Duncan and Douglas. Duncan died after being savaged by the family dog, a once amiable and placid rottweiler who turned into an unpredictable and cancer-ridden mutt, when he was just about seven years old. The boys had been playing about on the back lawn when their mother rushed indoors to answer the telephone, leaving an allegedly responsible sixteen-year-old sister to watch over them. Ordinarily not a problem, until an excited Duncan ran over to the dog and tried to jump on his back.

As a consequence, the mother lost all her maternal feelings, becoming elusive and bitter, and Douglas was thus cast aside, eventually being adopted by the Foster family. He never knew.

Douglas Foster (*previously Smythe*) married Rose, his biological aunt!

Her BMW was designed for speed and more often than not she had managed to adhere to the speed limits, unlike this moment when she didn't even know or care how many hours she'd been driving, where she was, what she was doing or even where she was heading.

Consequently she could never have expected to see the green Yamaha Virago with the leather-clad biker returning from visiting his daughter when she turned the corner, until she visualised those almost lightning flashbacks of him and herself, the last time he almost fell over her threshold, sobbing pitifully at her neck as he wallowed in life's knockbacks he'd suffered, like he was the only one who had ever endured hardships, craving satisfaction on the carpeted floor entangled together disregarding every sacred thing and a line that should never be crossed between a brother or sister-in-law.

The intense jealousy she felt the night she witnessed him wrapped around the young bimbo on his doorstep, pawing at her young body, blowing her kisses as she walked away under the romantic and alluring light of the streetlamps, realising he'd erased every single memory of his wife, his daughter, his family, and her.

Everything seemed to happen in slow motion as her foot eased off the accelerator pedal, too late, as they met head-on. She heard the screeching of her brakes first, then felt the thud of the impact. Seconds later came the indescribable pain which miraculously vanished in an instant.

She stood shivering with cold and shock at the side of her crumpled pride and joy, slightly aware of hearing her car stereo playing something indecipherable, confused to see herself slumped over the steering wheel with blood trickling down her forehead. And then she knelt by the unmoving leather-clad guy with the twisted limbs on the road, his face partially obscured because of the helmet he was wearing, the bike wheels still spinning in time with the music from her car, screwing her nose up at the nauseating smell of petrol, and held his leather-gloved hand.

She sat with him, trying to make sense of the scene before her, wondering why nobody was about to help them, where the ambulances were, constantly whispering to him words of reassurance that everything was going to be okay, and then she saw her parents walking slowly towards her, smiling serenely.

Meanwhile, back at her bungalow, her laptop beeped:

"Hey Suzanne. Are you there? I have something important I need to talk to you about. Does the date 6th February 2000 bear any significance to you? I know it was eighteen years ago, a cold, wintery Sunday in London, 4.03 a.m. precisely, but I feel sure you will remember. I'm hoping so.

Aaron."

EPILOGUE

Six Years Later...

As Margot lay on her bed reading *Pity my Sister* again with a pillow propped under her head, Rose was elsewhere, helping to gather the grapes with her kindly Italian neighbours. It was late September, but the sun was still making a welcome appearance and everyone was in high spirits. Huge swathes of black and red grapes were harvested and loaded into vats ready for George to make his gallons of organic red wine which he sold to the locals for a pittance. It was a backbreaking exercise, but Rose was more than happy to assist whenever she could as it afforded her more opportunity to learn the language.

For the first time in many years, she felt happy and relaxed. Italy was a brand-new start for her and, after selling Suzanne's cottage, she decided to follow her dream and buy a little place in the sun. She'd taken up painting, too. Something she used to love doing before becoming a mother and time disallowed such an indulgence. Now, though, she had plenty of time.

Margot had read all the books her aunt had written, ad-nauseum. She had been surprised, years back, seeing Aaron

Penfold's name in the acknowledgement section, considering it a coincidence that he had been at Greenlawns where she had been in residence, before the Kerry incident. Or was it a coincidence? She didn't believe in such a thing. She believed that everything was meant to be.

She had hated Aaron when he was first introduced to her, back in the days when she hated everything and everyone. Now she didn't feel any hate; Aaron had told her that 'hate' is a powerful word and the connotations didn't necessarily mean the same in every instance. In fact, she felt nothing for anything or anybody. She was completely devoid of empathy. She didn't even hate her own mother who was now out of the sanatorium and living in Italy after finalising her finances and receiving a comfortable income from the royalties of her sister's books.

Margot did listen to Krystal, though. That sad, pathetic, non-descript Krystal who talked about wanting a better life in heaven and couldn't wait to go there. Krystal, the fifteen-year-old arsonist who loved to pour paraffin through her classmates' letterboxes and then throw in a light and sit back to watch the glorious flames light up the darkness of the night. Those allegedly tough classmates that taunted and bullied her because of her bright red hair and her embarrassing stutter. Krystal had taken revenge after she had reached her own breaking point because no one had ever bothered to fight her corner.

Margot had forced herself to listen to her constant drone of wanting to 'jack it all in' and seek salvation in a more salubrious dimension and supported her decision. She practised perfecting the advice she was going to give her, over three months. Hanging, she promised, was the quickest and least messy way, and she would be there to help her. She could simply tie a belt to one of the overhead central heating pipes, loop another through it and fasten it around her neck, then take one simple step off the chair and voila! No more bullying to endure or the endless years at the Juvenile Detention Centre. She was doing her a massive kindness, releasing her from pain.

It was Friday afternoon, and as Margot lay reading on her bed, and Rose cut grapes from the vineyard, Aaron and Isaac were boarding the plane bound for Italy. He had paid his bi-monthly visit to Margot, mostly for his own benefit than hers, as she was almost the last link to a blood relative he would know. She had never acknowledged his stupid declarations that they were cousins, reminding him that they were nothing alike and she would have known if indeed her aunt had had a son!

Rose, on the other hand, was overjoyed to learn that she was an aunt to a wonderful and caring nephew, proud that he was following in her sister's footsteps and becoming an author in his own right, delighted he and his 'brother' were coming to visit her again to help repair a falling stone wall and rip out some of the far too many fruit trees on her little property!

Krystal waited in her room for Margot to come and assist. It was almost midnight, and everyone was sleeping. She waited and waited, becoming anxious that Margot wouldn't show. Then there was a little knock on the door.

As Krystal stood on the chair with her neck inside the belts which Margot had attached to the overhead central pipes, it became real to her, and she began to panic.

"Nonsense," reassured Margot, "you look like a beautiful crystal chandelier. This is exactly how it's meant to be, remember?"

"Marg, I'm frightened" she said. "I think I've changed my mind. Quickly, get me down."

Margot gave her chair a little kick and Krystal hung in mid-air, her legs kicking out frantically.

"Margot," she corrected. "My name is Margot!"

Acknowledgements

I love to be at this stage when the book is finally finished, and I get to thank all the wonderful supportive people who have enabled me to arrive at this point. It could almost be like writing an additional chapter, though unrelated to the book.

My ninety-one-year-old mother, Elizabeth Talbott, is the first person who gets to read every single chapter and woe betide me if I should overstep the mark!

Then I have my support team, Karen Tyres, Suzanne Bottomley, Patricia White. Each one has a specific role in ensuring I'm on the right track and believe me they pull no punches. The final editing goes to my ever-patient and supportive publisher, Mike Hurd at Lineage-Independent Publishing.

On this occasion I was extremely privileged to be able to use the photograph of John and Lisa Bond's daughter, Yasmin, for the front cover which, in my view, depicts a serene and sultry Margot.

I have never actually met Mike Hurd, my publisher, face-to-face, nor the Bond family. I haven't seen my team readers for years, either, but thanks to the internet and a bucketload of trust, I feel privileged to acknowledge them all as friends.

Lightning Source UK Ltd.
Milton Keynes UK
UKHW012057310122
397988UK00003B/984